DEADLY CHOWDER

Val went down the staircase to the kitchen. A hum of conversation came from the dining room. With her grandfather's chowder dinner well under way, she could sneak out the back door and go for a walk. She had her hand on the knob when a raised voice came from the dining room.

"Food poisoning! That's what it is."

Val restrained herself from zooming into the dining room and confronting the accusation head on. Doing that would expose her grandfather as a liar. To buttress his claim that he'd made tonight's dinner without her help, he'd doubtless told his guests she wasn't home.

She rushed out the back door and ran around to the front of the house. She risked annoying her grandfather by crashing his party. Too bad. He needed her, though he might not know it.

She opened the front door and called out, "I'm home, Granddad."

No one at the table even glanced at her as she approached the dining room. They all stared at the man with thinning blond hair. He groaned and pitched face-first into the chowder . . .

W9-ARR-945

Books by Maya Corrigan

BY COOK OR BY CROOK

SCAM CHOWDER

Published by Kensington Publishing Corporation

Scam
Chowder

Maya
Corrigan

KENSINGTON PUBLISHING CORP.
http://www.kensingtonbooks.com

KENSINGTON BOOKS are published by

Kensington Publishing Corp.
119 West 40th Street
New York, NY 10018

Copyright © 2015 by Mary Ann Corrigan

All rights reserved. No part of this book may be reproduced in any form or by any means without the prior written consent of the Publisher, excepting brief quotes used in reviews.

If you purchased this book without a cover, you should be aware that this book is stolen property. It was reported as "unsold and destroyed" to the Publisher and neither the Author nor the Publisher has received any payment for this "stripped book."

All Kensington Titles, Imprints, and Distributed Lines are available at special quantity discounts for bulk purchases for sales promotions, premiums, fund-raising, and educational or institutional use. Special book excerpts or customized printings can also be created to fit specific needs. For details, write or phone the office of the Kensington special sales manager: Kensington Publishing Corp., 119 West 40th Street, New York, NY 10018, attn: Special Sales Department, Phone: 1-800-221-2647.

Kensington and the K logo Reg. U.S. Pat & TM Off.

ISBN-13: 978-1-61773-140-2
ISBN-10: 1-61773-140-4
First Kensington Mass Market Edition: July 2015

eISBN-13: 978-1-61773-141-9
eISBN-10: 1-61773-141-2
First Kensington Electronic Edition: July 2015

10 9 8 7 6 5 4 3 2 1

Printed in the United States of America

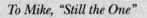

To Mike, "Still the One"

Chapter 1

"*Blech*. Ugly appetizer. I could add chopped roaches to it, and no one would notice."

Val Deniston agreed with her grandfather about the look of the olive-walnut-raisin spread she'd just made. "No matter how bad it looks, it's yummy on pita." But maybe too exotic for Granddad's guests from Ambleside Active Adult Village. Tonight's other appetizer would probably go over better with the older crowd—cherry tomatoes stuffed with herbed cheese.

Granddad pointed to the olive spread, his furry white eyebrows lowering. "Can you whip up something real quick to replace this?"

"I'm busy with the chowder." She stirred the pan and breathed in the fragrance of sautéed onions. The most expensive perfume couldn't compete with it.

"Well, don't dawdle. You gotta be out of here in half an hour."

"I know my role." She would cook and run before the first guest showed up. Then he would do his star turn, add the final ingredients to the chowder, and claim credit for the meal.

He donned his khaki apron emblazoned with CODGER COOK. "Did you remember to move your car?"

"Three blocks away. Your guests won't know I'm here, unless one of them is Sherlock Holmes." A glance at Granddad's apron would tell Sherlock that the codger had never used it to cook. He wore it only for photo shoots promoting his "brand" as the local newspaper's food columnist. He'd wangled that job by submitting Val's recipes as his own. She wanted no part of his ruse, but she could hardly expose her own grandfather as an imposter. On the plus side, his celebrity status in Bayport put a spring in his step and made him less crabby than at any time since she moved into his Victorian house.

He pointed to the two large pots on the stove. "Let's go over what I'm supposed to do. I put cow juice in one of those pots and fish juice in the other. Which is which?"

"Put the broth in the light chowder on the left. Add the cream to the white chowder, the pot on the right." Val turned off the heat under the onions. "Don't forget which one goes in which pot. Repeat after me: light left, white right."

"Left, white—no, light—right?" Granddad scratched his ear. The fringe of ivory hair above his ear stuck out like a tiny wing. "Call it creamy chowder, instead of white chowder. Then we can't confuse it with light chowder. I don't even know why we're serving light chowder."

"Because it's a traditional Chesapeake Bay recipe,

and it gives your guests a choice. Some of them may be lactose intolerant or have to avoid fat and cholesterol." As Granddad was supposed to do.

"Nobody was lactose intolerant when your grandmother made her creamy chowder. The day you were born, she invited all the neighbors for chowder to celebrate." Granddad gazed out the window at the big oak tree he and Grandma had planted as a sapling. "Hard to believe that was thirty-five years ago."

"Thirty-*two*." If anyone had told Val on her thirty-first birthday that a year later she'd live with her grandfather, she'd have laughed. A woman with a fiancé and an exciting job in Manhattan relocate to a rural area like Maryland's Eastern Shore? Impossible . . . until the fiancé and the job both went sour. Now, six months later, she had a new life in a tourist town near the bay and rarely thought about what she'd left behind. "You know when to put in the potatoes and how long they cook, right?"

"You told me, but I forgot." Granddad turned away from the window and peered into pots. "Can't you just sneak down the back stairs, finish the job, and leave me to entertain my guests?"

Given his track record, she'd like nothing better than to keep him away from the stove. Then she could stop worrying that he'd spill the chowder, scald himself, or blow up the kitchen. "I can do that, but if you're pretending you cooked dinner, you'd better excuse yourself and go into the kitchen once in a while. Even the great Codger Cook can't turn on the stove by remote control."

"Suppose someone wants to come with me? We need a signal so you have time to skedaddle up the back staircase." He snapped his fingers. "Remote control! I know what we can use." He opened the broom closet.

"What are you looking for?" She had visions of him creating an obstacle course of mops and pails to alert her of impending kitchen incursions.

He rummaged in a cardboard box and pulled out a gray plastic gizmo the size of a shoebox. "Our guard dog, RoboFido, will bark to tell you someone's going toward the kitchen."

She scratched her head. "How's that supposed to work? It's a motion sensor. Every time a guest moves, it'll woof, and you'll have to explain why you have a barking box in the house."

He pointed to his temple. "Use your noodle. Last time, we set up RoboFido inside the house and pointed it toward the outside. When it detected motion out there, it barked to discourage prowlers. This time, we'll set it up outside and point it toward the dining-room window." He reached into the cardboard box and pulled out something that looked like a car key fob. "And I'll carry this in my pocket."

She peered at the device. "I didn't know you had a remote control for Fido."

"Yup. When any guests pass through the dining room, Fido will bark. That's your signal to get out of here. They have to walk through the butler's pantry." He pointed to the cabinet-lined passageway between the dining room and kitchen. "That'll give you enough time to scoot up the back stairs."

She glanced toward the stairway. Within seconds, she could reach it and hide behind the wall that divided it from the kitchen. "Okay, but do your best to keep people out of here. When dinner's ready, I'll call the house phone from my cell phone, let it ring twice, and hang up. I won't come back in here after that, so you can turn Fido off."

"And if it's just me coming into the kitchen while you're still cooking, I'll turn off the sensor. Once I've gone past the dining-room window, I'll flip Fido's switch back on again."

She took the lettuce out of the refrigerator. "You know, hiding the fact that you can't cook is harder than actually cooking."

He grinned. "But it's more fun."

While she made the salad, he set up and tested his early-warning system.

He called to her from the dining room. "The remote works. Can you hear barking, Val?"

"Loud and clear." She looked up from scrubbing the potatoes as he came into the kitchen. "Who's coming to the dinner tonight?"

"Folks Lillian and I know from the retirement village, and a few others."

He used the words *Lillian and I* more and more lately. To attract Lillian, whose departed husband had been a gourmet cook, Granddad had hatched a scheme to prove that he too knew his way around the kitchen. Winning the contest to write the local newspaper's recipe column had apparently given him an edge over the other retired men vying for her attention. "Who else did you invite besides folks from the Village?"

"A woman who lives there is bringing her son. And a reporter from the Salisbury TV station is coming. The young, good-looking one. Junie May Jussup."

Granddad had a different definition of *young* than

most people. The reporter with dark hair and thick bangs was pushing forty. "Why did you invite a reporter?" And why did she agree to come?

"She called me about doing a TV interview. She wanted to see my kitchen and sample something I cooked. So I asked her to join us tonight. She's bringing a guest too." The doorbell rang. Granddad couldn't have looked more shocked if a meteor grazed him. "Oh no. Someone's early."

"It's probably Ned, coming to help you."

"I didn't invite Ned."

Val nearly cut herself with the potato peeler. "You invited other people from the Village and not your best buddy?" If it weren't for Ned, Granddad wouldn't even know Lillian.

"It's complicated." Her grandfather left to answer the door.

Complicated summed up Val's life ever since he'd assumed the Codger Cook persona. Bad enough that she had to supply recipes for his column. Tonight's dinner party embroiled her more deeply in his hoax when she already had enough weighing on her. Business had slackened off at the Cool Down Café in the last few weeks. Unless it picked up, the Bayport Racket and Fitness Club wouldn't extend her contract to manage its café, and she wouldn't earn enough to help Granddad maintain this big house.

She heard her grandfather talking louder than usual. "Thank you for bringing the bread, Lillian. I'll take it into the kitchen."

RoboFido barked. Lillian was coming to the kitchen too.

Val wiped her hands on her jeans and zoomed to

the staircase behind the wall. She sat on the fifth step, not daring to go farther up the creaky wood staircase until Lillian left the kitchen. Unlike the other walls in the old Victorian, the thin divider wall along the staircase barely muffled sounds.

"It smells wonderful in here," Lillian said. "And look at those lovely stuffed tomatoes. Can I sample just one?"

An image of the lovely Lillian with her short ivory coif sprang into Val's mind and morphed into a vision of a sleek white-haired cat.

"Sure. Go ahead and try the tomatoes," Granddad said. "They're from my garden."

His garden? Ha.

He'd done nothing with the garden in the six years since Grandma died. Val had dug it up in March, her first project after moving here. She'd planted the vegetables, weeded, and harvested without any help from him.

"Umm. Delicious. I'll just have one more," Lillian said. "And you've started the clam chowder. Two big pots just for the six of us?"

"Two different kinds of chowder. Instead of clam chowder, we should call it *scam chowder.*"

Lillian laughed. "For our guest of honor."

"I hate to give that crook any more of my good food than necessary. Let's spring the trap over the appetizers."

Val pressed her ear to the wall. A trap for a crook?

Why would Granddad invite a crook to the party and leave his friend Ned off the guest list?

"You may get better results by waiting until after dinner," Lillian said with a gentle, cajoling voice.

"The drinks, your delicious chowder, and a sweet dessert will soften him for the kill."

"And his mother might as well have a good meal before we lower the boom on him. If he doesn't do what I want, I'll get the cops after him. The chief of police is an old friend of mine."

"That rogue is slick enough to evade the law. If you want Scott to give the money back, you may have to promise you won't go to the police."

Val clutched the edge of the stair to keep herself from jumping up in protest. If Granddad had lost money to a crook, he should tell the police, not take Lillian's advice.

"Okay, I'll make a bargain with the Devil," he said.

How easily Lillian had persuaded him to do what she wanted. The plot to ambush a rogue named Scott at tonight's dinner made Val uneasy. She'd learned an important lesson about catching rodents during her ten years living in New York City—the trap could snap back on you. The same thing might happen with Granddad's rogue trap.

"I didn't see water glasses on the table," Lillian said. "Where do you keep them? I'll put them out and fill them up."

"Use the ones in the dining-room china closet. I'll bring you a pitcher of water."

Val waited until she was sure the kitchen was empty and went back to cooking. She peeled the potatoes and cubed them. The doorbell rang as she added them to the pots. Could Granddad keep the latest arrivals out of the kitchen? Two minutes later, RoboFido barked, and Val had her answer. She raced to the stairs and ducked behind the wall. A woman's voice drifted toward her.

"Oh, I just knew you'd have a homey kitchen like this. Painted cabinets, butcher block counters. Nothing fancy, just what everyone would expect of the Codger Cook." Junie May Jussup spoke with a broadcaster's precise diction and honeyed tones. "I'm so glad you invited me tonight, Mr. Myer. This is the perfect place to interview you. We'll position the camera here for a shot of the whole kitchen."

"You should film him cooking a recipe from his column." The suggestion came from a woman with a starchy voice.

Val stiffened. That voice couldn't belong to anyone but Irene Pritchard. The sixtyish woman had hair like steel wool and an abrasive attitude to match it. Val wouldn't have invited Irene the Irate to any party she was giving.

"Irene has such good ideas, Mr. Myer," Junie May said. "You won't regret letting me bring her along tonight."

Oh yes he would, and Val regretted not telling him about Irene's accusations a month ago. Disgruntled at losing the recipe columnist job to Granddad, the irate woman had accused Val of writing the column for him and of withholding evidence in a murder.

"I thought you'd bring a young man as your guest, Junie May," Granddad said. "We have four women and only two men tonight."

"We have an extra man coming," Granddad's girlfriend said. "The son of an old friend just texted me.

He's passing through town and wanted to meet me for dinner. I invited him to join us. I hope that's okay."

"Fine with me," Granddad said. "What's his name, Lillian?"

"Omar. I'll add another setting to the table."

Val ticked off the guests on her fingers. Four females—the lovely Lillian, the irate Irene, the reporter Junie May, and the mother of Scott, the reputed scammer. Three males—Granddad, Scott, and the late-arriving Omar.

"I'd like to watch the Codger Cook make tonight's meal," Irene said.

She wasn't above haunting the kitchen to make sure no one besides Granddad went near the stove, but he had enough riding on the Codger Cook hoax that he would keep her out.

"Not much to watch," Granddad said. "The chowder's just about done. Let's go to the sitting room and dig into the appetizers."

Val allowed two minutes for everyone to settle down in the sitting room and crept back into the kitchen. She opened the refrigerator and took out the clam liquor, the juice left over after Granddad shucked a hundred clams. He'd taken on the messiest part of making this meal.

Just as Val added the clam liquor to the pots, the doorbell rang. RoboFido barked a few seconds later. She rushed to her hiding place. She sat on her usual step, but this time couldn't hear anyone talking in the kitchen, only the floor creaking.

Someone must have gone into the kitchen while Granddad was occupied greeting new arrivals. Val stiffened, worried that a prying guest would catch her crouched on the staircase. She heard water splashing into the sink and then her grandfather's voice.

"Can I help you with anything, Irene?" he asked.

Luckily, Granddad had found Irene before she found Val.

"I just wanted a drink of water," Irene said.

Ha. Irene had spent a minute in the kitchen before turning on the faucet. Doing what?

Val returned to the stove only after she was sure Granddad had maneuvered Irene out of the kitchen. The doorbell rang one more time while Val finished making the chowders. She heard occasional laughter coming from the sitting room. The dinner party sounded as if it had begun well. But with Granddad and Lillian planning to trap a crook, and Irene trying to trap the Codger Cook, it might not end well.

Val turned off the burners and sampled a spoonful of creamy chowder. Good. The cream didn't overpower the taste of the clams. She filled a mug with the light chowder, figuring it would be less popular than the creamy one, and took it up to her room above the kitchen, the same room where she'd slept during the summers she spent here as a child. Intended as the maid's chamber when the house was built in the nineteenth century, the room had direct access to the kitchen, her favorite place.

She took out her cell phone, speed-dialed the house's landline number, and let it ring twice before hanging up to tell Granddad he was on his own. She shifted the cookbooks on the small table in her room to make space for her mug of chowder and James Michener's *Chesapeake.* Then she sat by the window overlooking the backyard and enjoyed the simple flavor of clams and brine. Whatever else happened at the dinner tonight, no one could fault the food.

She finished eating long before she finished thirty pages of *Chesapeake.* Then she went down the staircase to the kitchen. A hum of conversation came from the dining room. With her grandfather's chowder dinner well under way, she could sneak out the back door and go for a walk. She had her hand on the knob when a raised voice came from the dining room.

"Food poisoning! That's what it is."

Val restrained herself from zooming into the dining room and confronting the accusation head-on. Doing that would expose her grandfather as a liar. To buttress his claim that he'd made tonight's dinner without her help, he'd doubtless told his guests she wasn't home.

She rushed out the back door and ran around to the front of the house. She risked annoying her grandfather by crashing his party. Too bad. He needed her, though he might not know it.

She opened the front door and called out, "I'm home, Granddad."

No one at the table even glanced at her as she approached the dining room. They all stared at the man with thinning blond hair. He groaned and pitched face-first into the chowder.

Chapter 2

A woman across the table from the collapsed man yelped. "Scott! My poor boy."

Val rushed to Scott, intent on saving him from drowning in her chowder. She put her hands under his forehead and lifted his head from a nearly empty bowl. Not enough liquid in it to drown him.

He jerked his head, covered his face with both hands, and wiped away the trickles of chowder on his forehead and nose.

Lillian sat at the end of the table and looked askance at the man on her right. The henna-haired woman who'd called him *her boy* came around the table and peered at his face. "What's wrong?"

He looked up at her. "Feel bad, Ma. Sorry."

Scott's freckled nose made him look boyish, but the creases in his pale face suggested a man in his forties. Val glanced at the tall woman hovering over him and saw a slight resemblance between mother and son.

Junie May gaped at him from across the table. "He might have the flu."

Irene pushed her chair back from the table. "It's not flu season. Something he ate made him sick."

Junie May jumped up from her seat. "Where's my purse? I'll call 911. If it's food poisoning, they can pump his stomach at the hospital." She pounced on a leather bag near the sofa in the sitting room and pulled out a cell phone.

Scott's mother brushed her chin-length reddish hair back from her face. "Don't call an ambulance. Scott has ulcers and other tummy problems. Antacids usually help. I have some at the Village. We'll just go back there."

Granddad stood up. "*If* he's so sick, Thomasina, he's better off in the hospital. It's faster to drive him straight there than to wait for an ambulance."

Junie May fingered her antique cameo pendant. "Do you want to go to the hospital, Scott?"

He shook his head.

The reporter screwed up her face and crossed her arms, looking like a brat about to throw a tantrum.

She might have scored some airtime if the Codger Cook's dinner party had ended with an ambulance ride to the emergency room. A woman driving home with her sick son had no news value.

"Well, that settles it." Thomasina looked down at her son. "I'll drive us back to the Village. You can walk to the car, can't you?"

Scott moaned, clutched his stomach, and nodded.

A dark-haired man directly across from Scott maneuvered swiftly around the table to Scott's chair. "May I help you take him to the car?"

Val had barely noticed the trim, fiftyish man until now. He had to be the guest Granddad's girlfriend had invited at the last minute. Lillian had said his name. Something unusual. *Omar.*

Thomasina turned toward her host. "I feel so bad that we ruined your evening."

Val waited for her grandfather to absolve his guests of blame. When he didn't, she realized why. His plan to trap a crook had failed. *Tummy problems* allowed the rogue to slip the snare.

Scott got to his feet with two people supporting him. He walked with one arm around his mother's shoulder, the other in Omar's grip. The trio moved through the sitting room toward the hall. Scott swayed every few steps, and so did the leather purse hanging from Thomasina's shoulder.

Val and Junie May followed a few steps behind the sick man.

Scott paused in the hall, broke away from the two people supporting him, and rushed into the bathroom. Val winced at the sound of his retching. Granddad, Lillian, and Irene clustered at the archway between the hall and the sitting room.

Scott emerged from the bathroom after a minute or two, saying he felt better. He took deep breaths as if summoning strength and put one foot tentatively in front of the other.

Omar took his arm. "I'll help him into the car, Thomasina, and drive behind you. You may require assistance at the other end."

Scott pulled away from him and muttered, "No."

Thomasina gave her son a puzzled look. "Thank you for the offer, Omar. I'll call the aides at the Village to help me if he's still feeling poorly."

Scott took a step forward, leaning only on his mother. "I can walk."

Val slipped by them and opened the screen door. Scott stumbled. She reached out, and he grabbed her arm.

Omar sprang toward them. "Allow me to assist."

Scott's grip on Val's arm tightened. "I'm feeling better. Not much pain. I don't need help."

Yet he leaned on Val. She was glad Omar walked behind the sick man, near enough to break a fall if Scott's legs buckled.

Junie May shot a video with her smart phone while Val and Thomasina helped Scott into a black sedan parked on the street. Val waited at the curb until Thomasina drove off and then returned to the house, while Junie May stayed on the sidewalk, punching buttons on her phone.

Irene stood by the front door. She smiled at Val without showing any teeth. "All of us ate the appetizers and the salad. Scott was the only one who ate the creamy chowder. That's what made him sick."

Hard to believe everyone else wanted the light chowder. Given a choice between two types of chowder, most people selected creamy chowder, even in Manhattan, the home of red chowder. Not that it mattered which chowder Scott ate. "Getting sick after eating something doesn't mean getting sick because of it."

Irene folded her arms. "He was fine until he ate it."

Val's teeth clenched. "Food poisoning doesn't work that quickly."

"Don't be too sure of that."

Irene fancied herself an expert cook after running

a tea shop in Bayport until it went bankrupt last winter. If she didn't know how long food-poisoning symptoms took to develop, neither would most other people. She could spread her rumor around town without anyone disputing it.

Junie May came inside. "I hope you don't mind if I drive you home now, Irene."

"Not at all. I wouldn't want to eat anything else here." Irene kept her hands firmly against her body as if the walls in the house would infect her.

"I'll just go say good night to the Codger Cook." Junie May headed to the kitchen, her heels clacking on the wood floor.

The phone in the pocket of Val's cutoff jeans chimed. She excused herself from Irene and went into the study, the front room that the nineteenth-century builder would have called a *courting parlor.*

The phone's caller ID displayed Gunnar Swensen's name. Her spirits soared. "Hey, Gunnar. Good to hear from you. Where are you calling from?"

"From the mother of all traffic jams. There was an accident on the Chesapeake Bay Bridge, and I'm stuck on the other side of it. I started driving around dawn and made great time until now. I was hoping to see you tonight, but I think I'll just pull off the road, grab dinner, and wait for the traffic to ease up. That might take a while."

Though anxious to see him, she hadn't expected him to return from visiting his family in Indiana until tomorrow. And twice in the last few weeks, he'd scheduled visits to Bayport, only to cancel them. This time, with the Chesapeake Bay in sight, he might actually make it. "Do you have a place to stay tonight?"

"The B & B two blocks from you. The one on the water."

As a tourist town, Bayport usually didn't have unoccupied rooms on a Saturday night in July. If he'd arrived without a reservation, Val would have offered him a spare bedroom here, even though Granddad wouldn't have liked it. He hadn't yet warmed to Gunnar. "You scored a room at the River Edge B & B. Fancy place."

He laughed. "Not the room I have, the crow's nest, up in the attic. I got a bargain rate by taking it for a week."

"You'll probably be able to stand up without hitting your head if you stick to the center of the room."

"I hope so. If I have to stoop for a week, I'll end up your height."

"Being five-foot-three has its limitations, but I cope with them, and so can you." Val heard *good nights* coming from the hall and looked out the front windows. Irene and Junie May walked toward a silver compact car. Good riddance.

"How's your cookbook coming along?" Gunnar asked.

"It's more like a cook pamphlet right now. I finished the chapter on appetizers and the one on desserts. I'm just missing the middle. Can we get together tomorrow afternoon?"

"A real estate agent's showing me some places then. Why don't you meet me at the B & B around five-thirty? They have canoes and kayaks for guests. We can go out on the river and talk about how to spend the rest of the evening."

"Sounds great."

She hung up. How long would he stay in Bayport

this time, and could they really start over as friends? They'd agreed to that in June, after their brief and rocky romance ended. But his absence the last few weeks had left her wondering if he'd lost interest in a friendship.

She followed the aroma of coffee to the kitchen. Granddad, Lillian, and Omar stood in a tight group at the island counter.

The dishwasher, sounding like a waterfall on steroids, drowned out their conversation.

Val approached them and extended her hand to the dark-haired man. "We haven't met yet. I'm Val Deniston."

He shook her hand. "I am Omar, a friend of Lillian."

If Omar had a last name, he wasn't giving it up. "Nice to meet you, Omar." And it would be even nicer if he and Lillian would leave. Val couldn't expect straight information from her grandfather about tonight's dinner if his guests were hanging around. Time to nudge this party to a conclusion. "Junie May and Irene left, Granddad. It's just the four of us for dessert."

Omar raised his hand as if stopping traffic. "Please, not for me. I have a long drive ahead."

The wiry Omar didn't look as if he ever indulged in desserts. If he grew a straggly beard, he could pass for a hermit living off vegetation. A well-dressed hermit. His pressed white shirt, though open at the collar, cried out for a tie.

Granddad and Lillian saw Omar out. Val noticed how tidy the kitchen looked. No chowder pots on the stove. No spills, bowls, or glasses on the counter. The dishwasher at full blast. Granddad didn't usually clean up after a meal. Lillian must have done it, but she couldn't have managed it in such a short time without his assistance. Val could never get Granddad to help her clean up. Lillian obviously had more sway with him.

Val cut three slices of Key lime pie. She gave a plate with pie to Granddad and Lillian when they came into the kitchen. "You two go sit down. I'm making decaf coffee for Granddad. Would you like coffee or tea, Lillian?"

"I'll just have water."

Without hesitating, she opened the cabinet containing glassware, showing how well she knew her way around Granddad's kitchen. She took out a tall glass, filled it with ice, and added tap water.

Val brought the decaf to Granddad, who sat at the head of the table, facing the sitting room. She took her usual spot, the chair to his right. Lillian sat opposite him at the other end of the table. Grandma's chair. Resentment toward the woman taking Grandma's place left a bitter taste in Val's mouth.

Her first bite of the Key lime pie got rid of the bitterness. The pebbly graham cracker crust made the perfect foil for the smooth, sweet-and-tart filling. "I'm eating dinner in reverse tonight. Dessert now, but later I'd like some chowder leftovers."

"There isn't any leftover chowder. We finished the whole pot of light chowder. As for the creamy chowder—"

"Granddad, I'm not worried about eating the creamy chowder." She'd tasted it earlier without any bad effects. But Scott had eaten a whole bowl of it, which might make a difference. On second thought, Val would stick with the leftover salad.

Lillian closed her eyes and chewed slowly. "Umm. This is delicious."

Val opened her mouth to acknowledge the compliment.

Granddad beat her to it. "Thank you. It was easy as pie."

"Kudos to the chef." Val raised her plate like a wineglass in a mock toast. "Irene told me that only Scott ate the creamy chowder. I don't understand why. It's usually more popular than other kinds." Val looked to Lillian for an explanation because Granddad had just stuffed pie in his mouth.

"It was all so confusing. After your grandfather described the two chowders and went into the kitchen to dish them up, I asked who wanted which type of chowder. They kept changing their minds. I couldn't remember who wanted what, so I brought out one of each chowder and asked them to pass the bowls."

Granddad nodded. "Then they changed their minds again. Irene came into the kitchen to say that she and Junie May wanted a cup of each chowder instead of a bowl of one or the other. I decided to do the same. Irene said we should start with the light chowder because it would be less filling. I left the creamy chowder in the pot so it wouldn't get cold while we ate the light chowder."

"None of you got around to eating the creamy chowder?"

"When we finished the cups of light chowder, I took them off the table and ladled up the creamy chowder. I was bringing it to the table when Scott said he felt sick." Granddad chased a piece of pie around his plate with a fork. "Irene said it might be food poisoning. Nobody wanted to eat the creamy chowder after that. We threw out the whole pot in case there was something wrong with it."

Val lost her appetite. "And now there's no way to prove that there was *nothing* wrong with it."

Lillian frowned. "We just didn't want to risk anyone else getting food poisoning."

"Scott didn't have food poisoning." Val was afraid she'd have to repeat that often in the coming days. "Food-poisoning symptoms don't show up for hours or even days. Something other than the food made him sick."

Granddad pointed a fork mounded with pie at Val. "I think he faked it."

Val leaned toward him. "Why would Scott do that?" Maybe because he got wind of Granddad's plans to trap him. She took another bite of pie and waited for her grandfather to answer, but he just stuffed pie in his mouth. Val looked at Lillian. No response there either. "I saw Scott's face, Granddad. Unless he applied sallow makeup, he wasn't faking. And unless he's really good at sound effects, he was sick in the bathroom."

"Remember that syrup your mother gave you when she thought you ate poisonous berries? It made you upchuck really fast."

"Ipecac." Lillian cut off a dainty morsel of her pie. "It's off the market, but I'm sure it's still in a lot of medicine cabinets. Hardly anyone disposes of old meds."

Hardly anyone could name an off-the-market drug as fast as Lillian. Val had nearly forgotten about the berries and their aftermath, but hearing the

word *ipecac* brought the unpleasant memory back. "I
can't imagine anyone taking that foul stuff intention-
ally, unless they needed it." But she could imagine a
foul-minded person slipping it into someone else's
food and then claiming that food was poisoned.

Granddad pushed away his empty dessert plate.
"That was mighty good, if I do say so myself."

Lillian rested her fork on a plate that still had two
good bites of pie on it. "It's time I went back to the
Village."

Granddad reached for her hand. "Won't you stay
awhile? We can watch a movie."

"No, I suspect you're as tired as I am. Thank you,
Don, for the lovely dinner party."

Val nearly choked on her pie. A lovely party, when
one guest collapses in pain and the others scatter
without finishing their food? Lillian must have attended some brutal dinner parties in her life.

Granddad's girlfriend stood up, smoothing the
creases in her Capri pants. She had a trim figure for
a woman pushing seventy and could have modeled
in a jewelry ad. Rings with sparkling rocks encir-
cled the fourth finger of each hand. Gold chains of
different lengths glimmered against her powder
blue silk top. The jewelry looked expensive to Val,
but what did she know about such things? She'd
chucked the only pricey bauble she'd ever worn, a
diamond solitaire ring, flinging it at the feet of the
man who'd given it to her. She regretted some of her
impetuous acts, but not that one.

While Granddad saw Lillian to the door, Val stayed
in the dining room, wondering how to coax more
information from him about tonight's dinner. She'd

rather not tell him she'd overheard him talking to Lillian about trapping a con man.

She glanced toward the hall and saw him close the front door. "How about another sliver of pie, Granddad?" An offer he couldn't refuse . . . she hoped.

"Don't mind if I do." He returned to the dining room. "It might cheer me up."

She put seconds on his plate, delivered it to the table, and sat down. "Why did you invite Thomasina and her son to dinner tonight?"

Granddad's fork stopped on its way to his mouth. "She's one of the best-looking women at the Village, next to Lillian, of course. And Scott visits his mother on weekends. I couldn't leave him out."

He could have thrown the dinner party on a weekday and left Scott out, but not if the scammer was the guest of honor, as Lillian had said. "With all the excitement, I never introduced myself to Scott and his mother. What's their last name?"

"His name is Freaze, *F-R-E-A-Z-E*. Thomasina's name is Weal, *W-E-A-L*. I don't know if she went back to her maiden name after she split up with Scott's father, or if she remarried and got a new name that way."

"What kind of work does Scott do?"

Her grandfather dug into his pie and took his time answering. "Investment management. He gives seminars at the Village."

A good place to troll for investors to swindle. "Did you go to any of his seminars?"

"I've heard about them. Why are you asking me about him?"

Uh-oh. Granddad's guard was up. She'd better

drop the subject of Scott for now. "Just curious about your guests. Who's Omar?"

"A family friend of Lillian's. He was nearby and wanted to see her. We set an extra place at the table for him. And don't ask me his last name. I don't think Lillian said it when she introduced him."

"Where does he live?"

Granddad shrugged. "Thomasina asked him if he lived on the Eastern Shore. He said he was just passing through." He stroked his chin. "Odd thing. Scott kept looking at Omar like he was trying to place him. They didn't say anything about knowing each other."

"When Scott left the house, he shook off Omar's help and leaned on his mother and me." By then, he might have figured out how he knew Omar and wanted nothing to do with him.

Granddad scraped up the last of his pie and stood up.

Val followed him to the kitchen. She'd better warn him about Irene's hidden agenda. "I didn't expect to see Irene Pritchard here tonight."

"Me neither. Junie May asked if she could bring a guest. She didn't tell me who she was bringing."

"I can guess why Junie May contacted you and brought Irene with her tonight. Irene convinced her to interview you."

Granddad's mouth turned down in skepticism. "I don't think so. Junie May interviews prominent local people all the time."

"Prominent people around here live in waterfront estates that have names like English country houses. They're business tycoons, best-selling authors, and former cabinet members." The local rag's recipe writer was so far down the Eastern Shore's celebrity totem pole, he was buried in the ground. "Irene's a generation older than Junie May. They have nothing obvious in common. Yet they came here together because they had a common purpose—to expose the Codger Cook as a fraud."

Granddad dropped his dessert dish in the sink with a clatter. "What?"

"Irene wants to get back at both of us. She was slated to manage the Cool Down Café until I came along. Then when you won the contest for the new recipe columnist, she was furious because she expected to win. She went around saying you knew nothing about cooking and I was writing the column for you."

Granddad frowned. "Why didn't you tell me that?"

"I didn't want to upset you. She was on a rampage that day and even accused me of withholding evidence in a murder." Totally false, unlike Irene's claim about the recipe column. "What difference would it have made if I told you what she said? You weren't going to turn her away at the door tonight."

"I wouldn't have been so nice to her. You shouldn't keep secrets from me. How am I supposed to protect myself if I don't know who my enemies are?"

"Protect yourself or protect your Codger Cook scam?"

His face turned red, a stark contrast to his white fringes of hair. "It's not a scam. I'm not harming anyone or taking their money." He glared at her.

She opened the door to the dishwasher and stepped back from the blast of hot, moist air. "You keep secrets from me too."

The phone rang and stopped her from telling

him something that would have steamed him even more—that she'd eavesdropped on his scam chowder conversation with Lillian.

"I'll get it." He hustled out of the kitchen toward the front hall, the only place on the first floor with a landline.

She gave up on emptying the dishwasher until the plates cooled off. She walked past the hall toward the study and heard him say into the phone, "I'm sorry to hear that, Thomasina."

Val felt a sense of dread so strong it took her breath away.

Chapter 3

Granddad hung up the hall phone and swept his hand across his forehead as if wiping away sweat. "That was Thomasina. She says Scott's worse. In pain and upchucking."

Val released a relieved breath. She'd feared even worse news. "She called just to tell you that?"

"To find out if anyone else got sick. I told her they were all fine when they left." The skin around his eyes and mouth sagged as if gravity exerted more power than usual. "Irene had a chance to put that upchuck syrup in the chowder. She sneaked into the kitchen when Thomasina and Scott came to the door. I got away as soon as I could and found Irene in the kitchen by herself."

Val remembered how long she'd sat on the staircase after hearing the doorbell ring and the dog bark. "She had enough time to contaminate the chowder, but I tasted the creamy chowder after that, and I feel fine."

He pointed his index finger at her. "Maybe you

didn't get enough of it, or you ate it before her secret ingredient had time to dissolve. She wouldn't care how many people she made sick, as long as she wasn't one of them."

Val couldn't disagree with his assessment of Irene's character, but his scenario had a few weak points. "To contaminate a whole pot of creamy chowder, she'd have needed a lot of ipecac or whatever else—"

"She had a purse as big as a carpetbag with her, and she took it with her to the kitchen."

"But with no leftover chowder, we have no proof Irene added anything to it. Did you throw out the chowder or did Lillian?"

Granddad scratched his head and looked up at the ceiling as if checking for a leak. "I threw it out, but it was Irene's idea to chuck it."

Val believed the second half of his answer, but not the first. "Irene will look ridiculous if she keeps harping on food poisoning. I'm going to research foodborne illnesses on medical websites to prove she's wrong."

She went into the study while he stood near the sitting-room fireplace, staring into space. She sat at her computer and jiggled the mouse to awaken the display. The sites she checked confirmed what she'd told Irene earlier. "I was right, Granddad. Most types of food poisoning take a day or more to sicken people. Staph could appear in as short a time as two hours, but Scott's symptoms came on much faster than that."

A few more seconds at her computer should settle whether she or Granddad was right about the definition of *scam*. She brought up her favorite online dictionary.

Granddad came up behind her and leaned over her shoulder. "That's not a medical site. You looked up *scam*. What does it say? *A scheme to obtain money or something else of value through the use of false pretenses.*" He straightened up. "So you were wrong. The Codger Cook column is not a scam. No one's losing anything of value because of it."

Val could have said that the pittance the newspaper paid for the column gave him money that a more qualified recipe writer ought to receive, but she had a stronger argument. "See what else it says on the screen? *False pretenses include confidence tricks in which individuals misrepresent themselves as experts.* You've misrepresented yourself as a food expert and gained something of value, a reputation as a cook." She expected him to argue with her, as usual.

Instead, he said nothing. His shoulders slumped. "It's late. I'm going to bed." He shuffled out of the room.

Full of pep before the dinner party, he'd looked forward to impressing a TV reporter and outmaneuvering a con man. In the last two hours, he'd aged ten years, resembling a man in his eighties rather than his seventies. Val wished she hadn't added to his burdens tonight by labeling his column a scam.

She followed him down the hall to his room. "For a while, you were trying out my recipes before submitting them, but not recently. Go back to doing that. Before long, you'll *become* the cook you pretend to be."

He closed his door and probably his ears to her suggestion.

She returned to the computer and typed "Scott Freaze" in a search box. His investment business, located in a suburb of Washington, D.C., had dozens of clients that rated his services as "good," "very good," or "excellent." A handful of reviewers rated his services lower, saying their investments didn't do as well as they anticipated. Given that clients unhappy with a product or service were more likely to post an online review than those pleased with it, Scott had decent ratings. Of course, he could have paid people to write positive reviews.

Val tried a more specific search. Coupling Scott's name with *scam, swindle,* or *fraud* didn't produce any hits. If he only ripped off the elderly, though, he victimized the people least likely to complain about him online. Or maybe he wasn't a scammer after all.

The Cool Down Café at the Bayport Racket and Fitness Club had barely a dozen customers the following morning. Val couldn't attract breakfast eaters despite the enticing aromas of freshly brewed coffee and the vanilla-and-butter scent of baked French toast. No one was around to sniff those aromas on a beautiful Sunday in late July. Temperatures in the mid-eighties and uncharacteristically low humidity drove the fitness worshippers outdoors. Who'd want to climb on a treadmill or recumbent bike when they could jog or cycle in peace along the water's edge? Who'd want to sit at a rowing machine looking at treadmills when they could paddle on the river?

With the tennis leagues on hiatus until September, the club's courts attracted fewer players. Most of Val's tennis teammates had left town for vacation.

The morning's high point occurred around eleven o'clock when Val had two occupied bistro tables. Three women, who faithfully attended the Sunday-morning yoga class, sat at one table, a pair of college-age men at another.

Val was making a fresh pot of coffee when she heard footsteps. Her tennis teammate and café assistant, Bethany O'Shay, galumphed toward her in magenta clogs.

"So, Val, food poisoning at your house?" Bethany's voice matched her clothes—loud. Her bubblegum pink peasant top bloused over a cranberry red skirt. The colors clashed with her tangle of ginger curls. "How did the food get poisoned?"

"It didn't." Val glanced at the bistro tables. Her customers had given up talking and eating in favor of listening. Here was her chance to set the record straight, even if just for a small audience. She matched Bethany's loud tones. "A man came to dinner and got sick before anything he ate at our house could have bothered him."

Bethany approached the counter where Val stood. "So he ate something bad before he went to your house?"

"I didn't say that. He probably had a stomach virus."

Bethany sat at the eating bar. "I hope you didn't get anywhere near him."

The women at a bistro table pushed their half-eaten yogurt parfaits away and stood up. One of the young men eyed his quiche with suspicion. Val had to restrain herself from shouting, *My name isn't Typhoid Mary!*

She walked around the counter and sat on the stool next to Bethany's. With their backs to the customers, they could have a private conversation. "Where did you hear about last night's dinner?"

"People were talking about it outside the church."

"Does Irene Pritchard go to your church?" At Bethany's nod, Val continued, "She's the source of the food-poisoning lie. She's been dissing my grandfather for weeks."

"Then how come he invited her to dinner?"

"He didn't. Another guest at the dinner brought her along. I really appreciate your coming by and telling me what you heard." Earlier in the summer, Bethany had worked in the café from late morning to closing time at two. Val felt bad about hiring her as an assistant and then cutting back on her hours barely more than a month later. But with café profits down, she had no choice. "Want something to eat? Besides the usual lunch stuff, I have a lot of breakfast leftovers."

"Breakfast here is mostly grains and dairy. They're a no-no on my diet."

Bethany could use a few more no-no's in her clothes-shopping list. Her neon colors and ruffles suited the six-year-old girls she taught, but they made a generously proportioned woman like her look bulky.

"What kind of food is a yes-yes on this diet?" Val hoped it had more variety than Bethany's previous diet, which required downing cabbage soup at every meal.

"Lots of meat and some fruit and nuts. It's the caveman diet."

Val hadn't discouraged Bethany from going on the cabbage soup diet. Though unappetizing, it wouldn't do any harm. The caveman diet didn't sound healthy. "Cavemen had a life expectancy of thirty years. Let's say you follow that diet for five years. By then, you'll be thirty. A diet based on animal proteins and fats will take its toll."

"You're exaggerating."

A little, and Val should have saved her breath, given that Bethany's diets had a life expectancy of five days.

Val's cell phone chimed. She jumped off the stool, walked around the counter, and picked up the phone she'd left near the coffee machine. Her mother was calling. Odd. She usually called the land-line at the house rather than Val's cell phone.

"Hi, Mom. I'm at the café. Can I call you back later?"

"Don't call me from the house. I want to talk to you about something your grandfather shouldn't hear."

Val's curiosity kicked in. What did Mom want to hide from her own father? "Okay. Give me a second." She put the phone against her shoulder and said to Bethany. "Can you take over for a few minutes?"

"Sure." Bethany clomped to the food prep side of the counter.

Val took the phone to the café's far corner, where a table for six offered the most privacy. She sat on the settee. "What's up, Mom?"

"I found out something about your grandfather that worries me."

Could her mother, two thousand miles away in Florida, have heard about last night's dinner party?

News goes viral in a small town as fast as it does on the Internet, and Mom, who'd grown up in Bayport, still had friends here, aka spies. "What have you heard?"

"That he's taken up with a good-looking woman ten years younger than he is." Her mother's voice sounded as if she'd had to force the words through pursed lips.

Val released the breath she'd been holding. With any luck, rumors about last night's dinner would blow over before they blew south. "Who told you that?"

"Ned called me. Don't tell your grandfather. He might turn on his best friend for talking behind his back. Do you know anything about this woman?"

"Granddad's been seeing someone for the last five or six weeks. Her name's Lillian. I don't know if she's a whole decade younger, but she's close."

"Ned said she might be a gold digger. What do you think?"

Based on Lillian's jewelry last night, Val would call her a gold *flaunter,* but that didn't necessarily make her a *digger.* "Fortunately, Granddad doesn't have much gold to dig. He always says Ned's a worrywart."

"Don't let your grandfather's tightwad ways fool you. He has money squirreled away. Besides that, he has the house. What happens to it if he marries her?"

While her mother talked, a long-legged blonde in formfitting shorts and a top that bared her midriff came into the café. Spandex Barbie sat on a stool at the eating bar. Bethany approached her.

"What were we talking about, Mom? Oh yeah, the house. If Granddad marries Lillian, you probably won't inherit it, but you never planned on moving back anyway."

"This isn't about inheriting. Dad and I have enough to be comfortable, but Lillian may push *you* out of the house."

Keep that from happening, a little demon inside Val growled, but a sweeter voice reminded her not to be selfish. "Then I'll find somewhere else to live. If Lillian makes Granddad happy and he wants her to move in, it's none of my business."

"But will she make him happy? He's been glum since your grandmother died. If Lillian takes him for all he's worth or even drops him suddenly, he may go into full-blown depression. That's really dangerous for older people."

Val could dismiss all her mother's concerns except that one. "What do you want me to do?"

"Dig up what you can about her. I understand she's not from around there. Find out where she comes from and what brought her to Bayport."

"I'll look into it, Mom."

"And keep your grandfather busy so he has less time to spend with women. Make him cook instead of just modifying your recipes for his column."

"That would keep me busy too, cleaning up after his kitchen disasters. Speaking of busy, I'd better get back to work."

Val ended the call, stood up, and walked toward the counter. Bethany raised her chin at Val and flicked her wrist three times. Val checked her step. What did the pantomime mean?

The woman at the eating bar leaned down to rummage in her athletic bag. Bethany mouthed *no* and used her wrist again to shoo Val away.

Val shrugged, went back to the settee, and made a pretense of using her phone. Though the café alcove was small, the music blasting from the adjacent exercise room kept her from hearing anything said at the counter. That left her nothing to do but look at the back of the spandex woman's head and her hair woven into a French braid. Even if Val's hair suddenly uncurled itself and turned sleek, she wouldn't have the dexterity or the patience to plait it in such an intricate way. And it would take a lot of peroxide to turn her cinnamon-colored hair blond.

The woman held up her phone to Bethany, who peered at it and shook her head.

Two middle-aged men in athletic shorts and T-shirts seated themselves at a bistro table that gave them a good view of the woman at the eating bar. Val had often seen those same men pass the café alcove without stopping, but today the place had a new attraction. Unfortunately for them, it didn't last long. A minute after they sat down, the spandex woman left without having ordered anything to eat or drink. They followed her with their eyes. Val sprang up to wait on them before they followed the woman out like a pair of dogs. Bethany apparently had the same idea. She reached the men's table before Val did, explained the daily specials, and took their orders.

Val went back to the counter and made Bethany a lunch no caveman could resist—turkey and fresh fruit salad. She put the platter on the eating bar. "Thanks for taking over, Bethany. Go ahead and have lunch while I make the sandwiches those guys want, but don't keep me in suspense any longer. Who was the tall blonde, and why did you shoo me away when you were talking to her?"

Bethany sat on the stool the woman had vacated. "She thought her fiancé might be here playing tennis. When she asked for him at the tennis desk, Yumiko recognized his name and said the woman who runs the café played tennis with him a few times and might know where to find him. That's you, of course, but Blondie assumed I ran the café because I was behind the counter."

Val sliced an avocado for the sandwiches. "What's her fiancé's name?"

Bethany leaned across the eating bar as if she had classified information to share. "Gunnar."

Chapter 4

Val tried to digest the news that Gunnar's fiancée had shown up in the café.

Bethany speared a piece of turkey with her fork and gave Val a sympathetic look. "So you didn't know about his fiancée?"

"Gunnar told me he was engaged and his fiancée called off the wedding." Now that Val had seen the fiancée, she could understand the regret she'd detected when he spoke of that broken engagement. "What did you say when the woman asked for him?"

"I told her I never met anyone by that name. That's true. Of course, I knew you'd gone out with a man named Gunnar, but I didn't tell her that."

Val assembled the turkey and avocado sandwiches for the men at the bistro table. "Did she actually say they were engaged?"

"She implied it, and that's why I waved you off. I didn't want you walking into something awkward. But after we got to talking, she said she'd had a disagreement with him. She wanted to patch things up, but couldn't find him. He'd moved out of his apartment in Washington and quit his job. Someone gave her a forwarding address for him, a post office box here in town."

"So she drove here? Why wouldn't she just phone him or send e-mail if she wanted to reconcile?"

"Maybe she did, and he didn't answer. He's probably avoiding Blondie because he prefers you."

"Right. He prefers me to a woman with a Miss America body. Her hair is luxurious, blond, and obedient, whereas this"—Val tugged at her unruly curls—"has a mind of its own. Of course I didn't see Blondie's face. What word would you use to describe it?" Val hoped for *hideous*, but would settle for *interesting*, which covered a multitude of flaws.

Bethany squeezed her eyes shut, apparently trying to summon a vision of the woman. "Mouth too small, nose too narrow, eyes too close together, but otherwise she's not bad-looking."

"Describe that face in one word."

"Well, um, she's pretty. But you're cute."

"Cute. For most men, that doesn't cut the mustard, to borrow one of Granddad's phrases." Val heaped fruit salad on the sandwich platters she'd just made. "The two guys over there didn't come into the café for lunch or for cute. They came in for tall, pretty, and encased in spandex."

"I've never met Gunnar. Maybe he's different from most men, or maybe Blondie's looking for a different Gunnar."

"If Bayport has two tennis-playing Gunnars with former fiancées, I'll eat that spandex suit of hers."

Bethany giggled. "She showed me a photo of Gunnar on her phone. Dark hair, nice smile, crooked nose, and . . . well, he's not exactly handsome. No offense, Val."

"None taken. My ex-fiancé, total eye candy, cheated on me. I don't look for handsome anymore." Val delivered the sandwich platters to the two men and went back behind the counter.

Bethany finished her turkey and started on her fruit salad. "Tell me about your grandfather's dinner and why Irene talked about food poisoning."

Without saying she'd cooked the meal, Val described the dinner and its aftermath.

Bethany put down her fork. "I volunteer at Ambleside Village. I might know the two women who went to the dinner. What are their names?"

"Lillian Hinker, Granddad's girlfriend, and Thomasina Weal, who brought her son with her. He's the one who got sick."

"Haven't met them."

"What do you do as a volunteer?"

"I take Muffin there for pet-a-pet sessions. Most of the residents don't have pets, but they love playing with other people's dogs. I'm scheduled to be there tomorrow at two-thirty. I can ask the people who show up if they know Lillian and Thomasina."

Inside information—just what Val needed. "Can I go with you? I've never been to the Village, and I'd like to look around."

"You can't fool me. You want to find out about your grandfather's girlfriend. Shouldn't be hard. The people who live at the Village all know each other's business and love to gossip."

Sweet words. Val perked up as two more bistro tables filled with customers.

* * *

Val spent over an hour at the café after closing time, cleaning up and getting ready for breakfast the next day. On the way home, she stopped for groceries. It was after four by the time she steered around the corner onto her street. A cluster of neighbors and strangers stood on the sidewalk near the house and blocked the driveway.

Val's heart lurched. Had something happened to Granddad? She parked in front of a neighbor's house, jumped from the car, and skirted the knot of people blocking her view. Her grandfather stood between the sidewalk and the front porch. No EMTs attending to him, just the media.

Granddad wore his Codger Cook apron and beamed at a camera. Junie May, standing next to him, also faced the camera, but with a more somber expression.

At a nod from the cameraman, she spoke into her microphone. "This is Junie May Jussup outside the Bayport home of Don Myer, also known as the Codger Cook, the recipe columnist for the *Treadwell Gazette*. Mr. Myer, tell us how long you've lived on the Eastern Shore." She put the mike in front of Granddad.

"My whole life. I left to serve my country in Korea and came right back. I've lived in this house for more than fifty years." Granddad gestured toward the structure behind him, as if anyone could miss the behemoth Victorian.

Junie May tilted the microphone toward herself. "I'd planned to interview Mr. Myer in this house and tape him cooking in his kitchen. Today we're talking to him for another reason."

Granddad's grin disappeared faster than the Cheshire cat.

"We have breaking news about a man who was visiting his mother at Ambleside Village, located between Bayport and Treadwell. Early this morning, Scott Freaze went to the Treadwell Hospital emergency room, suffering from severe gastroenteritis. This afternoon, Mr. Freaze passed away in the hospital."

Val gasped. Granddad's jaw dropped. The neighbors murmured. Val wanted to tear the microphone away from Junie May and hit her on the head with it. Under the guise of publicity for the Codger Cook, she'd lured Granddad in front of a camera, only to ambush him.

Junie May held the mike close. "The unfortunate man ate his last meal at this house, a meal the Codger Cook prepared. I was present at the dinner during which Mr. Freaze became ill. One of the other guests suggested food poisoning as the possible reason for that illness. What's your response to that, Mr. Myer?"

Granddad grabbed the microphone from Junie May, his face red and his jaw set. He looked directly into the camera. "First, let me offer my sympathies to Scott Freaze's mother. No parent should have to suffer losing a child. I am very sorry for your loss, Thomasina."

Bravo, Granddad. Val would have applauded, except that she didn't want to attract attention and find herself in front of a camera.

Junie May leaned sideways to talk into the microphone, which Granddad held tight. "I second that sentiment. When we report the news, we get so caught up in the story that we sometimes lose sight of the human pain behind it."

Granddad stepped away from her, taking the mike with him. "Reporting news is not the same as broadcasting rumors. Now about that rumor you brought up, food poisoning can't explain what happened to that man. Its symptoms take longer to show up."

Junie May wrenched the mike from him. "That's true of the common foodborne illnesses—salmonella, botulism, and E. coli. But toxic-shellfish symptoms show up much faster."

Granddad closed the distance between them and bent toward her microphone. "I've been eating critters that come in shells for seventy years. Never got sick. Never heard of anyone dying from eating them."

Junie May nodded. "Improper handling can make fish toxic, but you're quite right. Death from shellfish poisoning is rare."

Val wondered if she'd heard right. She'd expected a "gotcha" from the reporter, not support for Granddad. But maybe Junie May was trying to lull Granddad before dropping another bombshell.

"According to our local food expert"—Junie May nodded toward Granddad without a trace of sarcasm in her voice—"Scott Freaze couldn't have died from the chowder he ate last night. Then how did he die? What killed him? The doctors must have some idea, but haven't released that information. I can only tell you what I *saw*. Shortly after Scott Freaze died, the police arrived at the hospital."

The onlookers gasped. Granddad's eyes bugged out.

Harvey, Granddad's sixtyish next-door neighbor, grabbed Val's elbow. "She shouldn't shock an old man like that. And some rubbernecking tourists trampled on my flower bed. Can't you get rid of those TV folks, chase them off the property?"

They would just decamp to the public sidewalk. Val fingered her car keys and fob. Maybe she could get Junie May to leave on her own. "I'm going to set off my car alarm, Harvey. If you turn on yours too, they might not be able to record good audio." Val pointed the fob toward her car and pressed the red button. Her car emitted raucous beeps.

Harvey reached into his pocket.

Junie May stared straight at the camera. "That noise you're hearing is someone's car alarm going off. Let's get Mr. Myer's reaction to the news—" She broke off as a series of whoops, beeps, and reverberating chirps came from Harvey's driveway, which abutted Granddad's. Junie May's mouth moved, but no one could hear her over the din. She turned toward the cameraman and made a throat-slitting gesture with her index finger. He lowered his camera.

Val caught Granddad's eye and waved her car keys at him. He gave her a thumbs-up. He fumbled under his apron, pulled out his keys, and discreetly aimed his fob at the Buick parked in front of the house. His car emitted a shrill wail. The cameraman near the Buick and most of the bystanders covered their ears.

Granddad disappeared into the house. End of interview. The audience dispersed.

Junie May and the cameraman drove off, leaving only Val and Harvey on the sidewalk.

Harvey silenced his car. "That was fun."

Val had never before heard him say anything was fun. Most of the time, he complained. "Thanks for helping, even though car alarms get on your nerves."

"I hate pushy people with cameras even more than I hate car alarms. Just don't set off your alarm at midnight, like you did in June."

He probably knew the exact date she'd done it. "Aye, aye, sir." She saluted and went inside. Like her father, Harvey had retired from the navy.

Granddad sat in the easy chair facing the bookshelves near the fireplace. He rubbed the bridge of his nose, his eyes downcast. "Scott's dead. What a disaster."

"He didn't fake his sickness after all. Why did you think he did?" Her grandfather had avoided answering that question the last time she asked it.

"He was a pro at faking, as crooked as a barrel of fish hooks. Ned invested with him. Now he'll never get his money back. And it's all my fault."

Val sank into the worn tweed sofa and folded the Codger Cook apron he'd left there in a heap. "I'm sorry Ned lost money on an investment, but how is it your fault?"

"He expected a nest egg from selling his house. He heard Scott's spiel and wanted my advice on investing with him. We checked Scott's business references. He sounded legit, so I told Ned to go ahead."

"What made you change your mind about Scott?"

"Lillian heard a man lost his life savings after investing with him. Ned doesn't know that. I didn't want to tell him without first trying to get his money back."

That explained why Granddad had left his buddy

off the guest list for last night's dinner. "How were you going to get Scott to give the money back?"

"Shame him into returning it. I figured with a newswoman here and his mother, he'd knuckle under and write a check to prove he'd done nothing wrong."

"Since when does a con man have shame? Why not report him to the police?"

"A fraud investigation might tie up Scott's money. I planned to go to the police, but not until after I got Ned's investment back." Granddad sighed. "With Scott dead, I don't know how to get that money."

"Ned should see a lawyer about that. You did what you could for him, Granddad." And wound up in a bad spot. He looked so despondent that Val wanted to cheer him up. "How about a piece of leftover pie?"

"I'm not hungry."

If sweets wouldn't improve his mood, maybe flattery would. "You handled the food-poisoning issue well during that interview and put Junie May in her place."

"I got the feeling she expected me to say that. She wasn't following Irene's lead about the food poisoning like you thought. And she wasn't doing a puff piece on me like I hoped." He straightened his bifocals. "What was the point of her interview?"

"Airtime. The local TV station would have no interest in a man who doesn't live around here dying in the hospital. Junie May needed a local angle. You were it—the food columnist and lifelong resident who served the dead man his last meal. That's enough to get her a spot on tonight's news. But what about tomorrow's news? She plants a seed—the police at the hospital—and hints at foul play in the man's death."

Granddad's mouth turned down at the corners. "She wouldn't make that up."

"I agree. The police went there, but we don't know why. Maybe an ambulance brought a road accident victim to the hospital and the police needed a statement."

"I hope you're right." Granddad took longer than usual to hoist himself out of the easy chair. "I'm going to the Village."

"To tell Ned about Scott?"

"To talk to Lillian. I can't face Ned yet. If Thomasina's there, I'll give her my sympathies. I sure hope she doesn't blame me for what happened."

Val walked with him to the front door. "Be careful driving. That interview was enough to shake anybody up."

"You had a clever way to cut it short." He held up his car key fob. "I'll be back before dinnertime."

And Val better have something ready for him to heat up in case she and Gunnar went out to dinner after their boat ride. On second thought, this wasn't the right night to leave Granddad alone. She'd just invite Gunnar for dinner.

The table in the hallway held the day's mail, most of it junk addressed to Granddad. Packets with discount coupons, sweepstake offers, come-ons for pills to restore youthful vigor. She had junk mail too, but targeted toward a younger demographic. Granddad had a few real letters. Though she'd set up automatic deductions for his electric and telephone bills, he banked the old-fashioned way. His bank still sent account statements by snail mail. He'd already opened an envelope from the bank, but the monthly bill for his newspaper subscription and a letter from a car dealer remained sealed.

Val glanced at the bank letter he'd left open on the table. The word *overdraft* popped out. Maybe Granddad's buddy wasn't the only one with financial woes.

Chapter 5

Val eyed the letter on the hall table from Granddad's bank. Until moving in with him, she'd played by the rules. She wouldn't have even considered reading someone else's mail. His more flexible ethics must have infected her, though, because she came up with justifications for reading his letter. She might have jumped to the wrong conclusion from reading just a single word. Maybe the bank had sent the letter to notify customers of a change in its overdraft policy. Reading the letter might ease her concerns about his finances.

She picked it up and felt a flutter of anxiety in her stomach. She read the letter. Yes, Granddad's account was overdrawn. He'd told her he kept a sizable cushion in his checking account. Gone now. What had become of it? The flutter inside Val turned into a knot. Ned might not have been the only one to invest money with a scammer. Granddad would be reluctant to tell her if he too had been taken in.

Should she share the bank news with her mother? Not yet. Her mother might overreact. No reason to start a family ruckus about an overdraft. A mistake by Granddad or even a computer glitch might explain the shortfall in his account. And a rapid response from Mom wouldn't make much difference in the final outcome.

Val went into the kitchen. Cooking something sweet would calm her. She set the ingredients for chocolate chunk cookies on the counter. Creaming butter and sugar usually put her into a trance powerful enough to take her mind off any troubles, at least temporarily. Not today. As she stirred in the chocolate chunks, one problem after another intruded on her thoughts. Gunnar's glamorous ex-fiancée arriving to claim him back. A man getting sick and dying after eating in this house. A possible police inquiry into that man's death.

She dropped the dough by spoonfuls onto the cookie sheet. She'd take some cookies to Gunnar later at his B & B. Did his former fiancée bake cookies? She couldn't possibly consume them and keep that svelte figure . . . unless she was one of those women who ate with abandon and didn't gain weight. If so, Val would envy the woman's metabolism more than her height or hair.

Val paddled vigorously to work off the cookies she'd eaten. Gunnar, the stronger paddler, sat behind her in the canoe's stern. He saw only her back, as she'd seen his ex-fiancée's back this morning, but what a different view. Instead of black spandex, Val wore khaki Bermuda shorts and a white tank top. Instead of upswept intricate braids of hair, she had whorls and spirals pointing in different directions.

Sitting tandem wasn't conducive to conversation. Gunnar talked about his plans to study acting, now that he'd quit his job in favor of part-time self-employment. As they paddled between the river's tree-lined banks, his voice washed over her like a melody, smooth and seductive, with a depth that suggested something dark. He'd never make a handsome leading man, but he could play the tragic hero.

Just short of the bay's open water, Gunnar laid his paddle in the canoe with a thump. "Forget paddling. Let's drift for a few minutes."

She took her paddle out of the water and turned around in her seat to face him. Her pulse kicked up at his smile. Over the last few weeks, she'd forgotten how that smile affected her.

Had his ex tracked him down? Val didn't want to bring up the subject, but maybe he would if she coaxed a bit. "How was your day? Any surprises?" Not exactly a subtle question.

"No surprises. I spent most of the day with the real estate agent. I asked to see small houses where I could have room for an office and living space."

"You'd know how to deduct a home office." With his accounting background and his former job with the IRS, he probably knew the tax code inside out. "Did you see anything you liked?"

He looked past her toward the wide expanse of the bay. "She showed me two places for sale that would work well, a small bungalow and a Cape Cod on side streets. But a rental would make more sense for me."

A change of plans? "Because you're not sure you'll stay in Bayport?"

"For the first time in my life, I don't have a safe job tying me down. I can open an accounting practice anywhere. Is this the right place to live if I also want to take up acting?"

"I asked you that question last month." He'd responded then with a firm *yes*. Where had that firmness gone? Maybe the slinky blonde had given him a reason to return to Washington. "You already miss life in the big city?"

"The pace here suits me better. I don't know whether anything else will pan out for me here. The business venture, the acting, and the"—he leaned forward and locked eyes with her—"the friendship."

That depended on how committed he was to just a friendship. Did he now want more than that? Did she? "You can't know how anything will work out unless you give it a try."

He put his paddle in the water. "Trying means renting, not buying a house."

She couldn't fault his commitment phobia when she suffered from it herself. "Six months ago, when I walked out on my life in New York and came here, I wouldn't have bought a place either. Fortunately, my grandfather had room for me."

"How's he doing?"

"He's fine physically, but otherwise iffy. It's a long story. I can turn around in my seat and go back to paddling, or I can tell you the story."

"Clever ploy to get out of paddling. Okay, you talk while I power us back to the B & B."

She told him what happened at the chowder dinner, leaving out her role in preparing the food.

He assumed, like everyone else except Irene, that the newspaper's recipe columnist could actually cook. While she talked about the allegations of food poisoning, Gunnar paddled rhythmically and listened without comment.

His paddle slowed when she mentioned the financial scam. "What's this con man's name? I'll try to do some research on him."

"Scott Freaze." Val spelled the name.

"Great-Aunt Gretchen nearly fell for a scam like that. Luckily, she asked my advice before she handed over any money."

Back in June, when Val questioned Gunnar's honesty, she'd doubted the existence of that aunt and the inheritance he'd received from her. "Your aunt went to the right person for advice. My grandfather advised his friend Ned to invest with the scammer, and may have even invested money himself."

"People who target the elderly are bottom-feeding lowlifes, almost as bad as child abusers." Gunnar wielded the paddle with a vigor that splashed up water. "Older people are easy marks for cons. They grew up when crime was rare. They respect authority, trust people, and want to please them. All those good qualities make them vulnerable."

"If all fraud victims respect authority, trust others, and try to please, I can rest easy." Val stretched out her legs. "Granddad doesn't have any of those traits."

Gunnar grinned. "You're hard on him. Those aren't the only traits of con victims. They also like to feel special and score a bargain."

"*Now* you've described Granddad. He always wants something for nothing. But I'd be surprised if he fell for a too-good-to-be-true scheme."

"Maybe he didn't. Safe investments these days don't pay as well as they used to. Your grandfather and his friend probably remember making ten percent on CDs. If the con man promised a return like that, they'd have less reason to suspect fraud."

Val hoped Gunnar's knowledge of financial scams encompassed how to recover from them. "How can a victim of investment fraud get the money back?"

"It's hard to prove financial fraud because it can look like bad investment advice. You can't put someone in jail or demand restitution for that."

"Even if it happens over and over?"

"A pattern of rip-offs would strengthen the case, but older people make bad witnesses because of their poor memory for details. Most of them don't even tell anyone they've lost money. They're ashamed or afraid their children will take over the purse strings."

Maybe Granddad had said his friend made a bad investment to avoid admitting he'd done it himself. Val made a mental note to talk to Ned. "You're not cheering me up, Gunnar."

"Would a dinner at the Tuscan Eaterie cheer you up?"

Val had gone there when the restaurant first opened and had left unimpressed, but maybe by now the chef had gotten his act together. She'd like to give it another try. "Yes, it would cheer me up, but I'd rather not leave Granddad by himself tonight. He's had a rough day." Gunnar's B & B came into view, a two-and-a-half-story Colonial with wings, one of the larger riverfront dwellings. "Why don't you eat with us? Nothing fancy."

He fingered his cargo shorts. "Does that mean I won't have to change clothes?"

"If you change into a tux, we'll do a *Downton Abbey* dinner. Otherwise, shorts and a T-shirt are fine."

He maneuvered the canoe toward the shore and climbed out where the water was only knee high. "Stay in your seat. I'll tug the canoe onto land."

Once she climbed from the canoe, they turned it upside down, next to the kayaks.

She pointed toward the top floor of the B & B. "You must have a good view if you're in the room with dormer windows."

"My window is on the front, facing the parking area. The view's not bad as long as I don't look down. Above the trees, I can see the turret on your grandfather's house."

As they walked from the B & B to the house, Val talked about her mother's concern that Granddad had fallen for a gold digger. "The woman he's seeing, Lillian Hinker, is younger than he is, good-looking, and in great shape."

"Your mother's afraid of a sweetheart scam. A lot of old, and not so old, people fall for that one."

She winced. "You missed your cue. You were supposed to tell me not to worry about Lillian."

"For years I tracked down the proceeds from criminal activities. You expect me to restore your faith in human nature?" He squeezed her arm. "I'll try. Women are usually the targets in sweetheart scams, not the culprits. Scams are the exception, not the rule. Widows and widowers often find mates who make them happy. How's that for upbeat?"

"I'm hungry for good news. I'll take whatever crumbs I can get."

"Who else was at the dinner besides Lillian, Scott, and your grandfather?"

Val put the phone down and looked through the screen door. Her grandfather climbed out of his white Buick, carrying a plastic grocery bag. She rushed out and met him on the sidewalk in front of the house. "You've been gone awhile."

"I didn't want to miss my interview on the evening news. Lillian and I watched it at her place. How did I look on TV?"

"I wasn't here to watch the news." She saw her grandfather's face fall. "Sorry. I saw most of the interview live. Did they cut anything?"

"Only the cars honking." He started up the path to the house. "Lillian said the camera didn't get me from my best angle. Next time, I'll stand on the other side of the interviewer."

May that next time be a long way off. "Did you get a chance to talk to Thomasina?"

"There was a please-don't-disturb note on her door. I can understand that."

Val eyed his plastic bag. "You went to the supermarket."

He stopped walking and planted his feet like a warrior defending a stronghold. "Do you know how long it's been since I had a nice piece of rare beef?"

"Well, I haven't cooked any for you since February." After moving in with Granddad, she'd followed her mother's directive to reduce his red-meat intake. "But you've gone to restaurants and eaten with friends since then. You must have tasted beef in the six months."

"Not as good as this." He held up the bag. "Tenderloin tips. I'm sure you'll enjoy it too, as a change from meat and fish. There's plenty for both of us."

"In order, from oldest to youngest. Scott's mother, Thomasina Weal, from the retirement village. A local woman, Irene Pritchard. Omar, a mystery man Lillian added to the guest list just before the dinner." Val ticked the guests on her fingers. "Junie May Jussup, a reporter for the Salisbury television station."

"The name sounds familiar. I must have seen her on the TV. Thin, late thirties, straight dark hair?"

"That's Junie May." Val peered down the street as they rounded the corner. Granddad's car wasn't parked in front of the house. "My grandfather's not back yet. When he comes home, don't say anything about the scammer or Lillian or my concerns about his money. Let's just keep it light."

"I'll check his video collection for a frothy film we can all watch."

"He's mostly into Hitchcock and film noir. You'd think, with all the femme fatales he's seen on the screen, he would have his guard up."

"Few men can resist an ego-stroking beauty."

The voice of experience? Val heard his rueful tone and saw the grim set of his mouth, maybe because she wanted to hear and see them.

They went inside the house and browsed for movies. Granddad's collection, the stock from the video store he used to run, filled half the shelves flanking the fireplace in the sitting room.

The hall phone rang. Val hurried to answer it and glanced at the caller ID. The Bayport Police. Her heart leapt into her throat. She had visions of Granddad in a smashed-up car.

"Hello, this is Val Deniston."

"Val, it's Chief Yardley. How're you doing?"

She relaxed. Earl Yardley wouldn't make small

talk if anything had happened to her grandfather, his childhood mentor. "I'm fine, and how are—"

"Your granddaddy there?"

The abrupt change in tone startled Val. The chief usually got what he wanted by letting a conversation develop rather than forcing it. "He should be home soon. Can I give him a message?"

Silence on the line. "Yeah, maybe it's better if you tell him. It'll be less of a shock."

Val's muscles tensed. "Tell him what?"

"One of his dinner guests, Scott Freaze, died."

"Granddad knows that."

"The death looked suspicious to the doctor at the hospital. There'll be an autopsy to determine the cause."

Val suppressed a groan. "What does the doctor suspect?"

"Something toxic."

Chapter 6

Val held the phone in a white-knuckled grip. Until the chief called, she'd clung to the belief that Scott had died of a natural cause, a rogue virus or bacteria. "What kind of toxin?"

"No one knows for sure until the autopsy res are in. Meantime, I'd like to talk to your grandd about the guests at his chowder dinner."

The guests and probably the food too. about talking to me first, Chief? There ar things you should know that Granddad m tell you."

"I'll be in my office at the station tomorr ing. Stop by. It'll be like old times."

Those times were only a month old. Sh him repeatedly in June, trying to refocu investigation on someone other than suspect. "Let's hope it's nothing like you tomorrow, Chief." She hung up.

She phoned Bethany and asked h café in the morning. Bethany agre ten and stay as long as necessary.

"I invited Gunnar to dinner. He's in the sitting room checking out your video collection."

Granddad rolled his eyes. "I thought he was gone for good. Well, I'm not giving up my beef. Go out for dinner with him . . . after you cook the steak." He climbed the three steps to the porch.

"I can stretch the meat you bought by making a stir-fry." She had plenty of vegetables to add to it. "With rice and a salad, we'll have enough for three."

"Hmph." He turned around and looked up and down the street. "Where's his little red car, the mini-otter. Did he get rid of it?"

"The Miata is parked at River Edge B & B, where he's staying. We walked from there." Val locked arms with her grandfather. "A stir-fry requires a lot of slicing and chopping. You and Gunnar can help me."

Meanwhile, she'd figure out how to tell Granddad about the autopsy without upsetting him too much. Bad news goes down better over a good meal.

Granddad suggested they eat at the picnic table in the backyard. Val nixed the idea, using mosquitoes as an excuse, and set the table in the dining room. Though sitting there would remind her grandfather of the chowder dinner, the joy of eating beef might counterbalance the bitter taste left by last night's meal.

He took his usual place at the head of the large mahogany table, with Val on his right and Gunnar on his left. Val tried a piece of beef. Perfect. Grand-dad couldn't complain about chewy beef. She'd taken extra care not to overcook it, easy to do with a stir-fry.

Gunnar dug into his food. "This tastes really good, Val."

Granddad nodded. "Almost as good as a grilled steak."

"A question for you, Mr. Myer. With all the great movies in your collection"—Gunnar pointed with his thumb toward the video shelves in the sitting room—"why are you keeping the ones on your top shelf? Most of them are mediocre and some are terrible, like *The Shrimp on the Barbie.*"

Granddad nodded. "That one is so bad it's almost good. It's part of my Alan Smithee collection."

Val didn't recognize the name of the movie or the man. When she cleaned the top shelves, she always used an extender on her dust mop. Without a ladder, she could barely see the titles up there and never bothered to read them. "Who's Alan Smithee?"

"The award winner for the most films directed by a person who doesn't exist," Gunnar said.

Granddad laughed and glanced at Val. "You don't get it? Has to be the first time you don't know trivia that two other people know."

Finally something that Granddad and Gunnar had in common—the movies. "Who's going to explain this private joke to me?" With her grandfather chewing, she looked toward Gunnar for an answer.

"Alan Smithee is the pseudonym directors use to disown films after someone takes over and messes them up. Suppose you started cooking a meal, and somebody else finished it. If it turned out good, you'd want the credit. If it turned out bad, you wouldn't want the blame."

Val exchanged a look with Granddad. Neither of them wanted the blame for last night's fiasco. "So

Alan Smithee appears on the credits instead of the real director's name?"

Gunnar picked up his wineglass. "Exactly. It's an anagram of *the alias men*. The Directors Guild allows an alias in the credits only if someone else's fingers got in the pie—a producer, an actor, or a second director."

And whose fingers had gone near Scott's chowder bowl? Depending on the autopsy results, the police might ask that question, and Granddad needed a ready answer. She'd better tell him the news about the autopsy before he and Gunnar became wrapped up in cinema trivia.

She speared a piece of broccoli. "Chief Yardley phoned while you were out, Granddad. There's going to be an autopsy on Scott Freaze to determine the cause of his death. They think he might have been poisoned."

Gunnar's blue-gray eyes widened.

Granddad laid down his fork, sighed, and leaned back in his chair. "By what he ate here?"

Val shrugged. "Maybe by poison that someone put into what he ate here."

"Do we have to talk about this now?" Granddad tilted his head toward Gunnar.

"I told Gunnar about the dinner party. He knows about financial frauds and may be able to help you track what Scott was doing. But it would help to know what the man was like. Did he behave oddly the night of the dinner?"

Granddad reached for his water glass. "I only met him a few times, but on Saturday night, he wasn't as talky as usual. He just shoveled in the chowder and stared across the table."

"Scott sat there." Val pointed to the empty chair

on Gunnar's left. "There were two chairs on that side of the table and three on this side. Scott's mother, Thomasina, sat where I am now. Junie May was in the middle seat, with Omar on the other side of her. That means Scott sat across from Omar and Junie May. Which of them was he staring at, Granddad?"

"I couldn't tell for sure. But I know where Irene was looking. She sat there." Granddad pointed to Gunnar's chair. "She kept craning her neck to see into the kitchen."

"She was hoping to catch me cooking." Val told Gunnar about Irene's grudge against Granddad for winning the recipe column contest. "Irene would like nothing better than to discredit my grandfather."

Granddad poked around the vegetables on his plate and speared a piece of beef. "She could have slipped something into the chowder pot during her sneak visit to the kitchen."

"She went into the kitchen as Scott and Thomasina were arriving, Granddad. She had no way to know which chowder Scott would eat."

"Maybe she passed it to him at the table and slipped something in it before that. If Scott scammed her out of some money, that battle-axe wouldn't hesitate to take him down."

Gunnar put down his fork. "How do you know he swindled anyone?"

Granddad pushed a piece of meat around in the sauce. "Lillian told me."

"Did he swindle her, Granddad?"

"No, she would have told me if he did." Granddad pointed to his wineglass. "Omar brought wine and walked around the table filling up everyone's glass.

He could have dropped something into Scott's chowder."

"Lillian invited Omar to the dinner. Lillian told you about Scott swindling people. Maybe he swindled Omar."

Gunnar made a time-out signal with his hands. "Anyone who lost money to a swindler doesn't get much out of killing him. Find out who profits from his death. To solve a crime, follow the money."

Granddad rolled his eyes. "Just what I'd expect an accountant to say."

Val had made the same remark in June when Gunnar suggested money as the root of another murder. This time, she wasn't as ready to dismiss the financial motive. "Ask not whom Scott swindled, ask who benefits from his death. Does Scott have a wife and kids, Granddad?"

"He's single, far as I know, and an only child. But if you think Thomasina killed her own son for his money, you're way off base. Parents love their children no matter how rotten the kids are. It's bred in us."

Gunnar swirled the red wine in his glass. "Someone else can benefit from a scammer's death besides his heirs—his accomplice. Let's say the two split the money, but the accomplice knows where it's stashed and wants it all. Or the accomplice wants to go it alone, figuring Scott's getting sloppy, will get caught, and turn in his former partner as part of a plea deal."

Val swallowed a piece of beef she should have chewed longer. "What makes you think Scott had an accomplice?"

"A lot of con artists do. The two work together, pretending to be strangers. The accomplice assures the victim that the fraudster is offering a fantastic deal that only an idiot would pass up."

Granddad groaned. "I said that to Ned about Scott's investment deal. I hope he doesn't think I was Scott's accomplice."

Chapter 7

Val tried to reassure her grandfather. "Ned knows you better than to think you'd swindle him. How much did he invest with Scott?"

Granddad reached for his water, took a long drink, and set the glass down. "Twenty thousand."

Gunnar leaned back in his chair, his plate empty. "Not enough to interest the Feds. They don't investigate if the case involves less than a hundred thou."

Val put her fork down, leaving food on her plate and space in her stomach for dessert. "If he swindles twenty thousand from five people, it amounts to the same thing."

"But it's complicated, like prosecuting five cases. The more witnesses you need, the more likely some can't or won't testify."

Val sipped the last of her wine. "So if you're rich enough to invest a hundred thousand, you get better service from the Justice Department."

"Hmph. Nothing new there." Granddad poked around his plate, pushing aside the vegetables in a vain effort to find meat hiding under them. "Maybe there's a way to make Scott's accomplice return the swindled money."

"Don't count on it," Gunnar said. "A smart financial crook would deposit investor checks in a business account and then wire the money to an offshore tax haven. Untraceable. Untouchable."

Val saw a glimmer of hope. "The money's out of reach unless the accomplice murdered Scott, gets caught, and agrees to restitution as part of a plea deal."

Granddad grunted. "Let's hope for that . . . and world peace while we're at it."

She stood up. "Time for dessert. You can have today's chocolate chunk cookies or yesterday's Key lime pie."

Gunnar opted for pie and her grandfather for a bit of both. Granddad's order reminded Val of Irene asking for some of each chowder. Did requesting a *bit of both* at the chowder dinner save others from poisoning, or did the poisoner wait until Scott's bowl was in front of him? The autopsy wouldn't answer that question, nor would any evidence from the kitchen, where the dishwasher had sanitized the bowls.

After dessert, Gunnar insisted on loading the dishwasher and scrubbing the pots, saying the cook shouldn't also have to clean up. No wonder his gorgeous former fiancée wanted him back.

Val dried the pans. "What are you doing tomorrow?" She hoped he wasn't planning to get together with a "friend" from Washington.

"Fishing in the morning. You want to play tennis in the afternoon?"

She nodded. "Late afternoon. I'll reserve a court

for four-thirty." That would give her plenty of time to get back from the pet-a-pet session at the Village.

With the kitchen cleanup done, they joined Granddad in the sitting room.

He was inserting a disc into the DVD player. "A day like this should end with *Casablanca*. It reminds you that your problems don't amount to a hill of beans in this crazy world."

The next morning, after Bethany arrived at the café to work, Val drove to the police station, a converted farmhouse at the edge of Bayport. She took the extra muffins she'd baked that morning into police headquarters.

On her previous visits here, the building had hummed with town police and sheriff's deputies working on solving a murder. Today the reception area was quiet.

The calm before the storm?

While waiting to see the chief, she paced in the reception area and rubbed her bare arms to stay warm. She'd forgotten how cold the building was. It didn't house a morgue, but if it did, the bodies would stay sufficiently fresh with no extra refrigeration needed.

Barrel-chested Chief Yardley greeted her with a smile and an outstretched hand. "Good to see you again, Val."

"Same here, Chief." She held out a sturdy paper plate piled with muffins. "I brought you some leftovers from the Cool Down Café."

He took the plate. "If this is a bribe, I'm taking it." He started down the hall leading to his office.

"Can we sit outside?" She remembered the bench under the trees behind the police station as more comfortable than the metal guest chair in his office. "I'd like to enjoy the last of the perfect weather. Hot and humid are coming back later today and staying awhile."

He pivoted toward the door leading to a fenced yard. For a large man in his fifties, he walked with a light step. "I saw your granddaddy on the news last night. How is he holding up with all this business about the chowder dinner?"

"He's upset, but managing."

The chief led the way to a shady bench. "What's he doing this morning?"

"Sitting at my computer at home, typing with two fingers. Monday's his deadline for submitting recipes for the Codger Cook column. It usually takes him most of the day."

"He sure never cooked when your grandmother was alive. I'm amazed he goes into the kitchen with you there." The chief put the muffin plate between them on the bench and loosened the plastic wrap. "Blueberry muffins. My favorite. I'd have offered you some coffee, but sludge is the only flavor we have here. Join me in a muffin?"

"I've already eaten more than I should have." She pulled a small wad of napkins from her tote bag, gave one to him, and tucked the others under the plate of muffins. "How long before you get the autopsy results?"

"Hard to say. Even a rush request can take until the end of the week. We might get the results sooner if the lab in Baltimore doesn't have a heavy load." He bit into a muffin.

She watched a robin tug a worm from the ground. She'd have to be just as persistent in tugging information from the chief. "The autopsy might show Scott Freaze wasn't poisoned."

The chief said nothing until he finished chewing. "I expect the results to tell us what kind of poison he had in his system, not that he died from something else."

"Could he have poisoned himself?" A long shot, but worth asking.

"You've heard of spies carrying cyanide pills. It's a rotten way to die, but you don't suffer long. Scott Freaze was in agony for nearly twenty hours. Most suicides don't pick such a painful way to go." The chief's second bite reduced the muffin to half its original size.

"There were rumors at the Village that he swindled seniors who invested with him. If he was murdered and the rumors about him are true, you won't lack for suspects." She told the chief what little she knew about Scott. "A swindler makes a lot of enemies. One of them could have poisoned Scott before Granddad's dinner party."

"The medical examiner may not be able to say when the man was poisoned or what he ate that contained poison. He died almost a full day after his last meal. The investigation will focus on what he did the day before he died, with emphasis on his food intake."

And special scrutiny of his final meal. "I'll give you a rundown on the guests at the dinner." She described them based on her own brief observations and what Granddad had said about them.

The chief polished off his muffin while she was

talking and wiped his hands on a napkin. "Doesn't sound like you know any of them except Irene Pritchard."

"I know Lillian Hinker slightly. Granddad's been spending time with her for the last month and a half, usually at Ambleside Village or in town. I met her for the first time when she came to our house two weeks ago." And not because Granddad had planned for them to meet. Lillian had stopped by the house briefly.

The chief pulled out a pipe and a tobacco pouch. "How come you didn't go to the dinner party Saturday?"

Much as Val wanted to hide her grandfather's ruse, she wouldn't lie to the police. "Granddad hoped to impress Lillian and take the credit for cooking the meal that I actually made. He wanted me to stay out of sight. But when I heard a commotion in the dining room, I crashed the party and acted like I'd just come home."

"Your granddaddy had nothing to do with the cooking?"

"He didn't make anything the guests ate, not the appetizers, the salad, or the chowder."

The chief filled his pipe with tobacco. "Did he serve the food?"

"He ladled the chowder up. Lillian brought the bowls to the table." Val told the chief her concern about the dwindling funds in Granddad's checking account and her mother's worry about Lillian as a gold digger. "I didn't mention any of this to Granddad, of course."

The chief drew on his pipe. "I'll try to get him

talking about Lillian. If anything sounds fishy, I'll warn him and make some inquiries." The chief tamped down the tobacco in his pipe. "Is that what you came here to tell me?"

"One more thing. I overheard a conversation between Lillian and Granddad. He doesn't know I eavesdropped. Please don't give me away." She told the chief about Granddad's plan to confront Scott and get Ned's money back. "Scott got sick before anyone could accuse him of swindling. His death makes it less likely that Granddad can help his friend recover the money."

The chief pointed the stem of his pipe at her. "Your granddaddy had no reason to want Scott dead. Is that your point?"

"Yes, but Lillian might have had a reason. She certainly had the opportunity to poison his chowder. When she took the bowls from the kitchen to the dining room, she walked through the butler's pantry. If she tampered with a chowder bowl there, no one would have seen her do it."

The chief drew on his pipe. "Did she set a bowl in front of Scott?"

"She *claimed* she put the bowls on the table and asked people to pass them. I'd want confirmation of that from other people at the table before I accepted it. You might also want to check on the mystery man, Omar."

"Whoever handles the investigation will check on everybody who was there."

Val sat upright. "Whoever handles the investigation? Aren't you going to—?"

"I have to step back. I've known your granddaddy

since I was a boy. He was like a father to me after my own daddy died. If the autopsy results suggest a crime may have occurred at his house, I gotta pass this to someone else."

The Bayport Police Department dealt mostly with traffic and safety issues. No one besides the chief had experience as an investigator. "Who'll handle the case?" Val tensed, fearing bad news.

"I'll turn it over to the sheriff's office."

"Oh no. Not Holtzman." The image of the detective with the shaved head and the sneering face sprang into her mind. "Please tell me it won't be him."

"He's the top investigator in the sheriff's department."

And Val's nemesis. "He was so nasty to me during the last murder case that I complained to his boss about him. Do you think he knows about my complaint?"

The chief chewed on his pipe. "If he knows you're the complaining type, he may treat you better."

Or worse. "He'll probably handcuff Granddad and me, and lock us both up."

"If he does, I'll get your granddaddy out. You, I might leave there, so you don't try to solve a murder on your own like last time."

"I wasn't trying to solve a murder on my own then, and I don't intend to do that now. If I find out anything, I'll report it." Reporting what she found out didn't guarantee the obnoxious sheriff's deputy would listen to her. Holtzman had come to all the wrong conclusions about the other murder. He would do that again, unless he'd had a brain transplant in the last month.

She stood up, thanked the chief for his time, and hurried to her car. As she waited to make a left turn from the police station parking area onto the road, a man trained a huge camera on her. Junie May was with him and hailed her, waving a microphone. Val didn't want to answer questions about her visit to police headquarters at all, much less on camera. She smiled, waved at Junie May, and pulled out onto the road.

Val drove back to the café. Customers sat eating at four of the bistro tables. Not a bad crowd.

Bethany took off her apron. "I'll come back for you at closing time, but you have to be ready to leave at exactly two. The pet-a-pet session at the Village starts at two-thirty."

"I'll be ready."

Usually Val stayed around for an hour longer, preparing what she'd need for the following day's breakfasts, but with business slow, she should have enough time to do the breakfast prep before closing at two. Nothing would keep her from going to the Village today. While there, she would try to track down Lillian. With Granddad working on the recipes for the column, Val would have a rare chance to talk to his girlfriend without him around.

A middle-aged couple Val had never seen before came into the café and sat at a table. She took their drink order. While they dithered about what they would order for lunch, she made their iced teas and glanced at the television hanging on the café wall.

Junie May appeared on the screen, microphone at the ready.

"This is Junie May Jussup outside Bayport Police headquarters. The county sheriff and the Bayport Police refuse to comment on the death of Scott Freaze or on reports that an autopsy will take place. Mr. Freaze died after suffering gastrointestinal distress. He was in Bayport at the onset of his illness. As I reported yesterday, Scott Freaze ate his last meal at a dinner party given by Don Myer, known to *Treadwell Gazette* readers as the Codger Cook. A short time ago, we filmed Mr. Myer's granddaughter, Val Deniston, who manages the café at the Bayport Racket and Fitness Club, as she left police head-quarters."

To Val's horror, she saw herself on television, smiling and waving from her car window. The clip, coming on the heels of the autopsy news, struck the wrong note, making her look heartless. Every-one in the café, except for a pair of teenagers in the corner, watched the television. As the clip ended, she felt the eyes of her customers on her.

Junie May appeared in close-up on the screen. "I knew Scott Freaze. I attended the same dinner as he did, his final meal. This story has a personal mean-ing for me. I will pursue the facts about his death and report them here. Stay tuned."

The reporter sounded as if she'd taken on a per-sonal crusade. She and Val might even trip over each other in their search for the truth about Scott's death, but Val certainly wouldn't broadcast her plans. With a murderer on the loose, she would keep a lower profile than Junie May.

"Excuse me." The middle-aged woman holding a menu beckoned to Val.

Val hurried to the table. "What would you like to order?"

"Are you the granddaughter the newswoman mentioned?"

"Yes." Val saw disapproval in the woman's pursed lips. "I went to the station to visit the police chief and give him some muffins. He's a family friend."

"I think we'll skip lunch." The woman stood up and tugged her male companion out of his seat. "We've got lots to eat at home."

Val groaned. If the publicity over Scott's death chased away customers, she could kiss good-bye to the café.

Chapter 8

Bethany's sweet mutt curled up in the backseat for most of the ride from the Bayport Racket and Fitness Club to Ambleside Village. Muffin resembled a cocker spaniel more than any other breed. The long hair on her droopy ears framed her face and matched Bethany's ginger-colored drapes of hair. On the off chance that anyone missed the resemblance between them, Bethany emphasized it by putting a pink bow on both their heads—her ribbon with white polka dots, Muffin's with images of little ivory bones.

The guard at the entrance to the Village glanced at the card Bethany held up and waved her car through the gate. Muffin popped up and thrust her head between Bethany and Val.

"Can you get into the Village without a pass?" Val said.

Bethany slipped the card into her wallet. "Sure. The guard asks who you're visiting and signs you in."

"Once I'm in the Village, can I check a directory to find out the unit where someone lives?"

"There's no directory. You go to the receptionist in the Village Center, the large building, and ask for the resident. The receptionist calls the person to find out if you can visit."

Too bad. Val would rather take Lillian by surprise. She studied the small houses along the winding street, all one-story in the same simple style, but painted in different shades of gray and brown. "This looks like your typical suburban community. I didn't realize there were individual homes here. I expected only apartments."

"These are all cottages. They have a bit of land around them and appeal to retirees who like to garden. There's more privacy here than in the apartments, but the activities are farther away in the Village Center."

Val wondered whether Lillian lived in one of these cottages or an apartment. "I'm going to look for my grandfather's friend Lillian while your pet-a-pet session is going on."

"That's fine. We have the pet-a-pet in the sunroom and usually run out of seats. Muffin is popular, aren't you, sweetie?" Bethany patted the dog. "Officially, the session lasts forty-five minutes, but I stay until everyone has played with Muffin."

Val seized her chance to pet Muffin while she had no competition. Muffin reciprocated with a warm lick.

They parked in the lot outside the Village Center, a four-story building with wings angling out on either side. Val followed Bethany into the sunroom off the lobby. The cheerful room had large windows on three sides. Striped chintz valences above the windows matched the pillows on the green sofas and the upholstery on the armchairs.

Val spotted Ned sitting on a sofa, reading the *Treadwell Gazette*. Though close to Granddad's age, Ned looked younger. He had more hair on top, and his dark eyebrows, unlike the hair on his head, hadn't yet grayed.

Val wasn't surprised to see him at the pet-a-pet session. Shortly after his wife died last year, his dog did too. Those two losses had prompted him to move from the house where he'd lived most of his life to the newly opened retirement village. The last time Val had talked to him, when he came to dinner in June, Ned had seemed happy enough, though not as jolly as she remembered him from years ago.

She sat on a chair nearest the sofa. "Hi, Ned."

He looked up from his newspaper, startled. "Oh, Val. What—what are you doing here?"

Not his usual warm welcome. "My friend Bethany brought her dog, and I came along."

He eyed the pet of the day and smiled. "Muffin. Nice dog." He rustled his newspaper and adjusted his reading glasses.

She couldn't miss the body language that told her he'd rather put his nose in the paper than talk to her. "Granddad told me he talked you into investing with Scott. He gave you bad advice and feels awful about it. I hope you don't hold it against him."

"Investments go in cycles. If they're down, you hang on until they go up again. That's not what I hold against him." Ned's eyebrows slanted downward toward his nose forming a V. "He didn't invite me to his dinner after all the years we've known each other."

Val was tempted to tell him he'd caught a lucky break. All the dinner guests except for the dead one might end up murder suspects. "You heard what happened at—I mean, after the dinner?"

"About Scott passing away? Yeah, I feel sorry for Thomasina." Ned took off his glasses and rubbed the lenses on his polo shirt. "I introduced your grandfather to her and Lillian one day in June when he was visiting me here. Now he invited them to dinner and left me out."

"He didn't mean to slight you. He was trying to help. Give him a chance to explain." Nothing Val could say would matter. Granddad had to soothe Ned's feelings.

Tail wagging, Muffin trotted to Ned and greeted him.

A grin transformed Ned's face as he hugged the dog. "You can always depend on a mutt."

A woman with a walker hobbled into the sunroom and looked around. Not many unoccupied seats.

Val motioned to the woman and stood up. "I don't want to take a space that the residents here need. Good talking to you, Ned. Do you know Lillian Hinker's unit number?"

Ned gazed into Muffin's dark eyes. "No, but it's on the fourth floor in this building, the south wing."

"Okay, thanks."

Val waited nearby until the woman with the walker settled into the chair. Then she left the sunroom and approached the counter in the lobby.

She smiled at the receptionist and said, "I want to visit Lillian Hinker. I remember she lives on the fourth floor, but her apartment number escapes me. Which unit is she in?"

The receptionist asked for Val's name and picked up the phone. "I'll check if she's in her room." Half a minute later, the woman shook her head. "No answer. She might be at afternoon tea in the garden. Oh, wait. Here she comes." The receptionist pointed to the building's entrance.

Lillian strolled into the lobby, dressed for a tee, not a tea. Her pastel-blue golf skirt matched the blue pom-poms at the back of her athletic anklets. Val hoped to look as slim and fit when she was Lillian's age, but she'd do without the pom-poms.

Lillian's eyes widened. "Hello, Val. Is your grandfather here with you?"

"No. I wanted to talk to you. Do you have a few minutes?"

"A few. Come up to my place." She headed toward the elevators.

Val read the activities list posted in the elevator as she rode to the fourth floor with Lillian and two other women. In addition to the pet-a-pet, today's activities included a bridge game, a trip to the outlet mall, and a current-events discussion.

Lillian pointed to a notice that this week's Brain Game would be canceled. "Too bad. That's one of my favorite activities here." The elevator doors opened.

She led the way down a long corridor. Chair rail molding divided the painted lower half of the walls from the upper half covered in floral wallpaper. Names on the doors identified the resident living in each unit.

"What do you do at the Brain Game?" Val said.

"Activities to exercise the mind. Word games, trivia, picture puzzles, math quizzes. It varies each time. I guess the Brain Dame, the woman who runs it, can't make it this week and couldn't find a substitute." Lillian stopped by a door identified with her name and inserted a key. "Thomasina never misses a Brain Game, though this week I'm sure she would have skipped it because of Scott."

Val went inside as Lillian held the door for her. "Did Granddad tell you about Scott's autopsy?"

"No, but his mother must have told someone here. The news spread as fast as a norovirus would in this place. Have a seat." Lillian gestured toward a barrel chair upholstered in tan synthetic suede. It looked showroom new. She stepped toward a kitchenette with a fridge, microwave, and sink, but no stove. "Can I get you something to drink? I'm having ice water."

"That's fine for me too." Val sat in the barrel chair. The compact living room had just enough space for a chair on either side of a love seat. She swiveled the chair toward the love seat and then toward a flat-screen TV on the opposite wall. A half-closed door off the living room gave her a view of a four-poster bed.

Six months ago, if she'd stayed in New York after breaking her engagement with Tony, she would have been happy to find an apartment of this size. But now, after spreading out in a two-story Victorian with high ceilings, she'd hate to live small again.

The drinks Lillian set on the glass-topped coffee table looked more like watery ice than ice water.

She sat in the chair exactly like Val's on the

opposite side of the table. "I'm a bit tight on time this afternoon. What do you want from me?"

Val could match Lillian's brusqueness. "Your impressions of the people at the chowder dinner, starting with Scott."

"Whenever I saw Scott here in the Village, he oozed charm." She made it sound like slime. "That night he looked ill at ease. I suspect he felt sick even before he ate the chowder."

An opinion she hadn't voiced the night of the dinner. "His stomach problems didn't keep him from wolfing down the creamy chowder," Val said.

"I think he was distracted. He fixated on Junie May the whole time. I'm surprised it didn't make her uncomfortable."

"My grandfather thought Scott recognized Omar and was trying to place him. Maybe Scott's eyes weren't fixed on Junie May, but on the man sitting next to her."

"No. Scott was at my end of the table. I could tell where he was looking." Lillian crossed her tanned legs. "I think Irene recognized Scott, but not vice versa. She obviously disliked him."

"She obviously dislikes a lot of people." Val counted herself among them. Lillian had done a good job of turning the focus from Omar to Junie May and then to Irene. But Val wouldn't be put off. "How do you know Omar?"

"His father was an old friend."

"I'd like to get his take on the dinner. What's his last name and how can I reach him?"

Lillian stiffened. "Your grandfather told me you solved a murder not long ago. I gather you'd like to solve the mystery of Scott's death too. So would Junie May. She asked me for the same information. I didn't give it to her, and I won't give it to you. You'll both pester Omar with questions."

"Junie May wants information to broadcast it. I want it to protect my grandfather."

"Does he need your protection? Or do you need his?"

Val felt the blood course through her veins fast and hot. Even the frigid water her hostess had given her couldn't cool her down. "What's that supposed to mean?"

"Young people in their twenties often move back home with their parents. You're past thirty, and you've taken refuge in a grandparent's house. If you plan to leave and go back to some high-powered career, you should do it sooner rather than later. The longer you stay, the more dependent he'll become on you."

"I don't plan to leave anytime soon, Lillian." *Or be sidetracked by a personal attack.* "You told Granddad that Scott was a swindler. How do you know that?"

Lillian looked at her gold watch. "Before deciding to move here, I visited other retirement communities. At one of them, I heard about a man who'd given financial seminars and cheated the residents who invested with him. Scott fit that profile."

She'd slandered him without proof. Yet, Val couldn't rule out Lillian's conclusion about the man. "What was the name of the retirement community where you heard about this?"

Lillian jiggled the leg that was crossed over her knee. "I can't remember. That was months ago, and these communities all blend together."

Val might have believed her, except for the jerky-leg motion that betrayed Lillian's discomfort with her own answer. "Why did you decide to move here?"

Lillian drew a circle in the air with her foot. "Ambleside stood out from the pack because of the golf courses nearby."

That didn't set Ambleside apart. She could have chosen almost any retirement community in the Mid-Atlantic states and found a nearby golf course.

Val caught Lillian looking at her watch again. No time for personal questions then. Focus on the dinner that ended so badly. "Did you throw away the creamy chowder or did Granddad?"

Lillian's eyes widened in surprise. "I did."

A quick answer. Granddad had hesitated before saying he'd tossed the chowder, possibly because he wanted to shield her from a charge of destroying evidence.

Lillian stood up. "I really must go." She ushered Val out the door.

As Val waited for the elevator, she ticked off all the things she still didn't know about Lillian—where she'd come from, if she had children, what type of work she'd done before retirement, and whether she cared a fig for Granddad.

Back on the ground floor, Val joined Bethany in the sunroom. Ned had already left. Bethany made one more sweep through the room so everyone could shake Muffin's paw a final time.

Once outside the building, she led the dog toward the shrubs edging the parking lot. "Muffin needs a short break before we climb in the car."

"She deserves it. Everyone really enjoyed petting her." Val followed her friend and Muffin to the al's heart thudded against her ribs. Somehow car hung on to the road. She gaped in amaze-nt at Bethany. "You just missed that truck."

'We'd have lost Lillian if that pokey truck came tween us." Bethany gave Val an apologetic smile. don't usually take risks on the road."

"I know why you took them now." Val punctuated er syllables with a raised index finger. "Because of he caveman diet. It's making you aggressive. You are hat you eat."

Bethany laughed. "That's silly."

"More intersections are coming up. I'll keep Lil-ian's car in sight. You focus on the road, and please don't try to outrun any more mastodons."

For the next ten minutes, every time Val spotted a strip mall or a big intersection, she expected Lil-ian to turn off the road. The white car kept going traight.

"Look, Val. She's turning onto Route 50."

"We should probably give up. We're going to hit eavy traffic."

"That'll make it easier to tail her without her oticing us."

"And easier for her to lose us." Val wouldn't mind Lillian eluded them. She'd never intended to end this long following the woman. "People always l me I'm dogged, but you're even more persistent, thany." Like Muffin refusing to let go of the cap.

'If you teach first graders, you learn persistence." hany turned onto the highway and zoomed into left lane. "I'll have to go fast to catch up with ian. You keep an eye out for her car."

hey passed two white sedans, neither with the

plantings at the side of the parking lot. "They also liked talking to you."

"They need to talk, especially the ones who don't have family or friends in the vicinity."

Val glanced through the shrubbery at the institu-tional building and felt sorry for anyone living there who had no one nearby to visit. At that moment, Lillian emerged from the building. Dressed in casual slacks instead of a golfing outfit, she crossed the parking lot, walking fast, and climbed into a white sedan. Where was she going? Probably shop-ping or to a doctor's appointment, but maybe to meet with the mysterious Omar.

Val pointed to the white car backing out of a park-ing space. "See the sedan with the yellow ball on the antenna? Can we follow that car?"

Bethany's face lit up. "I've always wanted to do that. Let's go."

Chapter 9

Val peered out the windshield of Bethany's silver Hyundai. Up ahead, Lillian's car rolled past the guard gate and turned onto the two-lane road that skirted the Village. Bethany caught up with the white sedan at an intersection with a stop sign.

Val put on sunglasses. "Don't get too close. I don't want Lillian to see me in her rearview mirror."

Bethany slowed down, glanced at Val, and laughed. "You'd better cover your curly mop too. Check the pocket behind my seat for a baseball cap."

Val reached into the pocket and pulled out the cap. Muffin chomped on the brim and wrestled her for it.

"Down, Muffin!" Bethany said. The dog relinquished the prize and lay on the car floor in the back. "Why are we following Lillian?"

Good question. Val tucked her hair under the cap and pulled the brim down low. "I'd like to know where she's going because I don't trust her. She invited a man to Granddad's dinner at the last minute and

won't even tell me the guy's last nan[...] at the pet-a-pet session know her or T[...]

"A few people knew them, not ma[...] moved in within the last few months. T[...] knew Thomasina talked mainly abou[...] sudden death." Bethany turned onto t[...] road that led from the Village to the m[...] "One person said Lillian must have mone[...] She rents her place month to month. Yo[...] pay a lot more that way."

"What do the other people in the Village[...]

"The ones who don't own their units lea[...] on a yearly basis. Either way, they pay lower f[...] the month-to-month renters."

Maybe Lillian planned to stay only long en[...] to find a widower like Granddad to take [...] "What about Thomasina?"

"She lives in a cottage. They don't allo[...] term leases for those. She moved into th[...] in the spring, April or May, about a mont[...] Lillian arrived."

The two women had moved into th[...] around the same time, one committing t[...] other arranging for a quick exit.

Val focused on the white car twenty y[...] and the intersection between it and [...] Hyundai. A farm truck approached the [...] from the right, made a rolling stop, an[...] into a right turn.

"Watch out for the truck!"

"I see it." Bethany leaned on her horr[...]

Val cringed. "Stop!"

Bethany swerved left around the tr[...]

distinctive yellow ball atop the antenna. A moving van moved into the left lane in front of them and blocked their view of the vehicles ahead in all the lanes. When the truck moved back into the right lane and Bethany passed it, Val spotted Lillian's sedan. "She's in the right lane up ahead. If you get in front of the SUV, that'll put us two cars behind her."

"Okeydoke." Bethany turned on her signal light and maneuvered into the right lane. "One of the residents at the pet-a-pet session who knows Lillian says she's always complaining about the food at the Village."

"She told Granddad her late husband was a gourmet cook." And from that tiny seed, the Codger Cook sprouted.

"The way to a man's heart is through his stomach. I guess that applies to women too."

"Anyone who thinks the way to a man's heart is through his stomach flunked biology." Case in point—Val's ex-fiancé who passed up her amazing dinners to "work" with a paralegal who had an amazing body. But an older woman would have different priorities. A man who could cook and owned a big house might sustain her interest, but for how long? Possibly only until a better catch showed up. "I wonder if Lillian hangs out with any men in the Village."

Bethany shrugged. "Ned says a lot of men in the Village would like to get to know her better, but she prefers your grandfather to them. She spends time with the older folks who can't get around well, the ones who don't have many visitors. That's a point in her favor."

"Maybe she hopes they'll make out a will in her favor."

Bethany's jaw dropped. "Wow. You *really* don't like her."

"I shouldn't have said that." Val had forgotten the lesson she'd learned from her foray into sleuthing last month—to set aside her prejudices and not attribute the worst motives to people she didn't like. From now on, she'd try to give Lillian the benefit of the doubt. Doubt was better than cynicism. "Did anyone say if Thomasina and Lillian are pals?"

"I don't know about pals. I heard they're rivals at the Brain Game. Some of the residents call them the Brain Queens and even bet on which one will come out on top each week."

Val had an unexpected brainstorm. "I read a notice that this week's session is canceled. Can you convince whoever's in charge to let me substitute as the Brain Game moderator? I used to run a bar trivia game in New York."

"I'll talk to the activities director. Why do you want to do that?"

"Sometimes the facts people know tell you what's important to them. You find out things they don't think to mention." Or prefer not to reveal. Val suddenly realized how long they'd been on the highway. "We're almost at the Bay Bridge. Why don't you look for a place to turn around? We don't have to keep following Lillian."

"I hate to give up after we've gone this far. Let's at least go over the bridge and see which way she goes. On a clear day like this, you'll have a great view of the Chesapeake."

Val couldn't remember the last time she'd enjoyed

that view as a passenger. She'd driven over the bridge regularly in the last fifteen years, but as the driver, she couldn't stare at the water.

Today the vast expanse of sparkling bay mesmerized her all along the four-mile length of the bridge. Everything from freighters and naval vessels to yachts and sailboats glided in the water. From high above, it looked like a world in slow motion. For the first time in two days, Val felt calm.

With the bay behind them, the pace quickened. The traffic grew heavier around Annapolis. Bethany's hands tensed on the wheel. Val's mental wheels rotated back to her preoccupations of the last two days—Granddad's finances, Scott's death, and Gunnar's ex-fiancée.

Gunnar! She was supposed to play tennis with him this afternoon. She looked at the dashboard clock. "Oh no. I was supposed to meet Gunnar ten minutes ago at the club." She pulled out her phone, paged through her contacts for his number, and called him.

"Hi, Val. Did you forget our tennis game?"

"No, but I had to do something, and now I'm stuck on the road."

"We can start a little late."

"We'd have to start a lot late. I'm an hour away." Or even more, judging by the eastbound traffic toward the tollbooths.

"Okay. I'll see if anyone's hanging around looking for a tennis game. If not, I'll go use the workout room. Thanks for letting me know."

Did she hear a hint of sarcasm in his thanks? "Sorry. Can we reschedule for later this week? . . . Gunnar, are you still there?" No answer. He'd hung up. She clicked her phone off and wished she'd never spotted Lillian leaving the Village.

Bethany looked sideways, frowning. "You stood him up with his fiancée trying to get together with him again?"

Val pressed her lips together to keep from saying what she was thinking. She would have met him for tennis if Bethany had listened to her about turning back earlier.

Unfair, Val's inner voice protested. She was behaving like Granddad, blaming someone else when the fault was her own. She shouldn't have forgotten her date with Gunnar. Usually, she controlled her impetuous streak. Today she'd given in to a whim and followed Lillian for no good reason. "I think it's time to turn around, Bethany. Get off at the next exit."

"That's exactly what Lillian's doing. We can't give up now. We're close to the finish line."

Val sighed. She'd created a monster by suggesting they follow Lillian. She only hoped Lillian wouldn't make a cross-country trip.

They lost sight of the white sedan in the narrow streets of Annapolis, but the yellow ball on Lillian's antenna served as a beacon that helped Val spot the car as it turned onto a side street.

Bethany made the same turn and followed Lillian's sedan, leaving a gap of half a block between them. They drove along a residential street with older houses and brick sidewalks, the historic district near the Naval Academy. As Bethany approached a stop sign, Lillian pulled into a narrow driveway in the block ahead.

"Stop here." Val pointed to an empty space at the curb, just shy of the intersection. From that vantage point, she watched Lillian walk to the front door of a brick Colonial house and let herself in with a key. "Hmm. I expected her to ring the bell. I want the address of that house, but we should wait a bit before we drive by it. She may be on the lookout for your car if she noticed it behind her during this odyssey."

"I'll take Muffin for a walk." At Bethany's words, the dog roused from her nap.

"But don't go too close to the brick house. Even if Lillian never went to a pet-a-pet session, she might have seen you in the Village with Muffin. I'll watch the house from here."

Bethany clipped a leash on the dog. "Come on, Muffin, we're walking in the ritziest neighborhood you've ever been in."

Val pondered possible explanations for Lillian letting herself into a house in an expensive neighborhood. If the house belonged to her, why was she staying in a tiny apartment at Ambleside Village? Maybe the property belonged to a relative or a friend who trusted her with the key.

When Bethany returned, she drove slowly past the brick house, and Val jotted down the address. With that information, she could look up the property records online and find out who owned the house.

It was almost seven when Val climbed out of Bethany's car at the club. She searched for Gunnar's Miata. No red sports cars in the club lot. She approached her Saturn and smelled something foul. The putrid odor turned her stomach. She sniffed around for the source of the stench. It was strongest near her car.

She peered in the side window. On the passenger seat lay a fish with a dull, milky eye. Yuck.

Val had left the windows cracked open three inches to keep the heat from building up. Someone had shoved the fish through the gap. Luckily, it was half-covered with brown paper, the kind used at the supermarket's fish counter. Val pinched her nose and opened the car door. Touching only the butcher wrap, she put the fish on the ground.

A man with salt-and-pepper hair emerged from the pickup truck parked three spaces away from her Saturn. He carried a tennis racket. "What's that stink?"

"Rotting fish." Val held her breath, darted past the pickup truck, and gulped air. Not sweet-smelling, but better than the air near her car. "Someone tossed a croaker into my car."

"Nasty." The man walked with her toward the club entrance. "I teach biology. I can tell you where the smell comes from. Fish amino acids break down into the compounds cadaverine and putrescine."

Val could do without that bit of trivia. Even the words made her feel queasy. "I wonder how long it will take to get rid of the smell."

"Once you clean the spot where the fish was, you'll probably have to keep the windows down for a few days."

"One dead fish came through a window cracked open. Wide open windows might net me a school of them."

The man laughed and opened the glass door to the club for her.

Val went into the café and gathered what she'd

need to get rid of the fish and its smell. Latex gloves, plastic bags, and rags. Water, white vinegar, and baking soda.

Back outside, she made a bandit bandanna from a rag, using a double thickness of cloth over her nose. She shoved the fish into a plastic bag, put the bag inside two other bags, and tossed the package in the Dumpster. While scrubbing the upholstery, she needed frequent breaks for fresh air. The stench lingered after the cleaning, but it wasn't as strong as before, or maybe she was just getting used to it.

She called her grandfather and blamed her lateness on the rotting fish. "It smells so bad! I may have to drive home with my nose out the window like a dog."

"Activated charcoal might help, the stuff you use to filter water in fish tanks. Harvey's got an aquarium next door. I'll see if he can spare some charcoal for your car. What about dinner?" Rough translation: what would she make him for dinner and when would she do it?

"We can have pasta with pesto if you harvest the basil leaves from the garden. I need two cups."

"Good. I'm in the mood for noodles." He called any form of pasta "noodles."

"Me too." Comfort food. "I'm on my way."

Half an hour later, she filled the food processor with basil leaves and chopped garlic, welcome aromas after the stench of decay. She'd already made the salad and boiled the water for the pasta.

Granddad came into the kitchen. "I put the charcoal Harvey gave me in your car. It should help absorb the odor. Teenage high jinks, throwing a fish in a car."

"I'd agree, except that the fish was bought, not caught. It was wrapped like fish from the supermarket. I don't think kids would buy a fish for a prank."

"You're right. They can catch fish easy enough around here." He rubbed his chin. "Whoever stank up your car has money to throw away and no fishing gear. A lot of folks at your racket and fitness club fit that bill."

She turned on the food processor and dripped oil into the chute as the basil, garlic, and pine nuts whirled around. "I can't imagine anyone walking through the club parking lot with a package of fish, hoping to find a car with open windows. I think someone targeted my car specifically."

Granddad set the table in the kitchen. "Someone you know?"

"Not necessarily. The cameraman from the Salisbury station filmed me in my car this morning. Junie May showed that clip on the noon news and identified me as working at the club. Anyone who saw the news report could have guessed my car would be in the club lot. It's bright blue and easy to spot." Her decade-old Saturn stood out amid newer models, most of them neutral in color.

"Nah. You're paranoid after last month's murder and Scott's death." Her grandfather poured himself a beer and her a glass of wine. "Vandalism's usually random. Just be thankful you got a fish in your car instead of a cinder block dropped from an overpass."

She nodded. "Cadaverines and putrescines are better than smithereens."

Her grandfather frowned. "What?"

"I can explain over dinner, but trust me, you don't want to know." She drained the linguini, mixed it with the pesto, and dished it up.

He tucked into the pasta. "Nothing like fresh basil straight from the garden. Too bad I had to wait this long to eat."

That gripe led to others about the miserable day he'd had. It took him hours to type his newspaper column with two fingers. Then he'd printed it, found mistakes, and had to correct them. Each time he printed, he found new mistakes. He barely got his column turned in by the deadline.

Val had finished most of her meal before his litany of complaints ended. "Did you talk to Chief Yardley today?"

"No time for that. I'll call him tomorrow." He put his fork down and watched her eat. "I have something important to tell you."

She dreaded what he would say. That he was going to ask Lillian to marry him? That he'd lost his life savings to a swindler?

Chapter 10

Val usually sipped wine, but anticipating bad news from her grandfather, she downed the wine that remained in her glass and reached for the Chianti bottle. "What's going on, Granddad?"

"After pecking away at a keyboard all day, I needed fresh air. I took a long walk and ended up on Main Street around six-thirty. I saw Gunnar there with a woman."

Val refilled her glass. "I'm guessing she's his real estate agent. He's been looking for places to rent or buy here."

Granddad picked up his fork and speared a lettuce leaf. "Agents these days work in hot pants?"

Probably not. "What did this woman look like, apart from the hot pants?"

"Tall, blond, curvy."

Gunnar's former fiancée. So much for the hope that she'd come to Bayport only for the weekend. "What were they doing when you saw them?" Val asked.

"He was parked in his car with the top down. She

was on the street with her arms resting on the driver's-side door. She was wearing one of them noodle strap tops, leaning way down, and giving him a good view. He's two-timing you, Val."

Val twirled linguini around her fork. "Gunnar and I are just friends."

"I'll bet he isn't just friends with that blonde." Granddad took a swig of beer. "I understand why he wants to be friends with you. You're like the girl next door. What I don't understand is why *you* want to be friends with *him*."

"You haven't liked him since the day you met him." Last night when Gunnar came to dinner, her grandfather had hidden his dislike well. She even thought he'd gotten over it. Apparently, he hadn't.

"I just don't want you hurt again. You trusted your fiancé in New York for years, and he was cheating."

"As you often remind me. That doesn't mean every man I talk to after Tony is no good."

"It means you gotta be careful because your taste in men stinks. *Smart women, foolish choices.* Isn't there a saying like that?"

"It's a book title." But she knew a saying that applied to his relationship with Lillian—*no fool like an old fool.* She swallowed the words and washed them down with her wine.

Granddad pointed his fork at her. "You should read that book."

"I could have used it before I got involved with Tony. Now that I'm living here, I don't need it because I have you to tell me about my foolish choices."

"It doesn't help. You pay no attention to me, but you believe Gunnar's story about some aunt who passed on enough dough for him to quit working.

He coulda left his job under a cloud. He coulda been fired for something illegal."

She laughed. "Do you know how hard it is to fire a government worker? A month ago, you tried to convince me he was a murderer. Now he's a corrupt bureaucrat. I suppose that's progress."

Granddad waggled a finger at her. "Make fun if you like. Just remember, I've had a lot of experience with people. There's something about him that rubs me the wrong way."

She knew what that something was. Her grandfather was suspicious of any man who paid attention to her. A voice inside reminded her that her attitude toward Lillian resembled his toward Gunnar. True, but unlike her grandfather, Val didn't have a lifetime of savings and a big house. Low financial assets had a silver lining—protection against gold diggers.

She pushed the linguini around her plate. The pasta she'd eaten with such gusto until now had lost its appeal. As long as Granddad was giving her advice, she had some for him. "I ran into Ned today at the Village. He's—"

"Why did you go to the Village?"

To grill your girlfriend seemed like the wrong answer. "Bethany takes her dog there and invited me along. I was curious about the Village. You never asked me to go with you."

"I didn't figure you'd want to. At your age, you don't have to think about living in a place like that. It's the last stop for most of the people there. Me, I'd rather make this house my last stop."

He'd joked about his age occasionally, but never mentioned the nearness of death until now. She stood up and refilled her water glass, blinking back tears. She would do her best to make sure he stayed at whatever last stop he chose for as long as possible.

She went back to the table. "I talked to Ned for a while, Granddad. He was hurt that you didn't invite him to the dinner party."

"I had a good reason."

"*I* know that, but *he* doesn't. He thinks you left him out because you like your new friends better than your old ones."

Granddad put the plate with his half-eaten salad on top of the larger plate he'd scraped clean of the pasta. "I'll go over there tomorrow morning and talk to him. Thomasina too, if she's up for company."

"I'd like to go with you, assuming Bethany can work at the café."

"What are you going to do there?"

"Give Thomasina my condolences." *And find out more about the woman who raised a swindler.* "I'll make myself scarce while you're talking to Ned. Are you going to see Lillian while you're there?"

Granddad shook his head. "She's away. She'll be back in a couple of days."

Half an hour later, with the kitchen cleaned up and Granddad watching TV, Val went into the study, sat at her computer, and searched for information about Lillian Hinker and Thomasina Weal. Neither had an online presence.

She navigated to a website for Maryland real estate tax records and entered the address of the house Lillian had driven to. The house belonged to Maxwell and Lillian Hinker and was valued at close to a million and a half. The website listed the last date of sale as twenty years ago. Who was Maxwell Hinker—a husband, a son? Val typed the man's name into a search box. No hits. Why was Lillian living in a small apartment in a retirement community when she shared ownership of a valuable property? Even half that house was worth more than Granddad's Victorian.

But suppose the Annapolis house was heavily mortgaged? An infusion of cash would help pay off the debt. Maybe Lillian hoped Granddad would "lend" the cash to her. Val closed her browser window and reminded herself not to jump to conclusions about Lillian's finances and her intentions without knowing the facts. First find out whether the Annapolis house had liens on it. She could ask Gunnar. With his background in financial investigations, he'd know how to locate the information. She could e-mail, call, or text him, but she wanted to see him, not just pick his brain.

Granddad was sleeping in his recliner. She slipped out the front door and strolled toward Gunnar's B & B. In the last six months, she'd given up her New York habit of looking over her shoulder when walking at night, except during that brief period in June when a murderer had stalked her.

When Val reached the riverfront B & B, she saw lights on in most of the rooms on the first and second floors. She looked up at the dormer windows. Gunnar had said the window in his top-story room overlooked the parking area. No light in that window. His Miata wasn't parked either in the B & B's parking spaces or on the street. *Darn.* He'd probably gone out with his ex-fiancée. If Val hadn't blown off the tennis game with him, he might have spent the evening with her instead of a blonde in short shorts.

On her walk back home, Val remembered some-one besides Gunnar who could tell her about prop-erty liens—a real estate agent who owed her a favor. She would call the agent first thing in the morning.

She went in the back door of the house, not want-ing to wake Granddad if he was still dozing in the sit-ting room. As she crossed the kitchen to go up the staircase to her room, she heard his voice coming from the sitting room. He must have a visitor. She tiptoed to the butler's pantry, heard another voice, and froze.

"I understand why people take justice in their own hands," Deputy Holtzman said. "The system fails them when someone commits a crime and gets away with it."

"I agree with you," Granddad said. "Folks who get away with crimes keep on taking advantage of others unless someone stops them."

Val had heard enough. She marched into the sitting room. "Deputy Holtzman, what are you doing here?"

From his seat on the old sofa, Holtzman turned his cold, protruding eyes on her. "Good evening, Ms. Deniston."

"He's working with the chief," Granddad said. "He stopped by to introduce himself."

No, he stopped by to look at what he believes is a crime scene and trick her grandfather into incrimi-nating himself. "He and I don't need any introduc-tion. Rather than *good evening*, Deputy, I'll say *good night*. My grandfather and I have had a long day, as I'm sure you've had."

Holtzman stood up. "Enjoyed talking to you, Mr. Myer. We'll do it again."

"Don't get up, Granddad. I'll let him out." She led the deputy to the door without exchanging another word with him, this encounter as frosty as their previous meetings. She returned to the sitting room. "Holtzman is the deputy who bullied me when he investigated the murder last month, and I complained to his boss."

"He seemed nice enough to me."

Mr. Nice Guy scared Val more than Mr. Bully. "*Seemed* is the correct word. He fed you a motive for murder. You swallowed it and said it was delicious. Getting Ned's money back isn't a reason to want a swindler dead, as I made clear to the chief this morning, but vigilante justice is. You just told a deputy that *somebody* needs to stop criminals who evade the law. Guess who he thinks that *somebody* is."

"He didn't warn me my words would be used against me, so he can't use them." Granddad shook a finger at her. "This is your fault. You went and told the chief why I invited Scott here, and you got on the wrong side of that deputy."

Val knew better than to argue with him when he played the blame game. "Good night, Granddad." The game always ended when she left him alone.

As she climbed upstairs to her room, Lillian's warning echoed in her mind. He would become more dependent on his granddaughter as time went by. For now, he depended on her as his scapegoat.

On Tuesday morning, Val and her grandfather drove to Ambleside Village, parked near Thomasina's cottage, and rang the bell. Granddad carried a plate of chocolate chunk cookies.

Thomasina opened the door, wearing a teal caftan and a heavy floral perfume that made her cottage smell like a funeral home. She thanked them for the cookies and led them to a living room twice the size of the one in Lillian's apartment. Large mirrors in gilt frames hung on three walls and reflected Thomasina's collection of antique glass bottles in myriad colors.

Val sat on a gold damask sofa. The down cushions plumped around her. Granddad had wisely chosen a side chair with arms he could use to hoist himself up when their visit ended. If he'd made the mistake of sitting on the squishy down sofa, he might have needed someone to tug him out. Thomasina, as one of the younger Village residents, was still spry enough to do that for her older visitors.

She leaned back on a velvet fainting couch amid fringed pillows covered in red and yellow silk. She put the cookies they'd brought on the table next to her.

She accepted Granddad's condolences with gratitude and without tears. "I've cried myself dry by now. No one could ask for a better son than Scott. He visited me whenever his schedule allowed."

Granddad nodded. "He was very attentive to you."

"Losing him is terrible enough. I can't bear to think they will cut my boy up." Thomasina grimaced.

Granddad lifted his chin toward Val, as if to say, *Your turn.*

Val could think of nothing comforting to say about an autopsy. "It's very hard on you, but it's the only way to find out what happened to Scott. It may make it easier for you to know that."

Thomasina shook her head. "It won't bring him back. It just prolongs the torture for me."

Granddad leaned forward. "Do you have family who can help you get through this, Thomasina?"

"Scott was my only family. Everyone here has been very kind." She gave him a weak smile. "I want you to know I don't hold you responsible at all, no matter what other people say. I'm afraid I may have brought this on."

Val exchanged a puzzled look with her grandfather. "Why would you think that?"

Thomasina's gold-sandaled foot traced a pattern in the Persian rug. "A few months ago, someone tried to kill me. I took precautions to keep them from trying again, so they went after my son."

Val glanced at Granddad.

He looked as startled as she felt. "Why would anyone try to kill you?"

"You think I'm imagining this, don't you? If *you* don't believe me, the police won't either." Thomasina's fingers fluttered and her feet tapped out a jerky tune. "Scott's father was involved with some shady men, gangsters. I didn't know that when I married him. I divorced him because I thought he was putting our little son in danger. Those thugs may be settling old scores."

And Granddad thought Val had bad taste in men. Much as Val liked a murder scenario that took the heat off him, she couldn't swallow Thomasina's theory. Sure, revenge was a dish best served cold. In this case, it would have needed cryogenic preservation for decades. Even revenge couldn't have much flavor after that.

Granddad crossed a leg and tied his shoelace.

Up to Val to keep the conversation ball in play, though Thomasina was lobbing it into cloud cuckoo land. "How did those thugs try to kill you?"

"Pushed me down the stairs. I lived on the second floor and never bothered to take the elevator for just one story. Someone shoved me in the stairwell. I was lucky the landing halfway down broke my fall. I moved out of there because I was afraid they'd try again. I was careful to get a place without stairs."

No staircase. What a deterrent for hit men. Val didn't mind feeding a fantasy that absolved everyone at the chowder dinner from blame. "If they're responsible for what happened to Scott, they must have gotten to him before the chowder dinner. Were you with him that afternoon?"

"No. He picked me up right before the dinner."

Val studied Thomasina for signs of drug use— watery, red eyes, pupils too large or too small—but saw nothing unusual. Maybe a drug prescribed to help her weather the shock of Scott's death made her imagine things. A peek in the medicine cabinet might reveal what kind of drugs the woman took.

Val stood up. "Do you mind if I use your bathroom?"

Thomasina pointed straight ahead. "It's the first door off the hall."

The tiny bathroom had a mirror, but no medicine cabinet. No makeup cases, not even a toothbrush. This must be the guest bathroom, and Thomasina's was probably off her bedroom. Val left the bathroom. The hall had three closed doors, the louvered one probably leading to a utility area. With Thomasina watching her from the couch in the living room, Val couldn't get away with snooping.

As she returned to the living room, her grandfather stood up. "Well, Thomasina, we've intruded on you long enough."

He again gave his condolences to Thomasina, who walked them to the door of the cottage and waved from the front porch as they climbed into his car.

Val buckled her seat belt. "Do you know where Thomasina lived before she moved here?"

"Another retirement place. I'll ask Ned. He may know where." Granddad started the car. "What did you think of her gangster plot?"

"As full of holes as Swiss cheese. Mobsters shoot victims at close range. They don't make their hits look like accidental falls or food poisoning. But suppose Scott was swindling seniors at the retirement place where she used to live? One of his scam victims might have shoved her, thinking she was in cahoots with him."

Granddad shook his head. "Nah. If you fall at her age, you're an old putz who lost your balance. If someone pushes you, you're the center of attention. I'm not saying she flat out lied. She convinced herself she didn't trip and it was someone else's fault."

No one understood scapegoating better than Granddad.

He parked in the lot at the Village Center. While he talked to Ned in the sunroom, Val introduced herself to the activities director, a man just below retirement age. He'd heard from Bethany about Val's offer to run the Brain Game this week. He gave her sample activity sheets from previous sessions to use as models and asked if she would run the session both this week and next. When she agreed, he provided a pass to get her through the security gate.

When she joined her grandfather and Ned in the sunroom, the two men were conversing. Granddad told Val to take his car. He would spend a few hours at the Village, and Ned would drive him home. Apparently, they'd patched up their differences.

Val drove directly from the Village to the club. Anyone planning to fish bomb her blue Saturn in the club parking lot would be disappointed. Instead of the blue car, she was driving Granddad's white Buick, and she wouldn't leave the windows cracked open today.

At a quarter to two, the last of Val's lunch customers left, and Yumiko, the club's tennis manager, bustled into the café, a clipboard in her hand and a smile less broad than usual. Yumiko talked fast for a speaker of English as a second language, as if she'd rehearsed and wanted to get through her part quickly without pausing for a breath.

"Hello, Val. I have three things to tell you. Number one, yesterday morning a woman called to ask if you were in the café, but you were not. Bethany said you would be back in the afternoon. I told the caller that you are usually here until three. But yesterday, you left sooner than that."

"Yesterday I needed to leave earlier than that." The caller had to be someone Val didn't know well. Her friends would have called her cell phone number. "Did you get the caller's name?"

"I am sorry. She hung up before I could ask."

Val cleared the eating counter of empty coffee cups. Maybe the fish vandal had phoned to find out when her car would be in the club parking lot. "Was there anything distinctive about the woman's voice?"

"She only said a few words, and the connection was bad. I also want to tell you that someone challenged you on the tennis ladder. The assistant manager took the message last night after I left."

"Great. I'd love to play. The ladder's been static lately." The players were ranked like rungs on a ladder, those on lower rungs challenging those above them. Val had climbed to the third rung from the top after joining the club six months ago and successfully defended her position since then. But if she lost a ladder match, the challenger would take her place, and she would go down a rung. "Who wants to play me?"

Yumiko consulted her clipboard. "Petra Bramling. She wanted to play tomorrow afternoon. The tennis camp has the courts reserved until three-thirty."

Val came from behind the counter to wipe the bistro tables. "I can play at three-thirty."

"Okay. I will phone her. Now for number three. This is not good news." Yumiko spoke in an undertone, though no one else was in the café. "Someone called to complain about the café. The front desk transferred the call to the club manager."

Val's hand stiffened. She stopped cleaning the table. "What kind of complaint?"

"A woman said she felt sick after she ate here last week. She said she saw cockroaches."

"What? I've never seen a roach here." And after ten years in New York, Val knew her roaches. With complaints about food and roaches, she might lose the contract to run the café. "I'll talk to the manager about this."

"Good idea, but you must wait. He left for a meeting and won't be back today." Yumiko patted Val's arm. "I know you have a clean place here. No bugs. Good food."

Yumiko left the café and Val sat at the bistro table, her chin cupped in her hand. She exhaled loudly. Between the rotten fish in her car and the bogus complaints about the café, she felt under siege. The fish vandal might not have targeted her personally, but the complainer probably had. You could ask the same question about a lie as you could about a murder—who benefits? Val knew of one person who'd like to see her lose the café contract—Irene the Irate. Irene would never admit to lying about the café, but her conscience might bother her enough that she'd answer questions about the chowder dinner. A phone call to her wouldn't do the trick. Irene could avoid conscience qualms and questions more easily on the phone than face-to-face.

Val stood up and rushed through the rest of the cleanup. Fifteen minutes after leaving the club, she turned onto Creek Road . . . and shivered. She wondered if she'd ever be able to drive on this street without the scene of a gruesome murder coming to mind. Last month, she'd found a woman murdered in a house on this peaceful street, the house next door to Irene's. Fortunately, Irene didn't know Val had suspected her of killing that neighbor. Even so, Val didn't anticipate cooperation from the woman who bore a grudge against the Codger Cook. Getting information from her would be like trying to make a gourmet dish from tough, dry meat.

Chapter 11

Val climbed out of the car in front of a yellow frame house, plain and sturdy like Irene and her husband, Roger. Orange marigolds and red salvia bordered the house. White and red impatiens flowered in the dappled shade of a tree to one side of the front lawn. A white picket fence behind the tree marked the property border. Along that fence, garden gnomes with grim expressions stood shoulder to shoulder as if facing a firing squad.

On the sunny side of the house, vegetables grew in raised beds. Val glimpsed a scarecrow standing sentry over the vegetables. She did a double take when the figure's wide-brimmed hat moved. Not a scarecrow, but Irene, in a straw-colored blouse and baggy Capri pants the color of mud. Irene harvested a bright red tomato and put it into a basket. She could have picked crops in the cool morning air or in the predinner hours when trees would shade the garden, so why garden in midafternoon on a hot day? Her relaxed posture and fluid movements, so different from her usual rigidity, suggested that she chilled out in the garden no matter how hot the temperature.

Val wiped sweat from her forehead and approached the vegetable patch with a plan—schmooze enough to make Irene feel guilty for complaining about the café and then dig for information. "Hi, Irene. I stopped to admire your flowers and noticed you working here. Your tomatoes look luscious."

Irene stiffened and turned her head slowly, her eyes like the ones on the falcon decoy that kept rodents from venturing near the crops. "Don't beat around the bush. You didn't come here to look at my garden."

After those blunt words, she whipped a far-from-blunt weeding tool from the gardening tote at her feet and looked more ready for combat than a guilt trip.

Scratch the schmoozing, Val told herself. *Move on to the backup plan. Give information to get information.* "I came to tell you that Scott Freaze didn't die of natural causes or food poisoning. Once the autopsy results come back, the police will interview everyone who went near him on Saturday. You may want to write down what you remember about the dinner while it's fresh in your mind."

"Are you suggesting my memory is failing?" Irene twirled the weeding tool in her hands. Its forked end glinted in the sun.

Val took a step back, ready to sprint in case Irene took her for a weed that needed uprooting. "Memories get hazy over time. With detailed accounts from everyone at the chowder dinner, the police may conclude that no one there could have poisoned

Scott's food. Then they'd focus their investigation on what Scott was doing before he came to dinner."

Irene shifted the weeder from one hand to the other and back again. "I saw him in town before the dinner. He was with Junie May at the Bean and Leaf Bar. They were sitting by the window, drinking fancy coffees with cinnamon sticks in them. They were gazing into each other's eyes and having a serious conversation."

Val's neck prickled. "How did they act at my grandfather's house?"

"Like they barely knew each other. I asked her about that afterward. She said she and Scott had discussed business in the afternoon, a private matter. They didn't want to answer questions at the dinner about how they knew each other." Irene stooped, plunged the weeder into the dirt, and ripped out a dandelion with its long root intact.

A more effective way to get rid of weeds than Val's approach of tugging and coaxing them from the ground. "Did Junie May give you any hints about the private matter?"

"No, but I can guess. He's a financial expert, and she has money problems. She talked about them while we were driving to the chowder dinner." Irene stood up and tossed the dandelion on her weed pile. "The upkeep on the house she inherited is eating into her savings. She'd like to make more on her investments so she can fix up the place and sell it."

Gossiping about Junie May's misfortunes had made Irene less hostile. Val might as well take advantage of the woman's surprising openness. "Are you suggesting she asked Scott for financial advice?"

"She might have already given him her money to

was forwarded from the station's system, probably to a cell phone. Junie May answered.

"Hi, it's Val Deniston. Can we get together for a talk? No camera and off the record."

"My camera guy's on his way to Salisbury. I just left the police station in Bayport, but I can turn around. If you're at home, I'll stop by there."

Not a good idea. Ned might bring Granddad back at any moment, and Val wanted to talk to Junie May without her grandfather around. "Why don't we meet on Main Street? For happy hour or high tea, whatever you like. My treat. Let's go someplace quiet."

"Bugeye Tavern has some booths way in the back. See you there in ten minutes or so."

At a fast pace, Val could walk there in ten minutes. On her way, she phoned Gunnar. He didn't answer. She left him a voice mail. He'd always called her back promptly in the past, but now that his former fiancée had come to town, Val might have to wait longer. Depressing, but what could she do if he preferred his ex to her? Nothing. Better to concentrate on something she might be able to change—the focus of the investigation into Scott's death.

The traffic on wheels and on foot moved slowly in the historic district. Tourists meandered along the sidewalks, walking in and out of wood buildings that dated back to the eighteenth and nineteenth centuries. Antique shops, small restaurants, and boutiques occupied narrow two-story buildings that shipbuilders and their families had once called home.

Val had just passed a wider and taller brick building, a merchant's residence turned B & B, when

Granddad called out to her from Ned's car. "Where are you going?"

"I'm meeting someone for a drink. I'll be home soon." She waved as Ned's car continued on its way.

Bugeye Tavern occupied a brick building at the far end of Main Street. Named for the type of sailboat used to dredge oysters in the nineteenth century, the tavern had offered beer and spirits for most of its history. The latest owners yuppified the menu and made the place inviting to twenty-first-century tourists by extending and enclosing the front porch.

Customers filled the converted porch even at four o'clock in the afternoon. The sunny eating area, frond rich with potted palms and hanging ferns, contrasted with the tavern's dark interior. Only a few patrons sat at the polished wood bar.

Val passed under an arch to a small brick-walled room and went back in time to a place where merchant mariners and fishermen had gathered to drink during their off-hours. The odor of beer spilled long ago rose from the dark wood floors.

Junie May sat in a booth, a tumbler of amber liquid in her hand, a laptop computer on the table. A red sandal, with a three-inch high heel, dangled from the foot of her crossed leg.

Even looking at those heels made Val's feet ache. Like her customers at the Cool Down Café, Val wore cushioned athletic shoes. Her feet would stage a protest if she switched to a job that required shoes like Junie May's.

"Hi." Val slid into the booth across from Junie May. The wood bench had a straight back and no cushions, hard seats designed for hard drinkers who wouldn't notice their discomfort. "Thanks for meeting me."

"No problem." Junie May clutched her glass, its edge imprinted with bright red lipstick that matched her scoop-neck shell. With her dark hair, she looked good in red. "I could use a break before hitting the road to Salisbury."

Val eyed Junie May's drink, a double scotch or bourbon, two for the road. "How about splitting an appetizer with me?" Or, better yet, two appetizers to sop up the alcohol. "Crab dip and some nibbles okay with you?"

"Sure. I didn't have time to stop for lunch." Junie May tucked her laptop into a nylon briefcase.

A young man in jeans and a black shirt took Val's order, a glass of sauvignon blanc, the dip with pita chips, and a snack platter with pretzels, nuts, dried fruit, and chocolate.

Junie May ran her fingers through her heavy bangs, which hid any lines she might have on her forehead. "I have a few questions for you."

"Likewise. We can trade answers."

"You're tight with the police chief. Did he tell you anything about the autopsy?"

"Only that it might take several days to get the results." Val noticed dark circles under Junie May's eyes that even heavy TV makeup couldn't camouflage. The reporter looked as if she hadn't slept much since the chowder dinner three nights ago. "How well did you know Scott? You acted like strangers at the chowder dinner, but you were with him before that."

"You've been talking to Irene." Junie May lifted her glass and peered through it. "Scott was helping me with a story. I like to keep my sources to myself. That's why we pretended to be strangers."

"He was your source, and now he's dead." Could that alone explain Junie May's vow to find out the truth about his death? Irene might have misread the relationship between the reporter and the dead man. Alternately, Junie May might be lying or admitting only part of the truth. "A story about what?"

Junie May gave her an aren't-you-naïve look. "Talking about my work before it's ready to go on the air is inviting someone to scoop me. Not even my boss knows. And I don't leave my notes lying around my desk at the station." She put a hand on the briefcase, as if to protect the laptop she'd stashed inside it.

The waiter brought the wine and the appetizers.

Val didn't need Junie May to tell her what kind of story Scott might contribute to. She could guess. When the waiter left, she pushed the crab dip across the wood table toward the reporter. "Help yourself. Given Scott's area of expertise, I assume your story has to do with money management." And maybe Scott was as much a target as a source for an investigative report. "I heard Scott's investments weren't legit."

"I researched him. He's—I mean, he *was*—a respected financial adviser. His clients say he gave them good advice." Junie May picked almonds and cashews from the bowl of nuts, leaving the peanuts untouched.

Similarly, she would also pick and choose what information to share. Val munched on a dried apricot while chewing over what she'd just heard. Junie May might be mistaken about Scott or even lying to protect his reputation. But suppose what she'd said was true and Scott hadn't been a scammer? Or suppose he'd given some clients good advice and others bad advice? He could have suppressed bad reviews, possibly with the threat of a lawsuit. Unsavory tactics, but not illegal.

Val ran her fingers along the pitted edge of the table. "Irene told me she attended Scott's money management seminar. She thought he was promoting risky investments."

Junie May mounded a pita chip with crab dip. "She thinks anything besides money under the mattress is risky. I understand why. Her husband made some bad financial decisions. They're not as well-off as she thought. Irene would stop him from making any new investments if she could, but they have an old-fashioned marriage. He handles the money." She plucked nuts from the small bowl on the snack board.

Val wondered how far Irene would go to keep her husband from making another bad investment.

Killing a scammer after he'd swindled money made as much sense as closing the stable door after the horses had bolted. On the other hand, putting a swindler out of commission to keep your husband from squandering the family nest egg made good sense. But was it a motive for murder? And how did Junie May know so much about Irene's family finances?

Val picked up her wineglass. "You sound like you know Irene well."

Junie May took a swig of her drink, apparently thirsty after eating every last almond and cashew. "She phones me regularly, wanting me to investigate wrongdoing of some sort. Most of it's in her head. Last month, she wanted me to investigate you."

No surprise there. "Because she thought I was hiding evidence in a murder?"

"Exactly. And your relationship with the local police was entirely too cozy and inappropriate. It turned out, though, you weren't hiding evidence. You were going out on a limb to catch a murderer." Junie May looked at Val over the rim of her glass. "Gonna do it again?"

"I'd rather skip the limb this time." Val reached across the table for a pita chip, loaded it with warm crab dip, and popped it in her mouth. She wasn't about to tell a reporter, who was also a suspect, that she was trying to uncover evidence before Deputy Holtzman got too far into the case.

"But you'd like to prove your grandfather blameless. Are you willing to share what you find out? The police clam up with anyone from the media, but you have a direct line to the chief, and your grandfather has friends at the Village. Between your sources and mine, we might figure out who killed Scott."

Join forces with a woman who vowed on TV to uncover the truth about Scott's death? "Doesn't that put both of us out on a limb?"

Junie May took a sip of her drink. "*I'm* out on that limb. You just have to support it."

"And stand under it when it comes crashing down. I can't protect myself unless you tell me what you know."

"Fair enough." Junie May banged her nearly empty glass on the table like a judge with a gavel. "I think I know how Scott was killed."

Chapter 12

Val leaned across the heavy wood table toward Junie May. "You have a theory about how Scott was killed?"

"I've been researching poisons. Arsenic is perfect to slip into food. It's colorless with a slight metallic taste, soluble in a hot liquid, and easy to disguise in chowder."

Or even in a cappuccino. Val had expected to hear how someone managed to poison Scott in front of other people, not what kind of poison was used. "The police haven't mentioned arsenic. What gave you that idea?"

"I'll answer that if you swear not to tell anyone about the arsenic." At Val's nod, she continued. "My sources at the hospital said Scott had neurological and other symptoms that suggested arsenic poisoning to one of the doctors. Something like that spreads fast in a small hospital."

"It could just be gossip."

"Of course. The autopsy should provide conclusive evidence about what killed him. I assume the police took the leftover chowder for testing."

Val's turn to provide information. "All the chowder went down the disposal before Scott died. Where do you even get arsenic? I would think it's banned or at least heavily controlled."

"It's banned now in rat poison and weed killers, but people keep that stuff for years. About six months ago, I did an investigative report about bottles of poison turning up in old houses. The bottles are sold at antique shops and flea markets around here." Junie May unwrapped a chocolate truffle. "At an online auction site, I've seen rat poison with arsenic for sale and even a bottle containing strychnine."

"I hope you didn't broadcast that in your report. It might give people with homicidal intentions ideas."

"You can buy arsenic from chemical supply houses too. It's used in glassmaking and leather tanning."

Val grabbed the last chocolate truffle before it disappeared. "Even glassmakers and leather tanners don't walk around with arsenic in their pockets. If arsenic killed Scott, the murder was premeditated, but we still don't know that he was the intended victim or exactly what contained the poison."

"True. I was just passing on my conclusions and hoping you would reciprocate. You and I have a lot in common. We both gave up city life and came to the Eastern Shore to help a grandparent. My mother died when I was young. When her mother was in an accident a few years ago, I was the only family member who could help her, but I didn't stay here long enough."

"What do you mean?"

"I set her up with a caregiver and went back to my job in St. Louis. The caregiver told sob stories about her family needing money. My grandmother *lent her money.*" Junie May put air quotes around the three words. "The woman emptied my grandmother's accounts, talked her into mortgaging her house to pay bogus bills, and then disappeared. My grandmother had no one to turn to except me. So I quit my job and came back here."

"Were you able to track down the caregiver?"

"I had leads, but the police and a lawyer told me I had no chance of getting the money back. My grandmother's memory was shot. She couldn't give a coherent statement. She died a year later, destitute and depressed. She left me a house with a mortgage that was way more than the house is worth now."

"That's rough. Can you sell the house?"

"I'll do better by holding on to it until the market improves rather than sell in a depressed market. I want a job at a station that pays better. I could rent a small place near the station and hang on to the house here for a few years. A big story would give me a shot at that kind of job."

Junie May claimed Scott was a source for a story she'd planned to write. Now his murder might give her an even bigger story to cover. Maybe Scott wasn't just a source to Junie May. Irene had seen them gazing into each other's eyes before the dinner. Lillian had noticed him fixating on Junie May during the dinner.

Val sipped her wine. "My sources suggested that you and Scott had more than a professional relationship."

"God, I miss the city where nobody pays any attention to what other people are doing. Even without living in Bayport, I'm the subject of small-town gossip." Junie May swirled the remaining liquor in her glass. "Scott said he loved me and asked me to marry him. I told him I'd think about it. I liked him well enough, a sweet, dependable guy, but too tied to his mother. Given time, I'd have probably accepted him. Now it's too late."

Val saw no sign of grief, just wistfulness about a lost opportunity. She bit into the chocolate truffle. "How did you two meet?"

"I was doing interviews in May at Ambleside Village for a report on the first anniversary of its opening. I saw a sign for Scott's lecture, went to it, and talked to him afterward."

Easy to understand why an unmarried man pushing fifty would fall for an attractive woman a decade younger. And he might not want to tell anyone about it until he was sure she reciprocated those feelings. Yet another reason to act like strangers at Granddad's dinner, especially with his mother present. "How well do you know Thomasina?"

"Scott introduced me to her after the lecture the day I met him. From then on, he and I got together in other places. I don't think she even recognized me when your grandfather did the introductions Saturday night. She must not watch local news." Junie May's fingers drummed on the table.

Val interpreted the tapping fingernails as a sign of impatience. She might as well tell Junie May what she knew and get reactions from her. "My grandfather and I talked to Thomasina today. She told us she'd been pushed down the stairs at the last retirement place where she lived. Did Scott say anything about that?"

Junie May shook her head. "What an odd thing for her to say. How did it come up?"

"In connection with her theory about the murder. Old friends, or maybe enemies, of her husband went after her and Scott." Val recapped the few details Thomasina had given. "It didn't make a lot of sense."

"Hit men on the Eastern Shore. Now that would make a great story." Junie May nibbled on a chunk of dried apple. "Maybe Thomasina blames everything bad that happens on Scott's rotten father. She's struggling to figure out why anyone would kill her son. So she concocts a motive for murder that makes sense to her."

"Leaving motive aside, Junie May, how could anyone have poisoned Scott at the chowder dinner?"

"The only way to guarantee Scott would die, and not some random person or persons, was to poison the bowl in front of him. Omar had the chance when he leaned over Scott's bowl to pour the wine. All he had to do was check to make sure no one was looking."

"My grandfather thought Omar made Scott nervous. Did you get the same impression?"

"Scott wasn't himself at the dinner. I doubt it had anything to do with Omar. It was weird how that guy went around pouring wine like it was a fancy restaurant. I know Omar brought the wine, but still the host usually pours, not the guest. It was one of the best wines I've ever tasted, a French white, perfectly chilled." The waiter appeared and asked if they wanted drink refills. Junie May declined a second drink and waved him away. "Lillian could have done it too. She was sitting at the end of the table next to Scott. Just as your grandfather sat down, a dog began barking right outside the dining-room window and wouldn't stop."

Oops. Granddad must have butt-dialed RoboFido.

Junie May scooped up the last of the crab dip. "Scott and Irene turned around to look out the windows behind them when the barking started, and the rest of us looked there too. Lillian could have reached over and poisoned Scott's chowder while everyone's attention was diverted."

Val suppressed a smile. That scenario made Robo-Fido an unwitting accessory to murder. "So Lillian brought arsenic with her in case a barking dog or some other diversion gave her the chance to poison Scott? You can't be serious." But if Junie May knew that Granddad could make a dog bark as a diversion, she might view him as a *witting* accessory.

"Okay, then Omar must have done it. Do you know his last name?"

"I asked Lillian, and she wouldn't tell me. She invited him to the dinner. If Omar poisoned Scott, she must have told him Scott would be there. Or else Omar carries arsenic with him in case he runs into someone he wants to poison."

"They worked it together."

Val figured Junie May had chosen the wrong career. She should have been a TV scriptwriter, not a reporter. "Why would Lillian and Omar want Scott dead? You can't possibly think they're hired killers."

"There's a motive. We just don't know what it is yet."

Val almost suggested retaliation against the swindler, but that motive wouldn't fly with Junie May, who believed, or said she believed, Scott to be honest. "We need to find out more about Lillian and Omar. Lillian hasn't been forthcoming with me. I'll tackle her again, but I can only go so far with her because she's my grandfather's girlfriend. You should work on this too, because you have research skills and contacts I don't have, and you don't have to go easy on her."

"I'll try to fit in the research tomorrow." Junie May pointed to the huge watch on her wrist. "Time for me to go. Still have to write something for the eleven o'clock news."

"One more question. How did you happen to bring Irene Pritchard to my grandfather's dinner?"

"When I told her I was going to dinner at the Codger Cook's house, she invited herself along. She expected me to prove your grandfather can't cook. I never intended to do that."

"Because you didn't believe it?"

"Because I didn't care. According to Irene, your grandfather used *influence* to win the contest for recipe columnist, and you actually write the column. I investigated the influence allegation. Nothing in it. He clearly writes the column. It sounds like him, not you. Maybe he started with your recipes, but it doesn't matter as long as they're good."

Val steered the conversation away from her recipes. "What about the cooking demo you want him to do on camera? That's asking a lot of a man in his seventies."

"Irene pushed for that too, but she doesn't know how it works. My cameraman and the video editor can make anyone look like a gourmet chef. Throw a party when the Codger Cook demo airs and invite

Irene. I'd love to see her face when your grandfather cooks like a pro on TV."

Nice try at blunting Val's opposition to the cooking demo, but it wouldn't work. The reporter and her team could do what they wanted once they had Granddad in front of the camera, including make him look ridiculous. "It's too stressful for him."

Junie May swept her hand across her bangs. "Relax, Val. The Codger Cook is a feel-good story. Pricking holes in it won't get me a better job. I need a more important story than that." She jotted on the back of a business card. "Let's compare notes tomorrow evening. Come to my house around six-thirty. Here's my address."

Val glanced at the card. "Where is this?"

"It's my grandmother's house in the woods, on a lane not far from the highway to Salisbury. See you tomorrow, and thanks for the happy hour." Junie May stood up.

Clad in red, she began a trip to her grandmother's house in the woods. A familiar story, lacking only a big, bad wolf.

Val finished her wine and paid the bill. She'd come to the tavern expecting the reporter to stonewall her. Instead, Junie May had disarmed her by sharing information, answering her questions, and recruiting her as an ally. But had Junie May told the truth? Maybe she'd made up the romance between her and Scott as a smoke screen for her partnership with a scammer. She could have a vested interest in convincing the world that Scott wasn't a swindler so that no one would go after the money the two of them had raked in.

Gunnar was the one person Val knew with the background to research someone in the financial field. He could ignore her phone calls, but not her presence. Instead of walking home, she detoured to the River Edge B & B. As she rounded the corner from Osprey Street onto River Avenue, she spotted a red sports car stopping in front of the B & B half a block away. Gunnar. Perfect. She could *bump into him.*

Gunnar's ex climbed out of the car on the driver's side, crossed the guest parking area, and walked past another red sports car—Gunnar's Miata. Val looked again at the car parked at the curb. Shinier than the Miata, probably newer.

How cute. They had his-and-hers red cars.

Val turned back toward Osprey Street, dejected. Her phone chimed. She fumbled for it in her fabric shoulder bag. Her cell phone often ended up buried in the expandable bag. She answered the phone seconds before her voice mail would have kicked in.

"Hi, Val. It's Gunnar. Sorry I didn't return your call. I've been busy. What's going on?"

She perked up. *So what if his ex was waiting for him in the B & B's reception area or climbing up to his attic room? He wasn't calling his ex.* "I was hoping we could get together. Maybe tomorrow night we could—"

"Why don't we try for tennis again? Does four o'clock tomorrow work?"

"That sounds good. . . . Oh, wait. I have a ladder match starting at three-thirty. It could go on for ninety minutes or even two hours. I guess we could play later. How about six-thirty?" That would give her time to shower and change.

"That's cutting it too close for me."

For evening plans that included the blonde? Val could suggest an alternate date. Thursday afternoon she'd offered to run the Brain Game session at the Village, but Bethany had agreed to work a few hours at the café that day. "Can you play on Thursday around noon? I have someone to cover the café."

"Thursday's tight. I'm busier than I expected this week. I'll phone you when I know more about my schedule."

Would he know more when he talked to his ex? Val might as well get information from him while she could. "Did you find time to check out Scott Freaze?"

"Not thoroughly. Online reviews about his investment business are mixed. People who complained about it had investments that didn't do well at a time when everyone's investments were going down. I'll research him more when I get a chance. A call's coming in on the room phone. Talk to you in a day or two." He clicked off.

Disappointed, she trudged home. Last weekend when Gunnar arrived in Bayport after nearly a month away, she'd anticipated spending a lot of time with him and getting to know him better after the shaky start to their relationship. In the past three days, they'd managed only a few hours together and the next few days didn't look more promising, especially if he was trying to fit both her and the blonde into his schedule. To be fair, Val had also been pressed for time ever since the chowder dinner.

A faint burning smell hit her as she opened the front door. *Not again.* Granddad often scorched his morning toast, but he didn't eat toast this late in the day. She raced through the sitting room and dining room.

From the butler's pantry, she saw water overflowing a pot on the stove, hissing and sputtering onto a red-hot burner. On the other back burner, round seeds crackled, popped, and flew into the air from a sizzling frying pan. She zoomed toward the stove.

Granddad backed away from it, stepped on a cookie sheet, which sat on the floor for some reason, and flattened cookie dough with his shoe. "Look what you made me do, storming in here like that!"

Val grabbed the lid lying idle next to the stove and clapped it over the frying pan full of mustard seeds. The seeds kept popping, hitting the metal lid like machine-gun fire. She moved the overflowing pot from the hot burner to one that wasn't glowing red and turned off all the burners. All the while, the oven gave off intense heat, its door open and covered with splats of dough.

Granddad pulled a metal spatula from a drawer and tried to scrape off the dough stuck to the open oven door. "Don't just stand around, Val. Help me out here."

She didn't know where to start. Inside the oven, dough globules hung from the center rack like Dali's melting clocks. "What happened here, Granddad?"

"Your stupid cookie recipe says to shape the dough into balls and space them out on the cookie sheet. When I went to put the sheet in the oven, the balls started rolling off. I tried to catch them and more of them fell off. I put the cookie sheet on the floor to get it out of the way."

"That's where I came in." His bright pink cheeks alarmed her. He looked as if he'd spent an hour under a sunlamp. "Your face is red from the heat." Or anger. Val took the spatula from him and pulled the trash can toward her. "I'll get the dough off the oven. What's in the pot with the boiling water?"

He straightened up. "Noodles."

"How long have they been cooking?"

"Ten minutes or so."

"Drain them or they'll turn to mush." If they haven't already. "The colander's in the cabinet next to the sink."

She bent down and concentrated on lifting off the dough before it baked onto the oven door.

"Doggone it. Half of the noodles went down the drain."

She stood up and checked the sink. Sure enough, pasta the size of rice had escaped from the colander. "If I'd known you were making orzo, I'd have suggested using the strainer." Of course, he could have looked at the size of the orzo and realized it was smaller than the holes in the colander.

"You should have known. The box is right there." He gestured toward the counter where a food processor, mixer, garlic press, juicer, and zester sat, along with myriad ingredients.

"How could I miss it? It's behind the flour and sugar, and surrounded by butter, lemons, maple syrup, parsnips, olives, and half-a-dozen other things. What happened to your five-ingredient limit on recipes?"

"I was making three five-ingredient recipes at once."

"Oh, it's the Codger Cook Three-Ring Circus. Focus on one recipe at a time."

"I was going to, and let you make the rest of the meal, but you were so late, I figured I'd starve if I didn't make more food." He gestured at the counter with his palm up. "This is what happens when I listen to you."

She was used to his finger pointing, but blaming her for a kitchen disaster that occurred when she wasn't even home took some fancy footwork. "How is this my fault?"

"You accused me of running a scam with the Codger Cook column. You lumped me with people like Scott. Well, you won't be able to call me a fraud once I get this cooking stuff down."

She had three strikes against her—her cookie recipe, coming home late, and calling his column a scam. Up until today, he'd needed only free access to her recipes. The cutesy names he gave them and his cornball writing style made her cringe, but until now his new career had made few demands on her time. If he really tried to cook, more kitchen disasters loomed, and more cleanups.

But how many men approaching their eighties tackled something totally new? She was proud of him for doing it. "I'll pay for my sins by cleaning up. You go sit down. Be careful not to slip with that dough on your shoes."

He didn't slip, but he did leave bits of dough along the path to the kitchen table. "All this work, and I haven't even started making the chicken. It beats me how cooks get everything ready at the same time."

She cleared away enough space on the counter to work. The longer he had to wait for dinner, the grumpier he'd get. "I'll cut the chicken in small pieces. It'll cook fast."

While it cooked, she made parsnips with mustard seeds, the side dish he'd chosen. She also salvaged the cookie dough that hadn't rolled away or gotten smashed under his foot.

When she put the food on the table, he dug in. Between bites, he told her how he'd spent the day— taking Ned to lunch to make up for leaving him out of the chowder dinner and then going to a movie.

"Was the movie any good?" she asked. Maybe she and Gunnar could—No, that wouldn't work. He was busy . . . with another woman.

"The plot was dumb, and the acting terrible. I don't know why they can't make good movies anymore. What did you do besides work at the café today?"

"Talked to Irene and Junie May. I found out that Junie May and Scott spent time together Saturday before the chowder dinner."

Granddad's white eyebrows jumped halfway up his forehead. "She could have poisoned him with something that wouldn't take effect until later."

If guilty, Junie May was playing a deeper game than Val could fathom. Why would she mention arsenic if she'd used it to poison Scott? "She said something that surprised me. The research she did on Scott convinced her he was a legitimate financial adviser with happy clients. Do you have any proof that Scott defrauded Ned? Does he have any paperwork?"

"He didn't get an account statement yet."

"All you have are rumors of Scott's dishonesty and no more facts than Irene had when she spread rumors about food poisoning here. Scott might not have been a swindler after all, but a victim of gossip."

Granddad rolled his eyes. "As usual, Val, your instincts about men are all wrong. Scott's worse than we thought. I found out something today that made my blood boil."

Chapter 13

Granddad put his fork down and folded his arms. "An eighty-year-old man committed suicide a few months ago after losing his life savings. He trusted a financial expert who gave investment seminars at his retirement community. I'd bet my Codger Cook apron that Scott was that expert."

Val pushed her orzo salad around the plate, her appetite gone. "That's terrible. How did you find out about it?"

"A woman at the Village told Ned and me. She heard it from a friend of hers at the retirement place where it happened, just outside Washington."

Thirdhand hearsay. "Can you ask the woman for the name of the place where the suicide occurred? If we have that, we can find out if Scott gave seminars there. And if he didn't, we'll at least know he wasn't the kind of monster who drives people to suicide."

Granddad raised one hand like a cop stopping traffic. "Why would we spend any time on that? We should focus on who killed him so I don't get blamed for it."

"We need to know more about Scott. The character of the victim was the key to solving the murder in June." Last month, she and Granddad had used each other as sounding boards for theories about that murder, but with him smitten by Lillian, Val doubted he could be objective about this crime. "When we talked about that last murder, you kept giving me lists of five suspects with motives. Can you do it again this time?"

"We had five guests besides Scott. I guess that means five suspects. Maybe Junie May was Scott's accomplice. He could have had a hold over her and forced her to vouch for him, or she might have wanted all the money they scammed for herself."

"That would give her a reason to insist on Scott's honesty and to plant the idea that someone else killed him. According to Junie May, Irene was afraid her husband would invest money with Scott and lose it."

"So Irene's number two on the suspect list. Omar's number three. I don't know what his motive could be, but Scott sure looked at him funny. I gotta put Thomasina and Lillian at the bottom. No motive."

Val was surprised that he put Lillian on the list at all. "We need to know more about Omar. What was he like at the dinner?"

"Overly polite and hoity-toity about the wine."

"What do you mean?"

"He brought two bottles of white wine. I told him we already had wine chilled for dinner. Then he said to use his wine instead, because it was exceptional.

He'd already chilled it to the perfect temperature in his car's wine chiller. The show-off even opened his exceptional wine with a corkscrew he carried in a leather case."

Val laughed. "Your corkscrew wasn't good enough." A funny story and a possible clue about Omar. Assuming he'd actually brought exceptional wine, an online search might narrow down places where he could have bought it. That might help Val track him down.

She put down her fork and jumped out of her seat. "Be right back."

"Where are you going?"

"To rummage in the recycling bin while it's still light outside."

An hour later, with the kitchen cleanup behind her and Granddad reading the newspaper in the sitting room, Val sat in front of her laptop in the study. She opened a browser window and typed in the multiword French name of the wine Omar had supplied. The hits that came up included reviews of restaurants serving wines from the vineyard listed on the label. She narrowed her search by adding *Maryland, Washington, D.C., Delaware,* and *Virginia* to the search box. Fewer matches came up, none for restaurants near the Eastern Shore. Val opened another browser window and typed *Omar* in the search box. One by one, she copied the name of each restaurant she'd found by searching for the wine and pasted it into the search box with Omar's name. Her fourth search produced a hit—a review of a restaurant that consistently placed among the top five eateries in

the Washington area. The restaurant's sommelier
was Omar Azamov. Bingo!

According to the review, the sommelier arranged
to import wines directly from small vineyards that
didn't sell to retail outlets in the United States. The
reviewer described the restaurant's five-course wine
dinner as the best meal he'd eaten paired with the
best wine he'd drunk in years. He suggested making
reservations a month in advance.

Val brought up the restaurant's website replete
with photos of beautifully arranged tables and food.
The sample menu did not include prices. Saturday
night had to be busy in a high-end restaurant like
that. Yet, instead of going to work last Saturday,
Omar had come to Granddad's dinner with the perfect wine to accompany chowder, not something he
could buy around Bayport. The wine clue might not
convince Granddad that his girlfriend had invited
Omar well in advance of the dinner instead of at the
last minute, but it convinced Val.

An online search for Omar Azamov gave Val his
address in a Virginia suburb of Washington, a link to
the review she'd just read, and one to his Facebook
page. That page didn't show his face, only hands
presenting a wine bottle. The page listed a Washington, D.C., restaurant as his current place of employ-
ment and three restaurants where he'd previously
worked, all in the Baltimore-Washington area. It also
gave the dates when he'd earned an Introductory
Sommelier Certificate, a Certified Sommelier Certificate, and, just a few months ago, an Advanced
Sommelier Certificate.

Val had met a certified sommelier in New York

two years ago during her former life as a cookbook publicist. He'd coauthored a cookbook focused on dinner parties with wine pairings. She looked up the sommelier's e-mail address on her contact list and sent him a message, reminding him who she was and asking if she could talk to him by phone.

Her cell phone rang and displayed the name of the real estate agent she'd tried to reach earlier in the day. Maybe by now the agent knew if Lillian's Annapolis house had a lien on it.

"Hey, Val. It's Kimberly. I wanted to call you earlier, but I was, like, totally swamped today." She had a high-school cheerleader's voice with enough volume to project to the top of the bleachers. "Sorry I can't help you. You have to contact a title search company or an attorney to look up liens on a property. You can do the search yourself at the courthouse, if you have the time."

Val didn't have the time or inclination to search through courthouse records. Maybe her mother would spring for a title search to find out if Lillian was a woman in financial straits and a possible gold digger. "I also had a question about the property owners. The woman listed on the tax records for that house said she's a widow, but a man with the same last name is listed as a co-owner. I suppose he could be her son. Can you access personal information like the age of property owners?"

"Not easily, but the name could be her dead husband's. If a married couple owns property with right of survivorship, the deed doesn't have to change after one of them dies. The one who's still alive just needs to show a death certificate to prove ownership when the house is sold."

The property record told Val nothing about who lived in the house. "Thanks for the info, Kimberly."

"No problem. I owe you for giving me a referral to Mrs. Z."

Everyone called the elderly woman with the long last name Mrs. Z. Val had met her once, after the last murder in Bayport, and remembered her and her macaroons fondly. "Did you sell her house yet?" She doodled a one-story house with as much artistic talent as any six-year-old.

"She listed the house with me, but then changed her mind like a week later and took it off the market. She wants to move closer to her son and his family in Chicago, but she's afraid of making a mistake."

Poor Mrs. Z, widowed after sixty years, unsure what to do next. Val had suffered the same indecision before her move to Bayport last winter. It had taken her a while to decide whether to stay. Now Gunnar was hesitating too, having trouble finding a place in Bayport, hearing the siren call of his former fiancée.

Aha! A possible solution to two problems.

"Hey, Kimberly, would Mrs. Z want to rent out her place?" Val turned her house doodle into a boat. Maybe Mrs. Z's house could serve as a mast holding Gunnar steady until his interest in the blonde waned. "She could try living near her son. If it doesn't work out, she can come back here."

"Most people want a year lease. She thinks that's too long. And she doesn't want to clear out all her furniture."

"I know someone who might welcome a shorter-term lease and even some furniture in the place."

"Really? I'll sound out Mrs. Z about it and let you know. See ya."

Val navigated back to the website for the restaurant where Omar worked. She jotted down the phone number and checked her watch. Nine o'clock. The dinner hour would still be in full swing at a fancy restaurant like that. Better to wait until the patrons thinned out and the sommelier had less to do.

Meanwhile, she could do other online research. She typed *arsenic poisoning* into a search box. The sources she skimmed distinguished between acute and chronic arsenic poisoning. She narrowed her search to acute cases and found out that even a quarter teaspoon of an arsenic compound was enough to kill a healthy person. Gastrointestinal symptoms could appear within half an hour after ingesting the poison or take several hours to show up, depending on the amount consumed and the individual.

That meant Scott could have been poisoned either before or after he arrived at the dinner. When his symptoms began, he'd finished his chowder, though the others hadn't. Unfortunately, the time required for the arsenic to take effect didn't rule out poisoning by chowder. Eating salad, passing bread, and conversing could have slowed down the pace of the meal. And given Scott's *tummy problems,* which Thomasina had mentioned, the poison might have affected him more quickly than the average person.

When Val finished reading up on arsenic, she phoned the restaurant where Omar worked and asked to speak to him.

He came on the line thirty seconds later. "Omar Azamov here. How may I help you?"

"This is Val Deniston. We met briefly on Saturday night before you left the dinner party at my grandfather's house. If you can spare a minute, I'd like to ask you a question or two about the dinner. Lillian invited you to my grandfather's house. Have you known her long?"

"A year or so."

Whatever he and Lillian had cooked up between them, they'd worked with different ingredients. Wouldn't she have known the son of an old friend for a longer time than that? "Did you know any of the other guests?"

"I'd never met them before that night."

A carefully worded answer. Perhaps he'd known *of* them without having met them. "With your experience—"

"Ms. Deniston, I really must return to my duties."

"Just one more question, which perhaps only you can answer. Having worked in restaurants, you may remember people's food preferences better than the others at my grandfather's dinner. Do you recall which chowder each guest wanted at first, before they changed their minds at the table?"

"Lillian and I asked for the light chowder. So did the gray-haired woman, whose name I've forgotten."

"Irene."

"Yes. The other guests requested the creamy chowder. Your grandfather did not tell us his choice. Truly, Ms. Deniston, I must put the phone down."

"Thank you for your help. I hope we can talk again."

"Good-bye."

Val hung up, satisfied with the phone call despite

its abrupt end. Someone less polite than Omar would have hung up on her sooner. Assuming what he'd said about his short acquaintance with Lillian was true, then what could have brought the two of them together? Omar didn't come across as someone who shirked his duties. Still, he'd spent Saturday night away from his job, prime time at any restaurant. Val would need to dig further to find out why and how Lillian had convinced him to show up at the Codger Cook's dinner party.

She'd done enough research for tonight. Tomorrow she'd have to get up early to buy café provisions at the market.

At six-thirty Wednesday morning, Val dressed in a turquoise T-shirt she could wear later for tennis and black Capri pants she'd swap out for white shorts to wear on the court this afternoon. She grabbed a package of peanut butter crackers to tide her over until she made coffee and a real breakfast for herself at the café. Her Saturn still smelled of dead fish, but the odor was far less pungent than two days ago. On her way to the farmers' market, she drove with her window wide open to let in the cool morning air.

The market opened for business at eight, but she'd made a standing arrangement to pick up produce, eggs, and artisan bread an hour before that. Today the market also offered fresh chickens raised on a local farm. She couldn't resist.

Her purchases filled four recyclable bags, one devoted to melons. She drove back along a country road toward Bayport. Before reaching town, she turned onto another rural road leading to the racket and fitness club. As usual this early in the morning, the club's lot was less than a quarter full. She toted the bags into the club, two in each hand. Rushing into the café alcove, she suddenly felt like an ice-skater. Her tennis shoes slid out from under her on the tile floor. She dropped the bags on her way down and tried to break her fall. The back of her head smacked against the floor.

Chapter 14

Val lay on the café alcove's hard floor. Her head hurt where it hit the floor, but nothing else did. She felt wet all along her back. Was her head bleeding? No, blood would be warm, and this wet stuff felt cold. She sat up in a puddle of water, surrounded by the cucumbers, peppers, and zucchini, which had fallen out of the bags. The cantaloupes and cherry tomatoes had rolled away after spilling as if in search of dry land.

She touched the back of her head and winced. She checked her fingers. No blood. She got to her feet gingerly, not wanting to slip on the way up. At least her pratfall had gone unnoticed. When the café was closed, the club members walking by had no reason to glance into the alcove.

She mopped up the water. Who had spilled it and left it there? Not the cleaning crew. They did their work at night. The club opened at six, the café not until two hours later. This early in the morning, people trickled in one by one. While the reception-ist behind the counter was looking the other way, anyone could have sneaked into the alcove and emptied a water bottle onto the floor. Whoever had done it must have targeted Val, usually the first person to arrive at the café. A dead fish in her car had annoyed her, but the water on the floor could have hurt her. Those pranks, plus bogus complaints about the food and bugs, equaled a campaign of dirty tricks against her. Whose campaign?

She crouched to pick up the scattered vegetables. As she tucked them back into the bags, a pair of bare, brown legs beneath running shorts came into view. She looked up at Althea Johnson, her tennis teammate. "You're back from vacation. How was it?"

"Great. You look like you need help." Althea bent down, picked up the melons, and put them on the counter.

Val stood up. "How about some coffee? I haven't made it yet, but—"

"I just have time to run on the treadmill before I go to the office." She adjusted the tortoiseshell glasses that had slipped down her nose. "The problem with vacations is that the work you left behind is still there, and more has piled up."

"Quick question. I know you focus on family law, but can you recommend a title company or property lawyer? I want to find out if there are any liens on a house in Annapolis."

Althea's jaw dropped. "Are you moving?"

"No. My grandfather is seeing a woman my mother thinks might be after his money. If this woman owns her Annapolis house free and clear, she's probably not interested in Granddad's money. Her house is worth a lot more than his."

"You know the property's address?" At Val's nod,

Althea took a smart phone from a zippered pocket in her shorts and punched in the address Val gave her. "I have a friend who's a real estate attorney in Annapolis. I'll let you know what she says."

"Thanks, Althea. When your workload lightens, let's set up some tennis. We can play doubles with Bethany and Yumiko."

"I won't have any free time until next week."

"The rest of the team should be back by then, enough of us for two courts."

"Way more fun than the treadmill." Althea headed out of the café.

Val washed the fruit and vegetables, cut away the bruised parts, and stowed them in the refrigerator. She mixed the dough for oatmeal breakfast bars, thinking about the last time someone had targeted her. A month ago, the *accidents* a murderer had set up for her could have killed her. By comparison, the complaints about the café, the fish in the car, and even the water on the floor struck her as merely spiteful and petty. Irene might act out of spite, still holding a grudge because she wasn't running the café as she'd expected. Maybe Granddad's girlfriend wanted to nudge Val into leaving Bayport. Lillian would recognize Val's car. She could have asked Granddad about Val's work schedule, bought a fish, and tossed it in the Saturn's window on Monday. Hard to believe women in their sixties would engage in such sophomoric stunts.

Ten minutes before the café opened, Val brewed coffee and took the breakfast bars from the oven, hoping the combined aromas would entice club members into the café after their exercise sessions. By eleven-thirty, she'd served the usual small number

goes to all the dance classes at the Village.
twork is better than the teacher's. Some
call her Twinkle Toes Thomasina. She was
of the talent show with her tap dancing. I
he must have been an entertainer."

ould test Ned's conclusions through some
estions. "Tomorrow I'm going to run the
ame at the Village. If you see Lillian or Tho-
encourage them to go. I'll come up with
edical and entertainment trivia to see if they
ore than the average person."

nasina may not want to go this week, but Lil-
probably be there. Me too. We're regulars."

ou socialize much with them?"

n keeps to herself. Thomasina goes to a lot
s. The Sunday ice-cream social and the
wine and cheese. I was there last Saturday.
me Scott was picking her up from there to
to your grandfather's house. That's how I
ut the dinner."

ound out Granddad had left him out. "Are
Granddad all squared away about that?"
good now."

cused herself from Ned, approached the
s, and asked if they were ready to order.
vanted a Cobb salad. Another one requested
butter and banana sandwich on walnut
ead. The girl opposed to *food fatism* asked
getables with a hummus dip. The two boys
am and cheese on pumpernickel and sweet
ips.

ned to go back to the counter.

get someone to wait on me here?" The

of customers for a midsummer morning. At least the number hadn't dwindled . . . yet. But it would, if word spread about bad food and bugs.

"Coffee smells good, Val. You got any left?" Granddad's friend Ned took a tentative step into the café. "I hope I'm allowed in here. I'm not a club member."

"You're always welcome here, Ned." Though he'd never come to the café before.

He sat on a stool at the eating bar. "I wanted to talk to you without your grandfather around."

Val poured Ned's coffee. He'd gone behind Granddad's back once before, when he'd alerted Val's mother that Lillian might be a gold digger. If he had more to say about her now, Val would love to hear it, but first she'd have to wait on the three middle-aged women at a bistro table. Five minutes ago, when she'd tried to take their food orders, they'd waved her off. Now they were giving her pointed looks.

She set a mug of coffee and a small pitcher of milk on the eating bar in front of Ned. "I'll be right back."

Val took the women's orders for two veggie wraps and a quiche. She went back behind the counter, sliced a piece of quiche, and put it in the oven to warm. "Would you like something to eat, Ned? A quiche or a sandwich? On the house."

"I'll eat lunch at the Village, but I wouldn't mind one of those." He pointed to a glass jar of biscotti studded with almonds. "Folks at the Village are saying your grandfather might have poisoned Scott's food. I know he wouldn't kill anyone on purpose. He could have done it by accident if he cooked the food. But I'm pretty sure you made the food and wouldn't poison it."

Val gave Ned two biscotti on a plate. He'd known her grandfather long enough to realize that the Codger Cook couldn't cook. "Someone might have poisoned Scott before he came to dinner."

"Or a guest at the dinner did it. The police should investigate Lillian and Thomasina."

If Val had antennae, they would have quivered. "I want to hear more about that. First, I have to get some stuff from the fridge." She hated to keep walking away from Ned, but she didn't want to keep her customers waiting.

Ned watched her put the hummus and veggies on the counter. "You may not know this, Val, but everyone out at the Village talks about what they used to do. Folks there know I ran a hardware store. If they have some small thing that needs fixing and they don't want to wait for the Village maintenance crew to get around to it, they come to me because I have the tools and skills."

"Uh-huh." Val wasn't sure what this had to do with Lillian and Thomasina. Maybe Ned just needed to talk, but she needed to work. She spread hummus on the two wraps.

Five teenagers came into the café, two boys and three girls. They shoved two bistro tables together and rearranged the chairs.

Ned dunked a biscotti in his coffee. "A lot of the women at the Village were teachers or nurses. The ones who didn't work for a living talk about what their husbands did. Well, Lillian and Thomasina never talk about the past. I don't know what they did for a living or what their husbands did."

Val tucked peppers, cucumbers, and sprouts into the wraps. "You think they're hiding something?"

"Could be. The police should l[ook] Your grandfather wouldn't like it into this and talked to the poli[ce] friend."

"He wouldn't like it any better [taking] the quiche from the oven. "I [told] mother your concerns about Li[llian] information to the chief. But c[ould] tell her about the chowder dinne[r] I don't want her worried."

"As long as you know and yo[u] don't have any reason to call he[r]"

Val delivered the lunches to the café and returned to the co[unter] her cell phone number. The ne[xt time] talk to her without her grandf[ather] it, he wouldn't have to drive to

"Hey, there's no burgers o[n] here. No hot dogs either." Th[e] teenage boys waved the café's [menu]

"Better than food *fat*ism," t[he other] him said.

Ned glanced back at the te[ens] brows almost met over the [bridge.] hope they never learn what f[ood] back to Lillian and Thoma[sina] guesses about what they use[d to] talk about herself, but she [talks about] news she's read. I think sh[e was in a professional] field."

"I got the same impressio[n, judg]ing how Lillian knew not [to] Granddad called *upchuck sy[ndrome*] had been off the market. "W[hy]

question came from a young woman lolling on the armless settee in the corner. She'd taken over the largest table in the café for herself. Val must have had her back turned when the woman came into the café. Otherwise, she couldn't have missed seeing her. The woman's black spiky hair had a streak of purple in it, her lips and nose had piercings, and she wore a white ribbed tank top resembling a man's undershirt, perfect to show off her bulging biceps. Instead of the caveman-diet food Val expected her to order, the woman chose a Greek salad.

Val went back to the counter. She made the Greek salad quickly and delivered it to the musclewoman in the corner. Then she tackled the teenagers' orders.

Ned cradled his coffee mug. "Your granddad asked me to find out more about the man who committed suicide at that other retirement place. I'll talk to the woman at the Village who told us about it."

"Ask her the name and location of that place. Thomasina moved to the Village from another retirement community, but she didn't say which one."

Ned stirred his coffee with what was left of his biscotti. "What are you thinking? That if Scott gave seminars there and bilked a man of his life savings, his mother might have lived in the community?"

"Right. Did she ever encourage you to invest with him?"

"She did the opposite. She told everyone Scott made a lot of money for other people, but she didn't want anyone at the Village to take his investment advice. She was afraid if the market went down, folks there might blame her."

That didn't sound as if Thomasina had been her

son's accomplice, but he might have had a less obvious partner in crime. "While you're at it, try to find out if Lillian lived at that other place, but don't tell Granddad I asked you to do that."

"Your secret's safe with me." He pushed his empty mug toward her on the counter. "Thanks for the snack. See you tomorrow at the Brain Game."

"Thanks for stopping by, Ned, and please come again."

She finished making lunches for the teenagers and delivered them to their table.

A shriek came from the woman at the corner table who'd ordered a Greek salad. "There's a worm in my salad!" She pointed to her plate.

Val zoomed to the woman's table.

One teenage boy beat her there. "Hey, look at that. It's green, with dark stripes and black bumps."

Val peered at the plate of tomatoes, cucumbers, Greek olives, red onions, and feta cheese. A yellowish green critter an inch long sat on a bright red tomato. "It's an earworm."

"Ew." The woman clapped a hand over her much-pierced ear as if expecting the worm to grow wings and fly into it.

"Not that kind of ear. When you shuck an ear of corn, you often find one near the tip. It's actually a caterpillar." And it would grow wings eventually. But how had it gotten into the salad? Val would have seen it when she was slicing the tomatoes and cucumbers. It certainly hadn't arrived with the onions, olives, and feta cheese. She reached for the plate. "I'll give you a new salad."

The woman pulled it away from her. "No, you won't. I'm showing this to the manager. And I don't want any more of your food with disgusting things in it." She marched out of the café. Val wanted to follow her and defend herself, but she still had customers—though she wondered for how long. The two women with veggie wraps opened them up and peered inside.

Val felt as if she'd stumbled onto the set of a play starring the musclewoman and her pet earworm. Act Three of *Café Sabotage*.

The boys at the teens' table were deconstructing their sandwiches, probably in search of crawling things.

The girl who'd ordered a Cobb salad pushed it away. "I really don't want to eat this. Could I have a smoothie instead?"

The chubby boy guffawed. "If there's a worm in the smoothie, it'll be chopped so small you won't even notice it."

Val had no choice. "Order whatever you like. Your lunch is free. All of you."

With that incentive, the five teens decided to risk drinking a wormy smoothie.

After the café closed, the manager came in with the plate the complaining woman had shown him, now minus the salad and the earworm. With a temperament as even as his perfect tan, he usually greeted people with a smile worthy of a tooth whitener ad. Today his mouth was closed in a grim line. He asked Val the origin of her salad ingredients.

He winced at her answer. "An organic farm market? No wonder. From now on, Val, check the produce from that market carefully or buy somewhere else."

If she argued that a total stranger had planted a worm in a salad, he'd ask why anyone would do that, and she had no answer. "Is the woman who ordered the salad a new member? I never saw her at the club before today."

"She bought a daily membership. But this isn't the first complaint I've heard about things crawling in the café."

Could she persuade him those complaints had been trumped up? "On Monday, I found a dead fish in my car. This morning, I slipped on water someone threw on the floor here. The complaints about the café are just part of a campaign against me."

His raised eyebrows conveyed skepticism. "Did anyone see you fall?"

"No."

Did he think she was lying, paranoid, playing for his sympathy . . . or all three? She couldn't tell. With a curt nod, he turned on his heel and left.

She envisioned her follow-on café contract slipping away. It was obvious who would benefit if she lost the contract—Irene. Maybe she'd hired the muscle-woman to plant a worm in the salad.

As Val put together a breakfast casserole to be baked in the morning, Bethany called to confirm that she'd work from ten to two tomorrow if Val still needed her. Val certainly did. Between playing a tennis ladder match this afternoon and meeting with Junie May this evening, she wouldn't have much time to come up with the questions for the Brain Game unless Bethany relieved her at the café. Val told her about the water on the floor and described the woman who'd claimed to find an earworm in the salad. Unless the purple streak in the woman's hair turned green and the piercings disappeared overnight,

Bethany would recognize her and watch out for trouble.

Val took extra care cleaning the café, making sure nothing was crawling around. When she finished, she had just enough time to change into her tennis shorts and rush out to the courts.

A pair of teenage boys played on one court. A woman stood alone near the net on the far court, a tall blonde in a body-hugging white tennis dress. That had to be Val's opponent, Petra Bramling.

As Val approached the court, she recognized the woman from her intricate French braid—Gunnar's ex-fiancée.

Chapter 15

Val and Petra introduced themselves and shook hands. They didn't mention their connection to Gunnar, but they didn't need to. Petra could have challenged any of the twenty women on the tennis ladder. Challenging Val was no coincidence.

Val couldn't control whether Gunnar returned to his fiancée, but she could control this match. So what if Petra had legs six inches longer? Most of Val's opponents had height in their favor. With good anticipation and stamina, she could prevail over taller players.

Trouble began early in the match. The first time Petra called Val's shot out when it was good, Val chalked it up to a mistake, possibly her own. After all, her opponent had a better view of where the ball had hit the court. The second time it happened, Petra was dead wrong. Val's shot had gone exactly where she'd aimed it—inside the line. But she didn't question the call and even gave Petra's shots the benefit of the doubt when they hit just outside the line. Experience had taught Val that generous line calls encouraged the opponent to reciprocate.

Other opponents. Not this one.

The third time Petra made a bad call, the ball was so far in the court that Val couldn't let it go. "Are you sure that ball was out?"

"Positive. I call the lines on this side of the net. You call the lines on your side."

Okay, no more charitable line calls for her. Competitive juices gushed through Val like a rain-swollen stream. She blasted shots across the net and made Petra work for every point, running her from one side of the court to another. She was so fired up that she sometimes overhit, giving away a point. The score stood at four to two in Val's favor when Petra announced it in her own favor and immediately served the ball. Val hit the return into the net, distracted by the incorrect score.

"You made a mistake in the game score," Val called out as Petra prepared to serve again. "You have two games. I have four."

"That's not true. I'm winning." Petra served the ball before Val could get into position to return it. "Now I'm ahead thirty-love in this game."

Val felt her blood pressure rising. She approached the net. "When I served the previous game, I announced the score as three-two. Then I won that game, making it four-two in my favor."

Petra joined her at the net. "I didn't hear you say that score, or I would have corrected it. And *I* won that last game, not you."

Val felt rattled. Could she have announced the wrong score? Possibly, but probably not. She'd never done that before. What's more, she remembered every point of the previous game. "I can refresh your memory about that last game. I won the first two points on the serve—"

Petra twirled her racket. "The score is four-two, thirty-love. Let's play . . . unless you're giving up."

Val's teeth clenched. "We have to agree on the score before continuing."

Petra looked down her nose at Val. "You might as well give up. You don't seriously think you can compete with me. I always win."

Not talking tennis here, are we? "I've seen how you win . . . by cheating." Val walked off the court, her racket tucked under her arm.

"Winning is winning," Petra said. "And you just defaulted."

Val went to Yumiko's office and told her what had happened. The tennis manager said she'd talk to Petra and try to resolve what must have been a misunderstanding.

Good luck with that. "No misunderstanding. She was cheating. She'll tell you I'm a sore loser and defaulted. You know me better than that, and you don't know her at all. So whose version will you believe?"

"She is the customer, Val. You work here. The customer is always right. If you cannot reach agreement, her name will replace yours on the tennis ladder." Yumiko pointed to the ladder list posted on her bulletin board. "You can speak to the club manager if you like."

Not a good idea, given how low Val's stock with the manager had sunk. "Don't involve him. I accept your decision." Val pivoted, took a few steps, and turned back to Yumiko. "When Petra Bramling first came to the club, she asked for Gunnar. You sent her to the café. Did you talk to her after that?"

"Yes, later that day. She said she went to the café and the woman working at the counter didn't know Gunnar. She must have spoken to Bethany. I told her your name and what you looked like. You were in the café too, she said, and heard her asking about Gunnar."

"I didn't hear her." Petra must have declared war on Val from that moment on. "I wish you had told me that the woman who challenged me was the one who asked about Gunnar."

"She did not give me her name the day she asked about him. I'm sorry the match turned out so bad for you."

Val went back to the Cool Down Café. She made a cranberry spritzer and took it to the corner table. The bad taste in her mouth from the tennis match disappeared quickly. The match had told what she couldn't have guessed earlier—that Petra hadn't succeeded in winning Gunnar back . . . yet. If she had, she wouldn't have bothered with the tennis confrontation. She'd acted out of frustration on the court, using tactics that couldn't possibly get her what she wanted, but revealed her character.

Petra played dirty. She would relish harassing Val, and all the dirty tricks had happened since Petra came to town. She could have found out what kind of car Val drove by following her to the parking lot after the café closed on Sunday. Easy to imagine Gunnar's ex thrusting a fish into a car, complaining about the café food, and throwing water on the floor, but Val couldn't pin the salad worm on her . . . unless the musclewoman was Petra's friend or even a relative. Both women had pinched features and steely eyes. Or was that just wishful thinking? Yes. Val was getting carried away because of her annoyance over the tennis match. She couldn't prove Gunnar's ex guilty of harassment.

She phoned Bethany and asked her to be on the lookout for both Petra and the musclewoman at the café tomorrow. Bethany said she'd keep her phone handy. If she saw the dirty-tricks suspects together, she'd snap a picture of them with her camera.

Val doubted the two would be stupid enough to hang out with each other anywhere at the club. Her phone rang a minute after she hung up with Bethany. The New York sommelier whose cookbook she'd publicized was returning her call.

"Hey, Val. Got your message. Yow!" Brakes screeched and horns blared. "I'm in a cab. Some idiot nearly sideswiped us. What can I do for you?"

He sounded in a hurry. She'd better get to the point fast. "Do you happen to know a sommelier named Omar Azamov? He works in the D.C. area."

"Omar. Yeah. He was in the Master Sommelier prep course with me. I'm sure whatever wine he recommends will be terrific."

"You know anything about his background or his family?" Val watched Gunnar's ex give the café a sneering glance on her way to the club exit. *Same to you, Petra.*

"His parents were immigrants. I don't remember where from. They died when he was young. He started as a busboy and climbed the restaurant ladder. That's all I remember, and the cab's about to let me off. How's your cookbook coming, Val?"

Slowly—thanks to a murder last month and another

this month. "I'm still working on it. Thank you for your help." And for being too rushed to ask why she wanted to know about Omar.

"Let me know when you're back in the city." He hung up.

What little she'd learned from him suggested Lillian had lied about knowing Omar's father. There had to be a reason for that lie.

Her phone rang again. This time it was her grandfather calling to ask when she'd be home.

"I'm meeting Junie May at six-thirty, Granddad. You can either wait until I get back to make dinner or microwave the chicken casserole that's in the freezer."

"I'll zap the casserole. I don't want to wait for you. Lillian and I are going to a movie tonight."

"I was thinking about her friend Omar. If it turns out someone poisoned Scott at your dinner, we'll need to find out as much as possible about every guest. See if you can get some information about Omar from her. She's the only one who knows him."

"I'd just as soon forget about that chowder dinner for a few hours."

Val couldn't blame him. After hanging up, she went to the locker room, showered, and changed her clothes. She looked forward to her meeting with Junie May. Maybe the reporter had dug up something new on Granddad's dinner guests.

Thanks to her aborted tennis match, Val had almost an hour to spare before driving to the reporter's house. She could spend the time poking around secondhand shops, where—according to Junie May—you might find old bottles containing poisonous substances now banned. Maybe Scott's poisoner had acquired arsenic locally.

Val didn't bother visiting the upscale antique shops in Bayport's historic district. They offered jewelry, coins, and decorative items made of precious metals. She'd have a better chance of finding toxic heavy metals at the secondhand shops on the outskirts of town.

The first two she tried, Old 'N Things and Must Haves, didn't carry vintage glassware or any apothecary items. The third shop, Cobweb Corner, had blue, green, and amber bottles with POISON embossed on them.

The grandmotherly shop owner watched her examine bottles. "A lot of folks like old poison bottles for the unusual colors and shapes. We have some three-sided and five-sided bottles. Now this here is one of my favorite shapes." She pulled a clear bottle off the shelf.

Val didn't recognize the contours until the woman laid the bottle on its side. "Oh, it's shaped like a coffin. That's appropriate."

"You see all the bumps, lines, and swirls in these bottles? The idea was that a person reaching for a bottle in the dark would know by feeling it that it contained poison, not cough syrup or a tonic, which came in smooth bottles."

The poison bottles at Cobweb Corner contained nothing except air now. "Do you ever sell antique bottles with the contents still inside?" Val asked.

The woman shook her head. "We clean everything first."

With no interest in clean, empty poison bottles, Val moved to a shelf displaying cooking vessels, including the copper pans and cast-iron pots that resembled her grandmother's. The ones in good condition had high price tags.

Her cell phone rang as she left the shop. Althea called to say her friend in Annapolis had been doing title searches today and researched the house Val had asked about. Lillian owned it free and clear, with no mortgage on it and no other obvious liens.

Granddad's sweetheart might have other debts not secured by the house, but at least she didn't have a mortgage company threatening foreclosure.

Val called her mother while she had good news to share. Waiting longer might mean she'd have to deliver bad news. She left a voice mail message, telling her mother not to worry about Granddad losing his money to his sweetheart. Based on the value of the property he and Lillian owned, he looked more like a fortune hunter than she did.

While Val tried to allay her mother's fears, she couldn't get rid of her own suspicions about Granddad's girlfriend. Owning an expensive house didn't mean Lillian wasn't after Granddad's money. Nor did it mean she wasn't a murderer.

Val drove to Treadwell and located secondhand shops more down-market than Bayport's.

She peered in the windows of several small stores, where the windows were clean enough that she could see they had no old bottles for sale. A shop named One of a Kind had dingy windows and assorted objects on shelves, tables, and the floor. Pictures and purses hung on the walls. Frying pans and suitcases were suspended from hooks in the ceiling. She went inside.

A Casablanca fan churned up musty air barely cooler than the outside temperature on a hot July afternoon. The only air-conditioning came from a single inadequate window unit. The shop had few customers—two middle-aged women examining teacups and a younger woman peering at jewelry in a glass case. A heavy, red-faced man stood immobile behind the counter. Wisps of his thinning brown hair fluttered in the breeze from the fan.

Val spotted glassware on the built-in shelves along the shop's back wall. Two shelves held dusty bottles, many with faded labels on them. After shifting three rows of glassware, she found a clear bottle of rat and mouse poison with a label listing the active ingredient as 1.5 percent arsenic trioxide. The bottle, embossed with a rat on the side opposite the label, had no cap on it and was empty. Behind it was another rat poison bottle, three-sided and containing liquid. Its yellow label listed the contents as 2.5 percent arsenic trioxide.

"Can I help you, miss?" the man behind the counter called out.

She turned to see him staring at her. She took the bottle with the yellow label to the counter. "This looks like something a friend of mine recently bought. I'm wondering if she got it here."

"Doubt it. Most of our stuff is one of a kind, just like the shop name. Except for candlesticks and such. You want to buy that bottle?"

"I don't think you should have this for sale. It's labeled poison, and the bottle isn't empty." She pointed to the contents listed on the label. "It says here that it contains arsenic."

He eyed her with suspicion. "It says on the cap that it's fifteen dollars. I'm not lowering the price."

"You're selling poison."

He shrugged. "Everybody's got poison under the sink and in the garage. That bottle will cost you fifteen dollars and ninety cents with tax. You want to buy it or not?"

A week ago, she'd have bought it as her good deed for the day, to prevent an accidental or a deliberate poisoning. She'd have put the bottle in the locked shed where Granddad stored dangerous items until the next hazardous-waste collection day. But now, after Scott's murder by poison, she wouldn't put arsenic in Granddad's shed. Nor would she even carry it. She had no way to dispose of it without arousing suspicion.

"No, sir, I don't want to buy it, and you don't want to put it back on the shelf. If I see it on the shelf again, I'll notify the police. Your fine for selling a banned and dangerous substance will be way more than the fifteen dollars you'd get for selling that bottle."

The man's face grew redder. "All right, I'll pour out the liquid. Will you buy it then?"

"No, and you won't pour it out because it isn't safe to dispose of arsenic that way. Keep it locked up until you can take it to the hazardous-waste collection site."

The man muttered something about her being a nut job.

One of the women looking at teacups approached the counter. "She's right. You can't leave poison sitting around."

The man fished a key from his pocket and put the bottle in a locked cabinet behind the counter.

Val checked her watch as she left the shop. She'd killed too much time checking out poison bottles.

Even if the traffic was lighter than usual, she would keep Junie May waiting.

The rat poison occupied Val's mind as she drove south on the highway. She had no idea if the bottle she'd seen at the shop contained enough arsenic to murder anyone, but it hadn't been hard to find. With patience and determination, a would-be poisoner could accumulate enough to do the trick.

Val turned off the highway onto a country road flanked by fields. Another turn took her to a lane where mailboxes at driveways provided the only clues that houses existed beyond the trees and bushes.

She found the address Junie May had given her on a mailbox and drove down a long gravel driveway toward a ground-hugging, one-story frame house. Junie May's silver compact car was parked in front of a detached garage. Val pulled up behind the car. The reporter had exaggerated in saying she lived in the woods. Though if she didn't get the bushes and undergrowth trimmed, she could soon say she lived in a jungle.

A paved path led from the driveway to the front door. It ran along the length of the house, under the roof overhang. Val approached a picture window. An armchair upholstered in a bold flower print was near the window, a lamp table between the chair and a powder blue sofa against an interior wall.

On the other side of the sofa, facing the window, Junie May was slumped in an armchair that matched the one near the window, her eyes unblinking, a hole in her temple.

Chapter 16

Val's heart thumped so loudly she could hear nothing else. She squeezed her eyes shut, convinced that they were playing tricks on her. When she opened them, the tableau framed by the window hadn't changed, but now she took in more details. The blood on Junie May. Her limp hand hanging over the chair's arm. Her fingers pointed toward a gun on the beige carpet.

Someone had shot her. Someone who might still be in the house or lurking around it.

Run! Val tried, but couldn't budge. Her knees locked. Her feet went numb. Trying to flee and getting nowhere—that happened in her nightmares. But this was real. A crow cawed in a tree behind her. Suddenly her legs worked.

She ran to her Saturn, put it in reverse, and zig-zagged back up the driveway to the lane. Across the lane, a woman emptied her mailbox. An SUV nosed out of a driveway in front of Val. A station wagon entered the lane from the country road.

Junie May's neighbors were coming and going,

like people in most neighborhoods at this time of day. These signs of ordinary life calmed Val. The car she'd seen at the house had been Junie May's. It didn't belong to her killer, who'd probably already driven off, the job done. Val didn't trust her own conclusion enough to return to the house, but she felt safe pulling over six houses from Junie May's, near where the lane intersected the country road. She reached for her phone and punched 911.

When the dispatcher answered, Val described what she'd seen at Junie May's house. The dispatcher took down her name, asked for her location and a description of her car, and told her to stay where she was. The emergency responders would arrive shortly. The sky was darkening by the minute.

Val hugged herself to keep from shaking. If she hadn't stopped at the secondhand shops, she would have arrived here early. In time to prevent a murder? Or would she have walked in on the murderer and be lying next to Junie May now? Val shuddered.

Her relief at being alive turned to anger as fast as the lightning forking in the distance. Junie May didn't deserve to die. Scott didn't deserve to die either, but Val had wanted to uncover the truth about his death only to prove her grandfather innocent. Could anyone possibly think Granddad had murdered Junie May?

The arrival of a county sheriff's car interrupted her churning thoughts. The car stopped across the lane from hers. A middle-aged deputy approached her Saturn. He confirmed that she'd made the 911 call and told her that he or a colleague would come to interview her shortly. In the meantime, she should stay in her car.

An emergency medical vehicle arrived next and more sheriff's cars. Some of Junie May's neighbors stood near her driveway. Val rested her head on the steering wheel. Junie May was going to dig up information today about the guests at Granddad's dinner. Did her search for the truth about Scott's death threaten his murderer and lead to her own death? Someone who'd murdered once had no reason to hold back a second time. Or a third. Val had asked a lot of questions about the chowder dinner. Did that put her next on the hit list?

Thunder rumbled, raindrops fell, and the neighbors near Junie May's driveway scattered.

A tap on the window startled Val. A deputy stood outside in the rain, tall, spruce, and broad-shouldered in a black-and-gray uniform. She cracked the window open.

He introduced himself as Roy Chesterfeld. He asked for her driver's license and took it to a sheriff's car. He must be checking whether she had a criminal record. Five minutes later, he appeared at her window again. His wide-brimmed hat did a good job of shielding his face and head from the rain, but the rest of him was getting wet.

He handed her the license. "Thank you. I'd like to ask you a few questions where neither of us will get rained on. We can use the sheriff's car, I can sit in your car, or we can meet at—"

"Please sit here." She gestured to the passenger seat.

He climbed into the seat next to her and took off his hat. His tousled blond hair contrasted with his otherwise neat appearance. "You mind putting on the air-conditioning?"

"Not at all." She hadn't noticed the heat in the car

until he joined her. She turned on the motor and put the AC on full blast.

"Your car has a weird smell."

"From a rotten fish. The AC will bring in fresh air from outside. If it bothers you, we can talk elsewhere."

"I'll get used to it." He gave her a reassuring smile. "What you saw at that house must have spooked you. Try to relax. From here on, it's all routine."

Maybe for him, but not for her. In answer to his questions, she told him where she worked and described what had happened from the time she turned into Junie May's driveway until she called 911. He was polite, respectful, and attractive, totally unlike Deputy Holtzman from the sheriff's office near Bayport . . . and therefore more dangerous. She'd never let down her guard with Holtzman, but with Roy, she felt herself melting, even calling him by his first name, at least in her mind. Holtzman had given her only his last name.

Roy took notes as she talked. "A deputy recognized the victim as a reporter for a local TV station. We don't want news of this to go public until we've contacted her next of kin. I'll ask you not to tell anyone what you saw here until we issue a statement." At her nod, he continued. "Were you a good friend of Junie May Jussup?"

"I barely knew her." Val wouldn't have met her except for the chowder dinner. Hard to believe only four days had passed since then. "The first time I talked to her at length was yesterday. We met for a drink in Bayport. She invited me to stop by her house this evening."

He looked up from his small notebook. "Why

her as more solid and rooted than Gunnar, who might hop into a red sports car, his or Petra's, and ride off into the sunset.

The deputy tucked his notebook with her phone numbers in his breast pocket. "Are you sure you're okay? Going to meet someone and finding them dead can be a shock."

And the aftershock could be even worse. A month ago, soon after Val came upon a murder victim, a killer had targeted her too. "I hope the statement the sheriff issues about this doesn't include my name. I don't want any attention from the media." Or from a murderer the police didn't believe existed.

"I understand. There's no reason to mention your name. I'll ask my boss if you can leave."

"Thank you." Her stomach rumbled as he climbed out of the car.

She usually had hard candy stashed in the storage bin between the front seats. Today the bin was empty. So were the pouches behind the front seats. She'd removed everything from the car in the fish cleanup.

The deputy tapped on her driver's-side window. She rolled it down.

"You're free to go. I'll bet you haven't eaten yet. Here's something to tide you over. I carry these in my glove compartment." He offered her a protein bar.

She'd tried a bar like that once, the closest she'd ever come to a mouthful of sawdust. A protein bar would tempt her only if she hadn't eaten in two days and there was no roadkill in sight. "Thank you, but I'll stop for a snack on the way."

Sadness nearly overwhelmed her on the drive home. Going in the other direction two hours ago, she'd looked forward to exchanging information with Junie May, convinced that between them they could solve the mystery of Scott's death and lift the shadow hanging over Granddad. Now Junie May was dead. Because of something she'd found out today? Or something she remembered about the chowder dinner?

Val told herself not to leap to conclusions and tried to imagine an explanation for the reporter's death that had nothing to do with the guests at the chowder dinner. Maybe a drugged-out burglar had shot Junie May for not surrendering her laptop. Unlikely, but possible.

To Val's relief, Granddad's Buick wasn't parked on the street when she arrived home. She didn't look forward to telling him about Junie May. He still hadn't returned from his movie date with Lillian by the time Val finished eating an omelet and a salad. She went up to her bedroom and phoned Chief Yardley.

She told him about the reporter's death and her interview with the deputy. "I'm just afraid the sheriff's department there will write off her death as a suicide without a full investigation."

"Between the crime scene unit, the medical examiner, and the forensic lab, they'll figure out what happened. Don't go around talking to anyone outside law enforcement about what you saw and what you suspect."

"Is it okay if I tell Granddad what happened?"

"Warn him not to go around saying his granddaughter found another body. If you're right about what happened to Junie May, you may have just missed seeing who killed her. The murderer would want to make sure the person who drove up didn't get a glimpse of him . . . or her."

"And I'll have to hope the murderer didn't get a glimpse of me."

It occurred to Val after she hung up that even without the police releasing her name, her bright blue Saturn might be enough to identify her.

She had trouble falling asleep, haunted by fears of a murderer gunning for her.

Before leaving for the café Thursday morning, Val knocked on Granddad's door.

He'd just woken up and was sitting on the edge of the bed when she went into the room.

She sat next to him. "I have bad news. I found Junie May dead when I got to her house."

"What?" He put an arm around her. "*You* found her? Are you all right?"

She leaned against his shoulder. "I barely slept."

"Why didn't you tell me last night?"

"Then we both wouldn't have slept. She had a bullet in her temple." Val felt her grandfather's grip on her tighten. "The first deputies on the scene thought she committed suicide. I think she was murdered because she found out something about Scott's murder."

"Someone shot her to keep her quiet. That makes more sense than suicide."

At least one person agreed with Val. "Yesterday she told me Scott was one of her sources. She was working in secret on a story she hoped would give her career a boost."

Granddad rubbed his grizzled chin. "Do you suppose whistle-blowing got him killed, not scamming?"

"I hadn't even thought of that." She glanced at her watch. "I'm running late." She'd spent the first half of the night restless and then zonked out for the second half, not even hearing her alarm go off.

"You gotta let the police handle this and not go around asking questions about Scott or Junie May."

"I'm happy to leave it to the police. The chief said we shouldn't tell anyone I was at Junie May's house." She stood up. "I'd better go to work or my customers will be in the café before I am."

"No more dead bodies, Val. This is the second one you found since you moved here. You keep that up, and folks here will run you out of town."

Arriving late at the café meant Val had to play catch-up for the first few hours. She was so busy brewing coffee, making pecan muffins, and serving customers that she forgot to turn on the wall-mounted TV until the regional news program was almost over.

The middle-aged anchorman recapped stories covered in more depth earlier in the show, one of them about Junie May. "Last evening, in response to an emergency call, sheriff's deputies went to the home of Junie May Jussup, a reporter for our affiliate station, and found her dead. No details are available yet about the cause of death, pending an investigation and notification of relatives. Ms. Jussup, who began working in southern Maryland two years ago, will be missed by colleagues and viewers alike. We'll bring more details about her untimely death as they become available."

Other recaps followed. The anchorman ended with a late-breaking bulletin. "A Baltimore man, Scott Freaze, died early this week at Treadwell Hospital after experiencing severe gastrointestinal symptoms. Criminal investigators from the state police, the county sheriff, and town police are cooperating on the inquiry into the man's death, tentatively attributed to arsenic poisoning. No further details are available at this time. Stay tuned for updates."

Stay tuned for updates repeated in Val's head. Junie May had said those words on TV a few days ago after vowing to find out what happened to Scott. Now she was dead. Val sighed.

She left the TV on, hoping for a news bulletin about the investigation into the reporter's death. An hour later, she was making crustless spinach quiche when two men in uniform strode into the café. Deputy Chesterfeld, blond, bright-eyed, and smiling. Deputy Holtzman, bald, eagle-eyed, and glaring. She recognized the classic setup. Unfortunately, the bad cop probably had seniority. The good cop might never get a word in.

They approached the counter as the club manager passed by the café alcove. He glanced at them, stopped cold, and then after two seconds continued toward his office.

Val gulped. On top of assorted complaints about the café, she'd have to explain visits from law enforcement.

Chapter 17

Val greeted the two men in uniform as if they were café customers. "Good morning, Deputy Chesterfield. Deputy Holtzman." She pointed to muffins mounded on a plate under a glass lid. "Care for a blueberry muffin and something to drink?"

Roy Chesterfield pulled a protein bar from his pocket. "No muffins for me, but the coffee smells great. I wouldn't mind—" He broke off at a frown from the deputy, who outranked him.

"Tap water for both of us." Holtzman surveyed the empty café. "We'll sit at that table in the far corner. Less chance of anyone interrupting us there. I have some questions for you, Ms. Deniston."

She brought their water to the table and sat on the settee. From there, she could see if anyone came into the café. "I'm expecting my assistant in fifteen minutes. Until then, I'll have to take care of any customers who come in."

"We'll wait if necessary. Last night, you told Deputy Chesterfield that Junie May Jussup was murdered. Well, you were right. Now how would you

glowered. "**Did** your grandfather know
nning to visit **Ms. Jussup?**"
 him at four yesterday and told him I'd
nner because I was meeting her."
ell him where you were going to meet

ed long enough to replay the brief con-
'd had with her grandfather and, from
Holtzman's face, to arouse suspicion.

xt fifteen minutes, Holtzman quizzed
ian and the other guests at the chowder
ld him what she knew without saying
he last three days digging it up. Roy
hrew in a few questions about Junie
ship with Scott.
cautioned her on his way out of the
k about what she'd seen at Junie May's
 know she's dead, thanks to the media.
 to announce how she died yet. We're
reaching her only relative."
ter the deputies left, Bethany arrived
e café until closing time. She wore a
dress in a leopard-spotted print.
seen that dress before. Something
 to match the caveman diet?
idn't think the flowered apron would
 so I bought this too." Bethany held
n with a reptile skin pattern. "Do you
 coming up with questions for the

the questions, but I could use help at
 really worked well with the people at

know that just from looking in the window? The first
responders who went into the room concluded it
was a suicide."

His interviewing techniques hadn't changed in a
month. He used veiled accusations to fish for information. In this case, he was suggesting she'd had
inside knowledge about the murder. "The first responders may have seen evidence the murderer
planted to suggest suicide, but I was too far away to
see that evidence. It never crossed my mind that she
would commit suicide."

Deputy Chesterfeld nodded. "You ruled that out
based on what you knew of her personality and
activities."

"You *said* you barely knew her." Holtzman's tone
implied Val had lied about that. "What was your
purpose in visiting her?"

"On Tuesday, we talked about my grandfather's
dinner. She thought one of his guests poisoned Scott
Freaze. She was going to dig up information and
share it with me."

"You told Deputy Chesterfeld she was secretive
about her research. Why would she share it with
you?"

A fair question. Val gave him points for picking up
on an apparent contradiction. "She wanted something in return. She expected me to tell her what I
learned about my grandfather's guests."

"Two Nancy Drews working together, huh? And
now there's just one."

Val didn't know what to say. Was he mocking her,
warning her of danger, or accusing her of offing
Nancy Drew?

A young woman came into the café, wearing a

red bandanna on her head and a long T-shirt over knee-length black leotards. She looked around.

Val stood up. "Excuse me. I'll deal with this customer and come back." She maneuvered between the bistro tables and checked her step when she noticed the customer's eyebrow and lip piercings.

Musclewoman must think hiding her biceps and her purple forelock would make her unrecognizable. She stared over Val's shoulder at the corner table, pivoted, and hightailed it out of the café.

Val turned around, wondering if the woman had recognized one of the deputies. Both had their backs to the café entrance. Their uniforms alone might have frightened off the woman. Val's small lingering doubt that musclewoman had planted a worm in the café disappeared. Val returned to the table in a better mood. The deputies had spared her from another dirty trick. They wouldn't be here together unless they were treating the murders in two different jurisdictions as possibly related.

She might as well lead them in the right direction. "The day before yesterday, Junie May said Lillian Hinker and Omar Azamov had the best chance to poison Scott's chowder. She even suggested they might have been working together. She was going to research those two."

"How would you have reacted if her research turned up something that incriminated your grandfather?"

"I'd have told her she was wrong. One thing I wouldn't have done is insist she was murdered. I'd have been happy for the police to assume she committed suicide." *Gotcha there, Holtzman.*

He sneered. "But if you knew we'd find out it was

---

murder, you would sa[...] take that as a sign o[...] grandfather's."

Roy Chesterfeld l[...] The mental contorti[...] pin crimes on Val d[...] while investigating [...] now he had even le[...]

She returned his [...] you and I sat acros[...] won't find my fin[...] scene."

"So you've neve[...] grandfather ever v[...]

Val stiffened. Th[...] tion without a re[...] looked hard at Dep[...] mastered the pok[...] her. Do you have [...] Junie May's house[...]

Roy Chesterfe[...] an obvious tell. W[...] there belonging [...] collect as eviden[...]

She stared at H[...] father sheds stra[...] His bathroom is [...] floor. It served a[...] der dinner. Any[...] collected a few [...] the last few days[...] Thomasina's co[...] those places to[...]

Chesterfeld [...]

Holtzma[...] you were pl[...]

"I talked [...] be late for [...]

"Did you [...] her?"

Val hesita[...] versation sh[...] the look on [...] "No."

For the n[...] her about Li[...] dinner. Val t[...] she'd spent [...] Chesterfeld [...] May's relatio[...]

Holtzman [...] café not to ta[...] house. "Peop[...] We don't wan[...] having troubl[...]

A minute a[...] to take over t[...] body-hugging[...]

"I've never[...] new?" Clothin[...]

"Uh-huh. I[...] go well with i[...] up a black apr[...] want any hel[...] Brain Game?"

"I'll manage[...] the session. Yo[...]

your pet-a-pet visit. Can you meet me at the Village before the Brain Game?"

"Okeydoke. Did you hear about the newscaster who died?" At Val's nod, she continued. "She was at your grandfather's dinner, like the man who was poisoned. That's scary. It's like that Agatha Christie where people die one by one until—"

"I know the ending." And the next step in the story—another murder. A chill came over Val. "See you later, Bethany. I'm heading home to work on those trivia questions." And to tell Granddad about the deputies' questions.

When Val arrived home fifteen minutes later, his Buick wasn't at the curb. As usual, she parked the Saturn at the side of the house. She had to squeeze past a pickup truck encroaching from the neighbor's half of the driveway. Whoever was visiting Harvey probably didn't expect another car to pull into the driveway at midday.

Granddad had left a note that he'd gone fishing. No point in calling him. He always turned off his cell phone while fishing, convinced that if it rang, the big one he was about to catch would get away. She sat at the computer in the study to work on the trivia questions.

She completed her questions in time to arrive at the Village thirty minutes early for the Brain Game.

Ned was sitting in a thick-cushioned chair on the front patio and motioned to her. "I got some information about the man who committed suicide at that other retirement community."

Val sat on the chair next to his. "On the Eastern Shore?"

"Nope. Near Alexandria, Virginia. A place called Spring Lake. The woman here who told me about the suicide put me in touch with her friend who lives there. I got the name of the man who died. Arthur Tunbridge. Here, I wrote it all down for you." He pulled a slip of paper from the pocket of his plaid shirt.

Val tucked the paper in her shoulder bag. She'd look up the man online as soon as she had a chance. "When did he die?"

"Around three or four months ago."

Just before Thomasina and Lillian moved here. "That's helpful, Ned."

His dark brows met over his nose. "Yeah, but I couldn't find out the name of the guy who gave financial seminars at the place. I told your grandfather all that when he called me this morning. Wanted me to go fishing with him. Wish I could have gone, but I had lunch plans with some folks here."

Fortunately, Granddad didn't mind fishing alone. "Did you ask the woman at Spring Lake if she knew Lillian or Thomasina?"

"She never heard of them. Then I called the main number and said I used to know some people who lived there and wondered if they still did. The gal at the switchboard didn't recognize their names. She looked them up on old rosters. No Thomasina Weal or Lillian Hinker for the last two years."

Darn. "Thanks for checking, Ned."

"Course if they were working with a con man, they coulda used aliases. It's easy to change your name."

"But harder to change your face." A picture beats

a thousand aliases. "I may take some photos at the Brain Game. I hope Lillian and Thomasina will be there."

"They told me they would be, but a woman who uses an alias may be camera shy." Ned tilted his head toward the reception area. "There's Bethany. She looks better in bright colors than animal designs. She gonna help you with the Brain Game?"

"Uh-huh." And with some photos, if Val could talk her into it.

"Don't forget to stop by the activity director's office to pick up the doughnut holes. We eat them before the session so we'll have the strength for all that brain work." He winked at her. "The winner gets to take the leftover doughnut holes as a prize."

"That's either an incentive to win or a reason to tank, depending on who made the doughnuts. See you there, Ned." Val stood up and went to the reception lobby.

Bethany beckoned to her. "I finally met Gunnar. He came into the café looking for you and introduced himself. I didn't say I recognized him from the picture his ex-fiancée showed me."

"That's good." Unfortunately, pretending Petra didn't exist wouldn't make her disappear.

"I liked him. He seems like a regular guy. I told him you'd gone home to work on questions for the Brain Game. You should call him."

"He cut short our last conversation."

"You're the one who stood him up for tennis."

Val put her hands on her hips. "Last month he went off in the middle of a date without any explanation. He had an excuse, which he eventually told me, and then he disappeared for a month. The guy has commitment issues."

"So do you. By the way, I kept looking for the musclewoman you described, but I didn't see her at the café today."

Without even waving a magic wand, the deputies had made the woman disappear at least for the day. Now to find out if Bethany's diet could still work its magic. If eating like a caveman had made her bold on the road three days ago, maybe it would turn her into a sneak photographer today.

Val lowered her voice, though no one in the lobby was close enough to hear her. "I want you to use my phone and take pictures of Thomasina and Lillian during the Brain Game, but without them knowing it."

Bethany rubbed her hands together. "That sounds like fun. But won't it click when I take a picture?"

"I can fix that." Val muted the sound and took a test photo. No click. She handed the phone to Bethany. "Take some practice photos while I stop by the activity director's office for doughnut holes."

"Just keep them away from me. Cavemen didn't do dough."

Val picked up the doughnut holes. They came in boxes from the supermarket. Bethany would have less problem resisting them than if they'd come from the Bayport bakery, which made airy, sugar-coated fried confections.

Bethany led the way to the game room. She and Val set the boxes on the counter near pitchers of lemonade and water. Assorted board games and decks of cards were stacked on shelves above a counter.

Though windowless, the room looked cheery, with three walls painted in lemon yellow and a seascape mural on the fourth wall. Padded club chairs on casters would seat more than thirty at five square tables for four and two round tables for six.

At each place, Val put pens and an answer sheet with lines numbered from one to ten. The majority of the trivia questions she'd made up dealt with local subjects that residents from the immediate area would find easy. She'd included challenging questions about medical and entertainment subjects to test Ned's theories about Lillian and Thomasina.

Bethany welcomed the Brain Game participants at the door and asked whether they'd like water or lemonade with their doughnut holes. Ned came early and offered to help serve the snacks.

Five minutes before the session was scheduled to start, Thomasina arrived in a black caftan. She came with a retinue, three women, also in black, apparently in mourning with her.

She frowned when she saw Val, as if trying to remember where they'd met, but then approached her with an extended hand. "Hello, again. I hope your grandfather's well. I didn't want to come today, but . . ." She looked toward her companions.

A thin woman with silver hair patted Thomasina's arm. "We encouraged her to get out of the cottage. She needs to be with people at a time like this." The other two women nodded in agreement.

The four of them took over one square table.

Four tables had already filled up by the time Lillian arrived. Her outfit was similar to the one she'd worn three days ago—a golfing outfit and pom-pom athletic socks, in pale pink instead of Monday's light blue.

She stopped dead when Val approached her. "What are you doing here?"

"Substituting for the Brain Dame. Thank you for coming."

Lillian joined another woman, who was sitting alone at a table for four. A minute later, a man in a wheelchair rolled into the room. Lillian moved aside a chair at her table to make room for him. Ned took the last empty seat at Lillian's table.

Val counted six men and fourteen women. "Welcome, everyone. I'm Val Deniston, filling in for the woman who usually runs the Brain Game. Please forgive me if I don't do everything the way she does. We'll start with some trivia. Please write your name at the top of the answer sheet in front of you."

"Oh heck." Bethany waved Val's phone. "I just got a new phone and it's so complicated, I can't get a text message I've been waiting for. It's totally frustrating."

Bethany sounded like a ham actress reading from a bad script, but nods from around the room showed empathy for her plight.

"Those newfangled phones are a real pain," the man in the wheelchair said.

"I second that," Ned said. "You gotta be a computer whiz to make a phone call these days."

"Sorry," Bethany said. "Just keep going with the trivia, Val, while I try to figure out this thing."

A good excuse for fiddling with the phone for the next half hour.

Thomasina rested her left arm on the table and crooked it around her paper, like an A student shielding her answers from roving eyes. Apparently, she didn't trust the friends she'd brought with her. Was she paranoid, or did these senior citizens cheat at the Brain Game? Amazing what some people will do for doughnuts.

"Is everyone ready?" Val saw heads nod. "Let's start. University of Maryland athletic teams share a name with the diamond-backed turtles native in this region. What is the name?"

All the men and half the women, including Lillian, immediately scribbled on their answer sheets, some probably writing *Terps,* the team's nickname. Only the full name, the Terrapins, matched the turtles' name. Thomasina pursed her lips, tapped her pen, and wrote something quickly as Val announced the second question.

"Which of these organs are not considered vital to life—the appendix, the liver, the gallbladder, the spleen? To get credit for the answer, you'll have to include all the organs from that list that people can live without."

All the pens in the room went into action. Val couldn't see the answer sheets, but she'd bet that everyone was writing *appendix.* How many of them would know the liver was the only vital organ among the four?

"Could you repeat the possible answers?" Thomasina said.

"Certainly. Appendix, liver, gallbladder, spleen—which can you live without?" From where Val stood, she could see Thomasina write something, hesitate, cross it out, and write again. "Question three. What married couple, both Oscar winners, starred in the

1973 TV movie *Divorce His, Divorce Hers* and, a year later, divorced in real life?"

Val had counted on most people forgetting this obscure Elizabeth Taylor and Richard Burton film if they ever knew it. Thomasina and a woman at another table wrote an answer immediately, everyone else more slowly. Lillian shrugged and scribbled something at the last second. As Val continued with the questions, Thomasina and Lillian glanced sideways toward each other's table frequently, apparently assessing the competition. Neither seemed to notice Bethany taking photos with the phone.

"We're almost done," Val said. "Question nine. The sweet taste of this antifreeze component makes it dangerous to animals and children who might drink it accidentally. Is it isopropyl alcohol, ethanol, ethylene glycol, or corn syrup?"

Both Lillian and Thomasina paused briefly and wrote something.

"Question ten." Casting around for entertainment questions earlier, Val had remembered the obscure fact Granddad and Gunnar had mentioned Sunday night about the director Alan Smithee. "What name was used by film directors from 1968 to 2000 when they didn't want their own name to appear in the credits? Was it Stacy Smith, Alan Smithee, John Smithson, or Sandy Shore?"

Thomasina smiled and wrote on her paper. The man in the wheelchair asked Val to repeat the question and answers.

When everyone stopped writing, Val asked the participants to pass their answer sheets to the table on their right for correcting and went over the questions again, asking for oral responses. No single question stumped the entire group of seniors. Lillian scored highest with seven correct answers. The man in the wheelchair and Ned got six right. Thomasina and three others scored five. To come out on top, Thomasina would have to make up her losses in the next game, Alphabits.

Val explained the rules while Bethany collected the trivia answer sheets and gave everyone a blank piece of paper. "I'm going to read a set of letters. You'll have five minutes to form as many words as you can from those letters. Your words have to be at least four letters long. You score a point for using all the letters in a single word and for any word that no one else has written."

When everyone was ready, Val announced the letters—*ACEEHLMNO*—and started the timer. When the timer dinged, she asked if anyone had used all nine letters in a word.

Only Thomasina raised her hand. "Chameleon."

"Great!" Val said. "That's worth two points. Anyone have an eight-letter word?" No one did. "How about seven letters?"

Thomasina had written *manhole,* but so had three other people. The woman at Lillian's table earned a point for *echelon.* Two of Thomasina's six-letter words, *menace* and *enamel,* were duplicates, but she scored a point for *enlace.*

Going through the shorter words took ten minutes and yielded few unique ones. Thomasina formed more words than anyone else. Though many were duplicates, her Alphabits score combined with her trivia score put her in first place. Lillian, Ned, and another man tied for second place. Thomasina claimed her doughnut prize and left with her entourage.

Once the room emptied out, Bethany gave Val the phone. "See what you think of the photos I took."

Val scrolled through them. She found an excellent full-face shot of Thomasina and a decent picture of Lillian. "I think you have a future as a paparazza when you give up teaching first graders."

Bethany laughed. "What are you going to do with those pictures?"

"I have a hunch one of our Brain Game rivals lived at a Virginia retirement community before moving here. No one there knows them by name. I want to drive there first thing in the morning and see if anyone recognizes either of them. Can you open the café for me?"

"I hate getting up early in the summer, but okay. I'll work as long as you need me tomorrow, but I have to leave right now. Muffin's waited a long time for her walk." Bethany hurried toward the door.

"I really appreciate your help." Besides paying Bethany for all the hours she'd worked, Val would invite her to a special dinner, but not until she could serve something other than caveman food.

Val took out her cell phone and checked her messages. She'd missed three calls. Granddad had left a message, saying he wouldn't be home until late afternoon. Either the fish were really biting, or he'd caught none yet and stubbornly refused to give up. The young real estate agent, Kimberly, had called to say that Mrs. Z liked the idea of renting her compact house for a few months and that Val's friend should call Kimberly to look at the house. Good news, but did Gunnar still want a place in Bayport? He, too, had left Val a message. He was sorry he'd missed her at the café this morning, hoped they could get together this evening, and would phone her later. Too vague a message for Val to guess why he was suddenly anxious to talk to her after being elusive for the last few days. She called him back, but only reached his voice mail.

She stuffed the score sheets in her tote bag and tidied up the room quickly, anxious to go home and search online now that she had the name of the man who'd committed suicide. She was about to leave when Lillian marched in.

"I want to talk to you." Lillian spoke through clenched teeth.

Uh-oh. Maybe she'd noticed Bethany sneaking a picture of her and held Val responsible. Val couldn't lie well enough to get away with denying it.

Chapter 18

Lillian ran a hand across her forehead and over her head, mussing up her usually neat hairdo. "I just found out Junie May Jussup is dead. The news reports aren't saying how she died. I called your grandfather to see if he knew, but he didn't answer the phone."

Val was relieved Lillian hadn't demanded an explanation of the sneak photos. "I'm not sure Granddad can tell you much. The police are keeping a lid on it."

Lillian sank into the nearest club chair, her face gray. "That means it wasn't an accident. It was another murder. Junie May announced on television that she would investigate Scott's death. She was asking for trouble."

A tremor of anger rattled Val. She stood tall and looked down at Lillian. "It sounds as if you're blaming the victim."

"No. I just don't want more victims. You questioned me, Omar, and no doubt everyone else at the chowder dinner. Don't you realize playing detective can put *you* in danger, like Junie May?"

Was that a warning or a threat? "Junie May kept her research to herself. I'll tell the police what I find out. No one will gain anything by harming me." The tell-all insurance policy for amateur sleuths, Val reasoned.

Lillian leaned back and folded her arms. "What did you find out about me?"

"That you own a nice house in Annapolis." Val took the chair opposite Lillian's at the square table. "I can't imagine why you're living in a tiny apartment here."

Annoyance flitted across Lillian's face. "People downsize, move to a place like this, and then regret it. Before I sell my house, I want to know if I can adjust to a different living arrangement. Is that so hard to understand?"

"Not at all." Mrs. Z felt the same way about selling her house. "My grandfather would have understood if you had told him. But for some reason, you didn't mention your house in Annapolis."

"Not talking about my financial assets is how I protect them from swindlers, fortune hunters, or anyone else who wants to go after them." Lillian drummed her fingers on the table. "Obviously, my financial affairs aren't safe from snoopers."

"I'll cop to being a snoop, but my grandfather's no fortune hunter."

"I know that. Did you do any research on Irene Pritchard? She and Junie May came to the dinner together."

And Junie May died four days later—hardly cause and effect. "I included everyone at the chowder

dinner in my research and my report to the police.
How long before the chowder dinner did you find
out that my grandfather invited Junie May?"

"A week. Scott was visiting Thomasina that weekend. I told them both. I didn't want him skipping
the dinner because he thought only senior citizens
would be there. He was definitely more enthusiastic
when he found out Junie May was going."

"So you used her to lure him there. And now
they're both dead."

Lillian covered her forehead with the palm of
her hand as if it were a cold compress. "My head's
throbbing. I've got to lie down." She trudged out of
the room.

Val had never before seen the cool Lillian so
upset. She looked almost frightened. Was she worried about her own or someone else's safety, or
worried that the truth would come out and impli-
cate her in two murders?

On her way out of the Village, Val drove past
Thomasina's cottage and slowed down. One of the
black-clad, gray-haired women who'd gone to the
Brain Game with Thomasina was carrying grocery
sacks up the walk to the cottage.

Val parked her Saturn. Though anxious to get
home and research Arthur Tunbridge, she couldn't
pass up the chance to hear Thomasina's take on
Junie May's death. She hurried up the path to the
cottage and rang the bell.

Thomasina's grocery-toting friend answered the
door and invited Val into the cottage. "I'm Edith.
You did a nice job with the Brain Game. This was the

first time I went. I only did it to keep Thomasina company, but I really enjoyed it."

"Thank you." The scent of Thomasina's floral perfume lingered in the empty living room and made Val long for a whiff of garlic.

She felt stifled by the velvet drapes and rugs on top of wall-to-wall carpeting. Between this overdecorated living room and the cold austerity of Lillian's apartment, a happy median existed. Granddad and Grandma had achieved it, in the clutter collected over the decades, the books on the sitting-room shelves, and sturdy, well-worn furniture. By contrast, this place had themed collections of brassware and glassware, but not a book in sight.

"Where's Thomasina?" Val asked.

Edith pointed to the hall leading to the bedrooms. "Changing clothes. Excuse me, I should put away the food so it doesn't spoil."

Val followed Edith into the kitchen. Black cabinets and appliances lined two walls. Thomasina's winnings, the half-full box of doughnut holes she'd carried away from the game room, sat on the counter. A round wrought-iron table and two chairs hugged one corner of the kitchen. Without a window to let in natural light, the room looked stark and gloomy. It contrasted with the plush living room, where Thomasina probably spent most of her time.

"Do you live nearby?" Val asked.

"A few doors down." Edith put a package of hamburger patties in the meat compartment and a quart container of half-and-half on a door shelf in the fridge. Packages of corn soufflé and macaroni and cheese went into the freezer. She set the other items on the counter. Hamburger rolls, a jar of salsa, and taco chips. "Well, that's everything on her list."

Not what the USDA would call a healthy diet. "Does Thomasina eat some of her meals at the main dining room?"

Edith shook her head. "Most of us in cottages don't bother going to the Village Center to eat. We have to pay extra for a meal plan. It's included with the apartments because they don't have full kitchens like we do."

"Who are you talking to, Edith?" Thomasina swept into the room in a green silk pantsuit that matched her eyes. "Oh, it's the temporary Brain Dame, but why are you in the kitchen? Come into the living room."

"I was putting the groceries away." Edith pointed to the items on the table. "I don't know where to put those things."

"I'll take care of it. I've already imposed on you enough for today. Don't feel you have to stay and do anything else for me." Thomasina looked pointedly at the living room.

Translation: Scram, Edith. Did that mean Thomasina wanted to talk to Val in private?

Edith looked more relieved than hurt. "Call me if you need anything else, Thomasina. Good-bye, Val. Will you run next week's Brain Game too?"

Val nodded. "I hope you'll both come again."

Thomasina saw Edith to the door and then whirled around to face Val. "As long as you're here, I'd like to talk to you about today's game."

"You did well today."

"Yes." Thomasina stroked the mahogany frame of

her couch. "Even though I won, I must say that your questions were too sexist."

Huh? "What was sexist about them?"

"Too much sports and science. That favors men, and you saw how few men go to the Brain Game. You should ask about things the women would remember, like songs and movies from the fifties and sixties."

In other words, more of what Thomasina knew. She didn't just want to win. She wanted to win *big*.

Val shifted her weight from one foot to the other and longed to sit on the down sofa that had enveloped her the last time she was here. But her mother wouldn't approve of her plopping down on the sofa uninvited with the hostess still standing. "When I work on the trivia for next week, I'll keep that in mind. How about if I include questions about cooking?"

Her hostess grimaced. "That would be sexist the other way."

And present a challenge for this week's winner, judging by her supermarket purchases. Val smiled. "I stopped by here, hoping you would have suggestions for improving the Brain Game, and you did. By the way, did you hear about Junie May Jussup?"

"I heard she was dead, and nobody's saying how she died. You know what that means?" Thomasina didn't wait for an answer. "She committed suicide. It's always hushed up for the sake of the family."

On the other hand, murder made headlines. *Zero details* plus *zero headlines* equaled *suicide* to Thomasina. To Lillian, they equaled *murder*. She'd assessed Junie May's character more accurately.

Val voiced her thought. "Junie May didn't strike me as suicidal. She enjoyed her work and had good career prospects."

Thomasina fingered a silk rose in the arrangement on her sideboard. "None of that matters if you're unlucky in love. She was crazy about Scott, you know, but he didn't feel the same way about her. That's why she murdered him and then committed suicide."

Stunned, Val couldn't speak for a moment. In Junie May's version of the relationship, Scott had pursued her, not vice versa. That version made more sense to Val, but Thomasina's idea intrigued her. "How could Junie May have poisoned him? She wasn't sitting near him."

"I don't think she did it at the dinner. Scott met her beforehand and told her to leave him alone. She poisoned him then. It just didn't take effect right away."

And she just happened to have some arsenic in her purse to do the dirty deed. Val had chalked up Thomasina's earlier theory about Scott's murder to a mother distraught over her son's death, unable to think clearly. The mother's revised scenario, like the earlier one, was long on fantasy and fuzzy on details. Both resembled B-movie plots.

"When I came to visit you with my grandfather, you didn't mention Junie May as someone who might have killed Scott. What changed your mind?"

"I was in shock then. Scott's death came soon after a murder attempt on me, and I connected them. Edith and my other friends convinced me I was wrong." She rubbed a brass samovar on the sideboard as if it were Aladdin's lamp. "I couldn't imagine who killed Scott and why, until Junie May died. Then it all fell into place."

When the news broke that Junie May had been murdered, Thomasina would have to go back to the drawing board—or the cutting-room floor—to make sense of her son's death. Would her next scenario involve Junie May poisoning Scott and a hit man shooting Junie May? Illogical to the point of being funny, but also sad. Thomasina was coping with grief in her own way. Her imagination shielded her from the ugly possibility that her son's swindling may have led to his murder.

"I won't keep you any longer, Thomasina. Thank you for your ideas on the trivia questions." At the door, Val added, "I also want to say again how sorry I am for your loss."

By the time Val arrived home, Granddad still hadn't returned from fishing. She sat at the computer in the study and pulled out the scrap of paper Ned had given her with the name of the man who'd committed suicide. She hoped he'd spelled the name correctly.

Her phone chimed. She dug it out of her bag and glanced at the display. Gunnar. Her heart did a cartwheel.

"Hey, Val. I know it's late to ask, but any chance you can join me for dinner? Nothing fancy, a picnic along the river."

"I've spent the whole day under a roof. Eating out, as in outdoors, sounds better than a banquet." And she'd get to listen to his melodic voice instead of the bluster of banquet speakers. "I have some news for you."

"I have some for you too."

His news might cancel out hers. If he'd decided not to stay in Bayport, no point in telling him about renting Mrs. Z's house. "What can I bring to the picnic?"

"Just yourself. I'll get the food and reserve the best seats on the lawn behind the B & B. Can you meet me there at seven?"

That would give her time to make dinner for Granddad, assuming he showed up soon. "See you then."

Val clicked the phone off and opened a browser window on the computer. She navigated to a page for *Washington Post* death notices and entered Arthur Tunbridge's name with a date range from March through May of this year.

The text of the notice popped up. Val skimmed it. Died April 9, Spring Lake Retirement Community. He'd worked as a restaurant manager in a suburb of Baltimore and, after retiring, volunteered as a mentor to small-business owners. Husband of the late Ann Tunbridge, survived by a daughter, Lucy Tunbridge Azamov, and two grandsons.

Azamov. Omar's wife? Val confirmed her guess on Lucy Azamov's Facebook page, which included photos of Arthur Tunbridge, his son-in-law, and his two grown grandsons.

If Scott's swindling drove Omar's father-in-law to suicide, Omar could have settled the score at the chowder dinner, abetted by Lillian. She hadn't exactly lied in saying Omar was the son of an old friend if *old* meant elderly rather than longtime, and Omar might well have called Arthur Tunbridge his father, having lost his own parents decades ago. But what connected Lillian to the old man and to Omar? What tie would be so strong that she would arrange a comeuppance dinner for Scott? Could Junie May have unearthed that link?

The front door opened. "Val? I'm home."

She popped up and met her grandfather in the hallway. His neat plaid sport shirt and tan pants surprised her. She'd expected a fishing vest and cargo pants. "Your note said you were going fishing."

"That's what I did. In Northern Virginia. Fishing for information." He whipped a folder from under his arm. The gold lettering on it read SPRING LAKE RETIREMENT COMMUNITY.

Chapter 19

Granddad held up the Spring Lake folder like a big fish he'd hooked. A current of excitement ran through Val.

She took the folder. "I was planning to go there tomorrow."

"Well, I beat you to it. Ned couldn't find out on the phone if Scott gave financial talks there. Figured I'd do better in person. I pretended I was looking to move there. Had to listen to the sales pitch and tour the place. Then they let me go off on my own and talk to the people living there." He went into the sitting room.

Why couldn't Granddad just tell her what he'd learned? Getting information from him was like trying to reel in something tugging on a line. It took a lot of maneuvering to find out if it was a fish or a waterlogged shoe.

She followed him into the sitting room and perched on the old tweed sofa. "Did you find anyone who knew about the investment seminars?"

"Yup, but they couldn't come up with the name of

the guy who gave the talks. Some folks thought his aunt or mother lived in the community. None of them knew her name either."

Darn. Just an old shoe. "So your trip was a bust?"

"Until the last minute. As I was leaving, a man I'd talked to earlier took me aside and said he remembered the financial expert's name—Freaze." Granddad raised his palm for Val's high five. "Scott was the one who bilked an old man of his savings."

"And drove him to suicide, according to some people. The pieces are coming together at last."

"Thanks to me. You're not the only detective in the house."

"I never claimed to be a detective, but I found out something about the man who committed suicide. He was Omar's father-in-law." She waited for Granddad to draw the obvious conclusion. When he didn't, she spelled it out. "Omar had two reasons to hate Scott. His family lost money they might have inherited if Scott hadn't swindled it. And Omar's wife lost her father, who was despondent over the swindle."

Granddad didn't look as elated as she'd expected. He rubbed his chin. "Nobody knew for sure why or even if the man committed suicide." He headed for the kitchen. "Been a long day. I could use a beer."

Val frowned. They'd reeled in a fish, not an old shoe, but now Granddad had thrown it back. Why wasn't he rejoicing that Omar's motive for murdering Scott had come to light? Then it dawned on Val. Maybe Granddad was wondering why Lillian had invited Omar to the chowder dinner. Possibly she'd urged him, like Granddad, to confront Scott. There was a chain from Lillian to Omar to his father-in-law to Scott the scammer. Granddad's girlfriend had kept the links in that chain secret, even after Scott was murdered.

Val had to give Granddad time to digest Lillian's deceit. Best to change the subject. She followed him to the kitchen. "I'm going out to dinner. I'll make you something to eat before I leave."

"I already ate. Cars were bumper to bumper going toward the Bay Bridge. I pulled off the road and stopped at a barbecue place until the traffic got lighter." Granddad took a beer out of the fridge and pried the top off the bottle. "You hear anything about Junie May?"

"The police have proof she was murdered. They're keeping it quiet until they reach her next of kin." Val pulled a tall glass from a cabinet near the sink. "I wonder if Junie May heard the rumors about the man who committed suicide. She might have gone to Spring Lake and discovered that Scott had given seminars there."

"Nobody told me about a reporter there, but I didn't ask."

"I can ask tomorrow. I want to go there to show Thomasina's photo around." And Lillian's, but Granddad didn't need to know that. "People might remember the face even if they've forgotten her name."

"You need a cover story to get through the guard gate. I'll go with you and say I want my grand-daughter's opinion before I move in."

Val filled her glass with water. How could she show anyone Lillian's photo if he went with her? "Once we get past the guard and the reception desk, let's split up. We can talk to more people that way."

"Good idea." Granddad took a swig of beer. "Here's our cover story. I'm a doddering old guy who doesn't recall the name of a woman he thinks lived there. That's why we're showing folks her picture. We should also ask if anyone remembers a woman falling down the stairs."

Val nearly dropped her water glass. A few days ago, he'd made fun of Thomasina's yarn about being pushed down the stairs. "I thought you didn't buy Thomasina's staircase story."

"I didn't buy that her ex-husband's underworld cronies pushed her down the stairs. But someone who'd lost money to Scott might have figured she was in on the scam and gone after her."

"You mean Omar?"

Granddad shrugged. "His father-in-law could have pushed her too. Or another one of Scott's victims. Where are you going for dinner?"

"To Gunnar's B & B. We're having a picnic by the river."

"He just got an inheritance, and he's too cheap to take you out? I retired years ago and I can afford to treat Lillian to a restaurant dinner now and then."

No point in telling him Lillian could better afford to treat *him*. Men of his generation didn't let ladies pay. But by bringing up his finances, Granddad had opened a door for Val to pursue that subject. "*Can* you afford it? I saw a notice from your bank about an overdraft."

Granddad flicked his wrist. "That was a mistake."

"A mistake by the bank?"

"Don't worry about it. I took care of it. Isn't it

time you started primping for dinner with your cheap boyfriend?"

Val wouldn't get any more information from Granddad about the overdraft. "I don't know about primping, but I'll change clothes. I'm also going to call the police and tell them what we found out today." Maybe they'd give up on the idea that Granddad had poisoned Scott. Omar made a much better suspect.

She went upstairs to her bedroom and pulled out her cell phone. She should tell Holtzman about Omar, but she didn't have a direct number for him. She phoned Chief Yardley and left a detailed message for him. He'd get the word to the deputy in charge.

As Val walked up the path to the River Edge B & B, a forty-something man on the front porch hailed her. "You must be Val. Gunnar told me to keep an eye out for a petite woman with fantastic hair."

"Hi, I'm Val Deniston." Gunnar's ex also had fantastic hair, but a different meaning of *fantastic* applied to Val's hair.

The man came down the porch steps and extended his hand. "I'm Ian Tallifer. I met your grandfather when my wife and I bought the B & B three years ago. How is he?"

"He's doing well, thank you."

Ian brushed his long hair off his forehead. "I noticed some work going on at his house. Roofing, painting. Fixing it up to sell?"

"He doesn't plan to sell anytime soon."

"It's a big house to keep up. How many bedrooms?"

That question didn't fall into the category of

chitchat. Maybe the Tallifers, or someone they knew, wanted to buy the house. If Granddad had gotten himself in financial trouble, he might welcome an offer. The thought disheartened Val.

"Four bedrooms on the second floor. One on the main floor." The B & B owner couldn't have missed Val's brusque tone. She'd come to eat dinner, not talk about real estate. "Is Gunnar here?"

"He's waiting for you out back." The B & B owner pointed to the path along the side of the house. "It's a great evening for a picnic. Enjoy."

The lawn behind the B & B sloped down to the river. Gunnar sat in one of the two Adirondack chairs closest to the river, his head of dark hair visible above the back of the chair. The neck of a wine bottle stuck out from a metal bucket on the table between the two chairs, and a large red cooler sat by his feet.

A refreshing breeze off the river ruffled Val's hair as she approached the picnic spot. "You snagged the best seats in the house, as promised."

He popped out of his chair and gave her a bear hug. "I hope you like prosecco." He reached for the bottle in the bucket and untwisted the wire around the mushroom-shaped cork.

"I never met an Italian wine I didn't like. Are we celebrating something with that bottle of bubbly?"

"The two of us together in one place for the first time in three days. That's worth celebrating." He eased the cork out of the bottle and took two champagne flutes from the cooler.

"I'll drink to that." He'd counted the days since he'd last seen her—a good sign.

She sat in the Adirondack chair, leaned back, and

savored the moment: the bubbles rising in the glass, the sunlight glinting on the river, and Gunnar's radiant smile.

He put a container of crabmeat dip and a tray of miniature bread sticks on the table. "I contacted the Treadwell Players to tell them I'd like to help out in their productions, build stage sets, learn lighting, whatever they needed. They were about to hold auditions for an October production. One of the guys in the company helped me get ready for the audition yesterday."

"You auditioned. Something else to celebrate." She clinked her wineglass against his for the second time. "You're here less than a week, and your acting career has taken off. Congratulations."

"It'll be a few days before the cast is announced, but I think it went well. Thanks for the vote of confidence." He twirled the stem of his wineglass. "My ex-fiancée showed up in Bayport this week."

What should Val say? *I knew that* or *No kidding?* She didn't like either of those. Having just stuffed a bread stick covered with crab dip into her mouth, she had a third option. "Mmm." She chewed vigorously and hoped he would keep talking.

"She's the one who called me a flake for even thinking of quitting my job and taking up acting." He downed the remaining wine in his glass. "Now she wants to get back together and won't take no for an answer. I couldn't figure out why, until I talked to a friend in Washington. He'd told her about the money I inherited from my great-aunt."

Val's arms and legs felt weightless, a wine buzz reinforced by her joy that he'd rebuffed his ex. "Now you're a flake with a bank account. That makes a difference."

He raised his empty glass. "To the departure of Petra Bramling."

"Petra Bramling." Val swirled the sparkling wine in her glass. "I met her, you know."

Gunnar's glass slipped from his hand to his lap. "You did? When?"

"She challenged me on the tennis ladder. We played yesterday afternoon."

"I'm sure you trounced her."

"I stopped the match because she was cheating. And she reversed our scores when she reported them, putting her above me on the ladder."

"Nothing could put her above you on any ladder. I don't know what I ever saw in her." He studied Val with blue eyes that reflected the sky. "I had blurred vision until I met someone I like a lot better."

Warmth spread over her. Despite her ornery hair and short—no, make that *petite*—stature, she'd trounced the tame-haired, long-legged blonde. "Blurred vision is a side effect of attraction. You see what you want to see. I had it when I was engaged to Tony, and Granddad has it about Lillian." Had Junie May or Scott also suffered from blurred vision?

Gunnar refilled their glasses. "You said you had news for me."

"I have a lead on a place for you to rent short-term. A small ranch on Maple Street." She described Mrs. Z's house and explained the reason for a short-term rental.

"Sounds perfect. A temporary solution for her and me."

They watched the river in companionable silence

for a few minutes. Then Gunnar took out the rest of the picnic food. Prosciutto sliced paper thin, a hunk of Asiago cheese, a loaf of crusty bread. Marinated zucchini, eggplant, and peppers. A salad of chopped tomatoes, cucumber, Greek olives, and feta. Chunks of fragrant local cantaloupe, softer, juicier, and lighter in color than the western cantaloupe.

She put a little of everything on her sturdy paper plate. "An antipasto picnic. I love it."

Gunnar sliced the bread. "I went back to my Mediterranean roots on my mother's side of the family. Next time I'll put together a Scandinavian picnic in honor of my father's side."

"You'll have a harder time finding the ingredients for that around here." She gestured toward the antipasto. "Where did you dig all this up?"

"The organic market and deli in Treadwell. I did some digging on Scott too. A client who gave him free rein to invest for him complained about a sudden downturn in his assets. The client planned to buy a new car. Between the previous account statement and the one that showed up when he wanted to liquidate, Scott had apparently shifted the money from winning to losing investments."

"Apparently? Are you saying he rigged the statements? How would he get away with that?"

"He could have had a *friendly* auditor. Still, client complaints would trigger scrutiny by regulators, especially if a pattern emerged. By the way, the client I mentioned was a retired man."

"He fits the pattern of Scott's investors." Val wrapped a piece of prosciutto around a melon chunk. "Granddad and his friend found out that Scott was running investment seminars at a retirement community in Springfield, Virginia."

"I only checked Maryland and the District, but I can expand my research to include Virginia." He took a sliver of cheese. "What's the latest on the murder investigation? I was so busy with the theater group that I didn't hear the local news."

"I'll give you the headlines. Scott died of arsenic poisoning. The TV reporter who was at the chowder dinner, Junie May Jussup, was shot dead."

Gunnar's jaw dropped. "*What*? Another murder?"

Val nodded, moving her fork aimlessly around her plate. "A murder masquerading as a suicide, though the police have yet to release that information, so don't spread it around. I'm sure the same person who killed Scott did it. Junie May was looking into his death."

Gunnar winced. "Please tell me *you're* not looking into his death . . . or hers."

"I'll leave it to the police, unless they suspect my grandfather."

"If they suspect your grandfather, you can hire a private investigator, but I wouldn't worry. The police aren't likely to take your grandfather for a gun-toting arsenic poisoner."

"You saw him toting a gun once."

"Don't remind me. Fortunately, he didn't pull the trigger." Gunnar reached across the gap between the two Adirondack chairs and covered her hand with his. "Promise you won't let any of those chowder dinner guests into your house or be alone with them anywhere."

She'd heard similar warnings from him after the murder in June, and she'd disregarded them. "Last month you told me I needed a bodyguard. I guess you don't think the danger is as great now."

"Last month somebody tried several times to kill you. No one's done that yet, or you haven't told me about it."

"No one's done it. Trust me, though, I'm looking over my shoulder."

"The guests at your grandfather's dinner are dropping like flies. Tell your grandfather to stay away from them too."

"I'll tell him, but I doubt he'll bar Lillian from entering our house."

Gunnar glanced at her plate and released her hand. "Let's talk about something else. This topic is an appetite-suppressant, and we still have lots of food. Bethany told me about the trivia game at the Village. How did it go?"

"Most of the participants enjoyed it. I'd like you to look at the questions and some answer sheets. See if you gain any insights into people based on what they know and don't know."

Val took a sheaf of papers from her bag and gave him the question list and Lillian's, Ned's, and Thomasina's answer sheets. "Here are the responses from three of the top scorers."

He finished the food on his plate while studying the answer sheets. "Can I see everyone's answers?"

She gave him the whole set, ate the rest of the food on her plate, and took seconds of the veggies and salad while he flipped through the answers.

He pointed to the question sheet. "Your Hollywood questions were difficult, and the health questions medium. Any conclusions about the multiple-choice questions are suspect because people might have guessed right."

"I had to give choices for some of the questions. Otherwise, they would have been too hard. I didn't want the participants getting depressed because they didn't know anything. I refused to spell the answers, though, figuring someone who knew the answer would spell it right and the guessers might not. So, do you have any conclusions based on who knew what?"

"Lillian is a local person who knows the health field. Thomasina isn't local and aced the Hollywood questions. Ned missed those, but got the sports questions, and named all three nonvital organs. Half the people there did that."

"The older you are, the more likely you know people who've had those organs removed. Everybody in the room got appendix right. Thomasina chose that and the spleen."

Gunnar took a sliver of cheese. "Lillian, Thomasina, and Ned all picked ethylene glycol as the antifreeze ingredient, and they spelled it right. The few others who put that down spelled it wrong."

"Ned knows what's in antifreeze because he probably sold it in his hardware store. With a health background, Lillian may know it because people show up in emergency rooms with ethylene glycol poisoning. Thomasina may have guessed which answer was correct, and she's a good speller. She made a nine-letter word out of a bunch of letters—*chameleon,* not easy to spell."

"She was the only person to spell Alan Smithee's name right. She knew that answer. A couple of others guessed it, but spelled it with a *Y* at the end."

Gunnar gave her back the answer sheets. "I'm not sure I helped you by looking at these."

"You confirmed my conclusions."

He stood up. "I'll get the cannoli out of the cooler if you're ready for dessert."

"I'd rather go for a walk. If we leave now, we can watch the sunset from the town dock."

"I'll take the cannoli with us so we can eat it while the sun's setting."

Gunnar stowed the leftover picnic food in the cooler and they set off, hand in hand, for the ten-minute walk to the dock.

They were eating the cannoli when Val got a call from Chief Yardley.

"Hey, Chief. Thanks for calling me back. You got my message about Omar?"

"I got it. Not calling about that. I'm on my way to talk to your granddaddy. He said you were out, but I'd like you to go home if you can. I have a few questions."

Chapter 20

Val and Gunnar walked hurriedly from the town dock to Granddad's house and made it in less than ten minutes. Chief Yardley's car was parked behind hers in the driveway.

"Do you want me to go in with you?" Gunnar asked.

"Better not. Granddad will be more comfortable without you there."

"I'll call you later."

Val went in by the front door and heard her grandfather's voice coming from the sitting room.

"I don't know how it got there. It's a plant."

She rushed into the room and found him and Chief Yardley both on the edge of their seats, Granddad in his unreclined recliner; the chief on the tweed sofa. "What's going on?"

The chief's mouth puckered as if he had a sour stomach. "Your next-door neighbor's brother was visiting today from Baltimore."

"I saw the pickup in the driveway this morning." Val turned toward her grandfather. "Why are you talking about Harvey's brother?"

Granddad took his bifocals off. "Harvey said if I had any hazardous waste, his brother would drop it off at the landfill near Baltimore. I threw some stuff from the shed into a box and took it over to him. Then his brother took my box to the police. Earl can tell you the rest." Granddad pointed his thumb at the chief.

"The brother heard on the news how Scott Freaze died. When he saw rat poison containing arsenic in the box that came from the shed here, he brought it to us. Your granddaddy says someone planted the arsenic in the shed."

Val was speechless, but only for the two seconds it took her to remember Junie May's investigative report. "I have an idea how it got there. Remember the junk you cleared out from the attic a few months ago, Granddad?"

"I remember when you nagged me into going up there and getting rid of stuff." He put his glasses back on. "Mystery solved. The poison came from the attic. I found a few bottles up there with a skull and crossbones on them. Old medicines and rat killer. The labels were faded so I couldn't read them in the dim light. I threw the bottles in a box and locked them in the shed. I didn't know there was arsenic in them."

"That makes more sense than someone planting the poison in your shed." Chief Yardley folded his hands in his lap. "You ever been to Junie May Jussup's house?"

"Never. My lady friends are a little older than that." Granddad's smile died when he looked at the chief's grim face.

"What were you doing yesterday between five and six?"

Val's stomach wound itself into a knot. Apparently, explaining where the poison in the shed originated hadn't taken her grandfather off the suspect list. He could have used the poison he'd found in the attic to kill Scott. Now the chief wanted to know Granddad's alibi for Junie May's murder.

Granddad gripped the arms of his chair. "Between five and six yesterday, I was cleaning up and getting dressed to take a lady friend to a movie. Why are you asking me these things? First the question about the rat poison. Now this. You know I'm not a murderer, Earl."

"I know that, but you will hear the same questions from people who don't know it. You'd best prepare yourself for that and get a lawyer."

"Why would I kill Scott?"

"You lured him here under false pretenses. According to his mother, you hinted that your other guests had money to invest so that Scott would come to the dinner. Is that true?" When Granddad nodded, the chief continued. "You also talked about stopping people who've gotten away with crimes."

Val threw up her hands. "Holtzman lured him into saying something like that. That doesn't mean Granddad took justice into his own hands."

"People are convicted, even with a weak motive." The chief stood up. "If the sheriff's deputies ask to talk to you, Don, tell them you want your attorney present."

Granddad leaned back in his chair, his eyes closed as if to shut out the world.

Val walked the chief to the door. "Thank you for stopping by and alerting us."

"I owe your grandfather a lot. Take care of him. Get him a lawyer."

Val went back to the sitting room and sat on the sofa near Granddad's chair. "I don't know what's making the police think you could have killed anyone, but I'll get to the bottom of it. I'll fix it."

"You're always trying to fix things. Fixing stuff just opens a can of worms. I didn't have to clean out the attic in the spring. All that stuff could have stayed there like it did for years."

"True, but that's not the only reason the chief came to see you. He also wanted to see if you had an alibi for Junie May's murder, and you don't." Val's cell phone chimed in her bag. "I'd better get that." She went into the study to take the call.

Gunnar's name appeared on the display. "Everything okay at your place, Val?"

"Uh-huh. The chief had some advice for my grandfather that I had to hear, to make sure Granddad follows it."

"Turn on your TV to the station where Junie May worked. Right before the last commercial, they promised breaking news about her case."

"Okay, thanks."

Val went back to the sitting room. She picked up the remote from the table next to her grandfather's chair. "There's something about Junie May on TV." By the time she tuned the remote to the right station, the news anchor had already launched into the story.

"According to the sheriff's spokesman, an investigation is under way into the suspicious death of our colleague Junie May Jussup, found shot last evening in her home. The sheriff provided no details. We have tracked down a teenager who visited a friend on the street where Ms. Jussup lived. Shortly before six yesterday, the teen noticed a white sedan race out of Ms. Jussup's driveway."

Granddad's jaw dropped. A vise squeezed Val's insides. Her grandfather and Lillian both drove white sedans. No wonder the chief had asked if Granddad had ever gone to Junie May's house and if he had an alibi. Val turned her attention back to the TV.

"The witness could not identify the car's make and gave only a sketchy description of the driver, who wore a dark baseball cap with white or light gray hair sticking out from under it. The witness couldn't say if the driver was a woman or a small-to-average-sized man. Police have requested that the driver of the white vehicle contact them. Sheriff's deputies have asked the media not to reveal the name of the witness."

Good idea. They'd want to keep the kid safe until they arrest the murderer.

"We'll bring you more as the story unfolds."

Granddad's face looked ashen. "You know what kind of car Lillian drives? A white sedan, same as mine. Whoever murdered Junie May borrowed or rented that car to frame Lillian or me."

Or Lillian killed Junie May. Val wouldn't say that to Granddad tonight. He'd already had enough shocks, and he might be right about someone framing him. "The driver could have been Irene, Thomasina, or even Omar with talcum-powdered hair or a wig."

"If we had pictures of them, we could have some

computer whiz put wigs and baseball caps on them.
Then the witness might be able to tell if any of them
were driving that car."

"The police may do that." Only they'd use real
people in a lineup.

"Where did you get the photo of Thomasina that
we're going to show folks at Spring Lake?"

"Bethany took pictures at the Brain Game."

Granddad pressed his lips together in a grim line.
"Did she take one of Lillian?" At Val's nod, he said,
"We should show the folks at Spring Lake her picture too. If we only show Thomasina's, it'll be too
obvious we're trying to get information about her."

Maybe he had suspicions about Lillian after all,
but couldn't bring himself to say it. "Good idea.
People might look more closely if they're asked
whether they know either of two women."

Granddad stared at the mantel with its collection
of family photos, a reminder of happier times. "The
chief thinks I need a lawyer."

"I'll phone Althea. She doesn't do criminal law,
but she knows other lawyers who do."

"*Criminal lawyers.* How did I get in such a fix that
I need one of those?"

Val put the blame for that on the chief architect
of the chowder dinner—Lillian.

At nine-thirty Friday morning, Val pulled up at
the guard gate for the Spring Lake Retirement Community. Her grandfather told the guard he'd visited
the community yesterday and was coming back for a
second look. The guard waved the car on.

She drove Granddad's Buick along a tree-lined

street flanked by brick buildings three to five stories high. "This looks like a college campus. Those are the dorms."

"Not as much partying as in colleges. Take the next left to the campus center and park in a visitor spot. Yesterday I spent all my time in the Woodview Lounge there. Today I want to go to the Lakeside Lounge on the other side of the building. I'm hoping for a different crowd."

Inside the four-story building, they stopped at the reception desk. Artificial flower arrangements and precise chair groupings made the reception area look like a hotel lobby. She signed the visitors' log and looked up to see an African-American woman staring at her. "Fayette?"

The woman broke out in a smile. "The William and Mary coffeehouse. That's where I know you from."

Val introduced Granddad to her. "We managed a student-run coffee shop for a year. Fayette also played guitar and sang there."

"And your granddaughter ran the trivia nights. What brings you two here?"

Val would let her grandfather answer that one. He could lie more glibly than she could to her old friend.

"I'm looking into options for when I move out of my house. I heard the sales pitch and took the tour here yesterday. I liked it so much I wanted Val to see it."

"It's a great place. I should know. I work here as the director of community relations. If you have any questions, I'll be glad to answer them."

"I just want to talk to some folks who live here and

see how they like it," Granddad said. "You two can catch up while I go to the Lakeside Lounge and get to know people."

"Great idea." Fayette checked her oversized watch. "I'm free for the next half hour."

"I'll join you in the lounge, Granddad, when we're finished talking."

"Okay. Nice meeting you, Fayette." He left with a wave.

"He's so darling, Val. That's where you get your cute genes, and you haven't changed a bit in the last decade."

"The extra five pounds don't count?"

"Not to someone who's put on fifteen. I get to blame my two kids for that. Let's go to my office." Fayette led the way through a corridor to a small room with a big desk and three leather armchairs grouped around a glass-covered wood table.

She sat at the table with Val and talked about her marriage and children. A military wife, she'd worked as a troubleshooter in a variety of volunteer and paid positions over the years. She described her current role in the senior community as a problem solver for residents and their family members.

Val talked about being a cookbook publicist in New York, her move earlier in the year to her grandfather's house on the Eastern Shore, her current work as a café manager, and her hope of publishing her own cookbook.

"If you publish it, Val, I'll buy it. It surprises me that your grandfather is looking at a retirement place so far from where he's been living. Does he have family or friends in this area?"

Val hesitated, hating to lie but seeing no way around it. "He thought two women he knew lived here. Yesterday when he was here, he mentioned them to the receptionist and the other residents. No one had heard of them. Of course, his memory for names isn't as good as it used to be."

"I can relate to that. Faces stick in my mind. Names? In one ear and out the other."

"I have pictures of the women. You mind looking at them?" Val handed her a print of Bethany's photo of Lillian.

"Looks familiar. Not a resident. A visitor." Fayette closed her eyes and popped them open after five seconds. "I know who she is. A geriatric care manager. It's been months since I've seen her here."

"What do geriatric care managers do?"

"They're hired, usually by the family, to check on elderly relatives. They alert us and the family of any needs that aren't being met."

They could also alert con artists about elderly clients with money and no family members watching over the finances. "What kind of background do geriatric care managers have?" Val asked.

"Most come from nursing, social work, or psychology. They usually have training and experience in eldercare." Fayette waved to a woman passing by her door. "Hey, Nina, got a second? Look at this photo and see if you recognize this woman."

A fiftyish woman came into the office, donned glasses that hung from her neck, and examined the photo. "Mr. Tunbridge's care manager."

Omar's father-in-law. A surge of excitement shot

through Val. At last, she'd found what connected Lillian to Omar.

"Mr. Tunbridge. Right." Fayette stared at the ceiling as if trying to summon a memory from above. "Didn't he move here from another retirement community?"

Her colleague nodded. "In Maryland. The family wanted him nearer to where they live. The woman in the photo was his care manager there, and they kept her on for continuity." She put an index finger on her pursed lips and gave Fayette a pointed look.

Val could interpret the silent message, though it wasn't intended for her. *Don't talk about the man who killed himself here.*

"Thanks, Nina." Fayette handed the photo to Val as Nina left the office. "Your grandfather may have run into this care manager at that other retirement community in Maryland and mistaken her for a resident there."

"That's possible. There was another woman he thought lived here." Val gave her Thomasina's photo. "Do you recognize her?"

Fayette studied it, frowned, and made a circle with her thumb and forefinger around Thomasina's face. "If I block out the hair, she looks like Shawna Maliote, who was a blonde. She moved out a few months ago after being here half a year. If your grandfather knows her, my best advice is to keep him away from her. She was a bit off." Fayette tapped her temple.

"In what way?"

"Delusional. Paranoid. She claimed people here were stealing from her and trying to kill her. She threatened to sue us. We let her out of her contract, happy to return her money just to get rid of her."

That paranoia may have led her to change her name to Thomasina Weal. "Did her family support her decision to leave?"

"That I don't know. It wouldn't matter anyway. She came here as an independent resident, responsible for her own decisions and finances." Fayette returned the photo to Val.

"I've probably said more than I should have about her, given current privacy laws, but I wanted to warn you. Your grandfather shouldn't get involved with her."

"I'll just tell him she isn't here anymore. How does she spell her name?" Val jotted Shawna Maliote's name on the back of the photo. "Thanks."

"I'm guessing you're thinking of moving around here. Is that why your grandfather's looking at this place?"

"He's just trying to get a feel for different communities." Enough said about their motives for visiting this community. "At the retirement village near us, a TV reporter recently interviewed residents for a story and embarrassed some of them. Have you had reporters here too?"

"Not lately. We don't let the media bother the residents, though some of them like the attention."

"Do you have educational programs, guest speakers, that sort of thing?"

"Occasionally. And we have so many clubs and activities, your grandfather's bound to find something that interests him." Fayette glanced at her big watch. "If you have any other questions, don't hesitate to call me."

Val took the hint and stood up. "Great talking to you, Fayette."

"I'll walk you back to the lobby and set you up with a tour. Let me know if you want to visit again. We'll have lunch."

For the sake of Granddad's cover story, Val had to go on the thirty-minute tour. With that out of the way, she checked her phone messages. Only one had come in, a text from Althea with the contact information for three criminal lawyers. On the way to the Lakeside Lounge, Val passed the elevators and the door to a staircase. She opened it and walked up one story, twenty concrete steps in all, with a landing halfway up, where the staircase turned. With a shove from the top of the stairs, Thomasina would have hit ten steps before the landing broke her fall. Ouch. Hard to imagine she could have avoided serious injury, unless she'd grabbed the handrail before falling far. Or maybe, as Granddad suspected, no one had pushed her. She'd just stumbled down a few steps.

Val went into the Lakeside Lounge. Based on the view from the room, *Pondside Lounge* would have been more accurate, but she was spoiled by living near the Chesapeake. It made bodies of water smaller than oceans, seas, and the Great Lakes look puny.

She found her grandfather on a sofa facing the puny pond. Three women sat in chairs grouped around the sofa.

He gestured with a sweep of his arm toward Val. "This is my granddaughter, ladies. Meet my new friends, Val."

"He's been telling us all about you," the tiny

woman with ash-gray hair said. "You're so lucky to
have a grandfather who cooks for you."

Val smiled through clenched teeth.

"And he's lucky to have a granddaughter with experience in book publicity," the robust woman with
yellow-gray hair said. "You'll make his cookbook a
best seller."

Val felt herself getting steamed, and not just because the temperature in the building was five degrees warmer than she liked. Had Granddad managed
to do anything but lie about his cooking? Had he
passed around the photos?

The lanky woman with frosted gray hair stood up.
"It's almost time for bridge. So nice to meet you,
Don, and you too, Val. Come visit again."

The other two trailed her out of the lounge, the
largest woman commenting, "Maybe he can do a
cooking demonstration, and we can sample the
food."

"A cookbook, Granddad?" Val kept her voice low.
"You can't be serious."

"Why not? It's the next step after a recipe column.
Stop looking like you just drank battery acid. I got a
lot out of talking to those ladies."

Something besides a boost to his ego? Val sat next
to him on the sofa. "What?"

"You first. Your friend tell you anything?"

"I found out the name Thomasina used here."

"So did I. Shawna. The ladies recognized her
from the picture, but didn't know her last name."

"Shawna Maliote." Val could contribute at least
something to what he'd learned. "Did they say anything else about Thomasina/Shawna?"

"They said she carried on about being pushed

down the stairs. She bought pepper spray and things
like that to protect herself. The tall one said Thomasina made up the story about being pushed in order
to get out of her contract. The little one swallowed
the story and won't go near a staircase. The third
one took Thomasina's paranoia as a sign of Alzheimer's. Now I've known a few people suffering
from that awful disease, and it's true they did turn
paranoid."

"Yes, but you can be paranoid without having that
disease. Alzheimer's destroys your memory, and
Thomasina's memory worked well for the trivia
game."

"Folks with Alzheimer's can recall something
from fifty years ago, but not from five minutes ago."

Val thought about the trivia results. Yes, memories
from the distant past could have given Thomasina
the answers to the Hollywood questions. Random
chance could explain her other two correct answers,
given that she'd made a stab at every multiple-choice
question. "Thomasina is going by a totally different
name than the one she used a few months ago.
Could someone with dementia change names without getting confused?"

Granddad shook his head. "Nah. Let's rule out
Alzheimer's. What about the idea that she used her
fall on the stairs to wiggle out of her contract?"

"It tallies with what Fayette said. Thomasina's false
name makes me wonder what else is false about her."
Val lowered her voice. "You didn't like the idea that
a mother would murder her son. Suppose she's not
Scott's mother, but his accomplice? She moves into
a retirement community and vouches for his expertise. For that, she gets a cut of the money. She has to

move out before anyone catches on to him. Maybe she was tired of the setup, but he wouldn't let her quit."

Granddad shook his head. "You only saw her and Scott together for a minute. He was devoted to her."

"That's exactly how a con man would behave."

"I can tell the difference between real and fake affection."

But could her grandfather tell the difference with respect to Lillian's affection for him? "Did you show anyone here Lillian's photo?" Val asked.

"Yup. No one recognized her."

Not a surprise. Lillian wouldn't have necessarily met any residents except the one she was hired to visit. "Fayette and another woman who works here recognized Lillian from the photo." She told Granddad about Lillian's role as geriatric care manager to Arthur Tunbridge.

Granddad gazed out the window at the pond. "She must have felt terrible when he committed suicide. I suppose she found out that Scott bilked the old guy. That's why she warned me against investing."

And also why she'd arranged to confront Scott at the chowder dinner, backed up by someone from the dead man's family. "She didn't tell you about Omar's connection to the man who committed suicide."

Granddad polished his glasses on his shirt. "I'll ask her why she didn't mention it."

"I want to be there when you ask her." Not only because Val would like to hear Lillian's excuse, but also because she didn't want Granddad alone with a suspect. His girlfriend had two possible reasons to murder Scott—to avenge her client's death by suicide, or to eliminate her accomplice in scams against the elderly.

Granddad stood up. "We got what we came for. It's a long ride home." He held out his hand. "Give me the keys. You drove here. I'll drive back."

"There's a ton of traffic on the beltway."

"I drove both ways yesterday." He waggled a finger at her. "Stop treating me like a baby."

She didn't baby him, but sometimes she acted like an overprotective mother of a teenager. She surrendered the keys. While he was driving back to Bayport, she would call the chief and tell him what they'd found out. Granddad would have no choice but to listen again to all the things Lillian had kept from him. He might even get past his blind spot about her.

Chapter 21

Val watched the traffic while Granddad drove on the beltway, or more accurately, the speedway around Washington. When he left the urban congestion behind, she relaxed and phoned Chief Yardley. She told him what they'd heard at the Spring Lake Retirement Community.

"Did you drag your granddaddy there this morning to snoop with you?"

She turned her face toward the side window and covered her mouth. "I planned to go alone. He insisted on coming along."

"It's bad enough you're playing detective. Now you're both at it. You'll need to tell Deputy Holtzman what you just told me. Go to the county sheriff's substation outside Treadwell and make a statement."

"Okay. Granddad and I are in the car and can swing by there on the way back to Bayport. Where exactly is it?"

He gave her directions to the substation. "Go there alone. Your granddaddy shouldn't talk to the deputy without a lawyer present."

She clicked off her phone and relayed the warning to Granddad. "Althea sent me the names and phone numbers for lawyers. I'll copy them for you." She wrote the information on the outside of the Spring Lake folder the tour guide had given her.

"I'll call them when I get a chance."

"You'll have a chance. When we get to Treadwell, we'll stop at a coffee shop. You can have lunch there while I go to the substation and tell the deputies what we found out this morning."

Val rifled through the Spring Lake folder, located an information sheet printed on one side, and turned it to the blank side.

Granddad glanced at her. "What are you doing?"

"Making a diagram of the dining-room table, showing where everyone sat Saturday night and the type of chowder they first requested and eventually ate."

"What's that going to tell you?"

"Possibly nothing, but I won't know until I finish it."

It was late morning by the time Granddad stopped at a coffee shop. Val drove his Buick to the county sheriff's substation. As she backed into a parking space, a neatly dressed man with dark hair walked out of the barracks-like building and donned sunglasses.

She jumped from the car. "Omar!"

He stopped and frowned as she approached him. "Yes?"

"Remember me? I'm Don Myer's granddaughter,

Val Deniston." She met him at the edge of the parking lot, where a large tree provided shade even at noon.

The lines in his forehead deepened. "Yes. How is your grandfather?"

"He's good." No thanks to Omar and his crony Lillian.

Omar took off his designer sunglasses. "Please tell him I'm deeply sorry for taking advantage of his hospitality and not explaining my presence at his dinner."

"I assume your presence at the dinner—" His formal way of speaking was contagious. Val started again. "You were there because of Scott. Why did you want to sit at the same table with him when his actions may have brought on your father-in-law's death?"

Omar jerked back as if she'd hit him, apparently surprised at what Val knew about his family. "I wished to shame him in the presence of his mother, appeal to his conscience, and possibly prevent another family from suffering what mine did. He was worse than a killer, Ms. Deniston. Murdering a man takes away his life. Driving him to suicide takes away his life and his soul."

"Are you sure Scott was responsible for that?"

"My father-in-law left my wife a rambling voice mail, full of despair over money he'd lost on risky investments. He gambled his entire life savings, hoping to bequeath more to our sons. My wife was distraught at not receiving his message until it was too late. He didn't realize we all valued him for himself, not for his money."

Such a sad story. Val's eyes stung. "I'm sorry for

your family's loss. After your father-in-law's death, did you go to the police?"

"With what?" Omar held out his hands with his palms up. "He'd lost the early account statements that showed gains and prompted him to invest more and more money. The latest ones, which came after he requested some money back, showed losses. I left several phone messages for Scott. He never returned my calls."

But he'd probably listened to them. "Scott must have recognized your voice at the chowder dinner. He was afraid of you. He pulled away when you offered to help him."

Omar shrugged. "He had the chance to avoid me. Shortly after we sat down, his mother said she didn't feel good and wanted him to take her home. He didn't do it. When he got sick, I assumed they'd both eaten something earlier in the day that gave them food poisoning."

"But then it came out that he was deliberately poisoned."

"And I didn't care if his killer was caught. Now I fear the same person murdered the woman reporter. Her death convinced me to tell the authorities what I know. I suspect you are here for the same reason." He took car keys from his pocket. "My best to your grandfather."

With a back as straight as the knife-edged crease in his trousers, he walked to a shiny black SUV. A trim man, shorter than average, he could have been mistaken for a woman by someone who glimpsed him in a fast-moving car. He could have rented a white car to go to Junie May's house, but why would he have killed her? She wouldn't have told him she'd dug up proof that he'd murdered Scott, and she wouldn't have let him in her house. Even though Omar made an unlikely culprit in Junie May's murder, it was worth checking his alibi. Val would ask Roy Chesterfeld about it if she saw him inside the substation.

She hurried into the building and came face-to-face with Deputy Holtzman. After she explained why she was there, he ushered her into a small room and turned on a recorder.

His face remained stony as she reported what she'd discovered at Spring Lake. When she suggested Thomasina might not be Scott's mother, he rolled his eyes.

"From our previous talks, Ms. Deniston, I know you lack confidence in the police. At least give them credit for checking on a murdered man's next of kin. He was her son, and she had her reasons for their name changes."

Could he have swallowed Thomasina's story about her husband's criminal past catching up with her? Maybe if she'd shed tears when she told the story. In the last murder investigation, Bethany had earned Holtzman's sympathy by crying when he questioned her. Val had roused his suspicion by keeping her emotions in check.

She snapped back to the present as his last three words echoed in her mind—their name changes. "So Scott used a false name too?"

"I wouldn't call it *false*. People can change their names as long as their purpose isn't to defraud. They don't even have to file a name-change petition with the court. They just use a different name. Actors and writers often do." He leaned toward her across the table. "Name changes for the purpose of cashing in on someone else's fame might land you in court. So don't hang out your shingle as *Nancy Drew*."

Her turn to roll her eyes. She left the interview room, confident that he would investigate this murder as he had the last one, ignoring facts that didn't fit his preconceived theory of the crime. She asked a deputy standing near the substation exit whether Roy Chesterfeld was around. He wasn't. As she climbed in the car, she thought of a way to check on Omar's alibi herself.

She phoned the restaurant where Omar worked and said she'd had a wonderful wine with her dinner there on Wednesday evening, but had forgotten the name of it. The restaurant's wine expert had suggested it and might recall it. "I can't remember his name, but I'd like to speak to him if he's there now."

"You probably mean our sommelier, Omar. He isn't in the restaurant at the moment," the woman on the phone said. "I can ask him to phone you if you leave your name and number."

"Would he have been the man who helped me choose the wine on Wednesday? I ate there quite early."

"He usually comes in around five."

Usually didn't suffice for an alibi. "Were you working at the restaurant Wednesday evening?"

"No. Omar will be happy to call you back."

"I'll phone again this evening, unless I remember the name of the wine before then. Thank you." Val clicked off her phone.

Omar's usual work schedule would have put him

two hours away from Junie May's house at the time of the murder. No point in asking him if he'd been at the restaurant that evening. He could simply lie about it. The deputies would surely check his alibi, but they might not tell Val what they learned.

Granddad steered into the club parking lot at one o'clock to drop Val off at the café.

"Why don't you come inside the club and wait for me, Granddad? I'll be finished in an hour. Then you and I can drive to the Village." And talk to Lillian together.

"I'm supposed to sit around twiddling my thumbs for an hour?"

"The club has today's newspapers and a bunch of magazines. You can read them or watch the TV in the café. I'll make you a smoothie."

"Hmph. You just want to keep an eye on me." He parked and unbuckled his seat belt. "You're the one who needs watching, not me."

Val reached behind her for her shoulder bag and climbed out of the car. "We have each other's backs then."

Granddad pointed to the club entrance. "Look who's heading inside. They make a nice couple, don't they?"

She looked, turned rigid, and forgot to breathe. Not a couple she expected to see. Gunnar and Petra, both in exercise clothes, were climbing up the steps to the club. He opened the door for her.

Val took a deep breath. She didn't believe Gunnar had lied to her last night. So what could explain those two together today? Unlikely that they'd run into each other by chance outside the club. More likely, he'd changed his mind overnight. "Whoever says women are fickle should meet Gunnar," Val muttered.

"I could say *I told you so,* but I won't. I know how it feels to find out that someone you like a lot hasn't been straight with you."

A wave of sadness engulfed her . . . for both of them. She hugged Granddad, her eyes stinging with tears. The first man who'd interested her since Tony, the first woman who'd interested him since Grandma—both disappointments. "We'll get through it."

"Smoothies will help."

They went inside the club. Granddad found a fishing magazine and sat on a sofa in the reception area. Val went into the café, noticing out of the corner of her eye that most of the tables were occupied. A good sign. Maybe the summer slump was over.

Bethany broke into a smile. "So glad to see you, Val. Too bad you didn't come in sooner."

Val joined her behind the counter. "Has it been hectic?"

"I've had no problem with the lunch crowd. The musclewoman arrived with a new dirty trick."

Val groaned. After a promising start, this day was going downhill fast. "What happened?"

"She came in early this morning and ordered coffee. After she left, I noticed the nutmeg shaker wasn't with the other coffee condiments. I went to the pantry, found an empty shaker, and filled it with nutmeg. By the time I did that, the first shaker was back, but the stuff inside looked more reddish than nutmeg. I confiscated it." Bethany pointed to the corner of the food prep counter. "It's there. Don't touch it, or you'll mess up the fingerprints."

Only an idiot would tamper with it and leave fingerprints. Val sniffed the shaker top. Definitely not nutmeg. A different, yet familiar, smell. "It's Chesapeake Bay seasoning. Great on crabs and shrimp, bad in coffee. Thanks, Bethany. You saved a customer from a peppery mouthful."

"Is that all? After what happened at your house, I figured it was poison." Bethany looked disappointed. "Oh, I almost forgot. Irene Pritchard's at the corner table. She asked for you."

A chat with Irene the Irate—just what Val needed to brighten her day.

She pasted a smile on her face, squared her shoulders, and marched toward the corner table, where she'd sat with the deputies the day before. "Hi, Irene. I hope you enjoyed your lunch." She must have, based on the few crumbs remaining on her plate.

"It used to be enough to mix mayo and celery with tuna fish. *You* put in lemon juice and chopped-up olives and red peppers. Not bad tasting, but more trouble to make."

Val sat down, facing the older woman. "That tuna salad sells well here. What can I do for you?" Irene probably wanted a list of popular menu items so she'd know what to serve when she took over the café contract.

"I feel terrible about Junie May. I want her murderer caught." Irene banged her glass of iced coffee on the table. "I've talked with the sheriff's people already, but you did more than the police to catch the last murderer. How can I help?"

Irene had stonewalled four days ago, possibly out of animosity for Granddad or fear of being a murder suspect. Did she come here today to help or to plant misinformation?

Val might as well hope for the best. "When was the last time you talked to Junie May?"

"The night of your grandfather's dinner."

"I'm still trying to figure out exactly what happened at the chowder dinner. Maybe you can help with that." Val took the sketch she made in the car from her tote bag. "Based on what I've heard from other people, I made a diagram of the table. Would you look it over and tell me if it's correct?"

Chapter 22

Val gave Irene the table diagram. "I put down the kind of chowder each person requested and crossed it out if they ended up eating a different type."

Lillian
light

Omar
light

Scott
creamy

Junie May
~~creamy~~ both

Irene
~~clear~~ both

Thomasina
~~creamy~~ light

Granddad
both

Irene put an index finger on her own name and pointed to each of the other names. "Yes, that's where everyone sat. When we first went to the table, your grandfather was in the kitchen and Lillian was going back and forth from the kitchen to the dining room."

Now for the key question. "When Lillian started serving, where did she put the chowder bowls?"

"She put the light chowder by me and the creamy chowder by Thomasina."

"But then both of you changed your mind about what kind of chowder you wanted."

"Yes. I wanted to try small portions of both chowders. I passed the light chowder to Scott. He set it at Lillian's place. Thomasina said the creamy chowder looked so rich that her gallbladder might act up and she'd be better off with the light chowder. She passed her bowl to Junie May, and I went to the kitchen to tell your grandfather and Lillian about the change."

Val pointed to Junie May's name on the diagram. "When did Junie May switch to a cup of each chowder?"

"She called out to me while I was going to the kitchen. By the time I returned to the table, the creamy chowder was in front of Scott."

According to Irene's version of the traveling-bowl tale, her hands never went near Scott's chowder. No surprise that she would give the story that slant. The surprise was that the creamy chowder had gone to Junie May before it went to Scott. Junie May hadn't mentioned that to Val, talking instead about who could have poisoned the chowder once Scott had it. Maybe Junie May had poisoned Scott, as Thomasina claimed, but why would she have waited until the chowder dinner instead of doing it when they met for coffee in the afternoon? Possibly because she'd had no chance to slip anything into his coffee. And if she'd poisoned Scott, who had killed her? Thomasina would have had a motive, avenging her son's death, but wouldn't she have tried to keep that motive secret? Instead, she'd described a scenario involving Junie May as Scott's killer.

Val rubbed her temples, feeling as if she was going in circles. "You saw Scott and Junie May in town on Saturday afternoon. Where and what time?"

"They were drinking coffee at the Bean and Leaf around four-thirty. Half an hour later, on my way back to the car, I saw them go into the vintage jewelry shop on Main Street."

Val remembered Junie May fingering a cameo pendant on Saturday night. Maybe it had come from that shop. The clerk there might remember her and Scott if they'd bought anything or browsed for a while. Val foresaw a trip to the jewelry shop in the near future. She'd enjoy that more than poking through dusty bottles at thrift shops or visiting retirement villages.

She glanced toward the counter to see if Bethany needed help, but a woman entering the café caught her attention. *Petra.*

Val stiffened. "Excuse me, Irene. Gotta see someone." Or rather, see her out.

"If you have any other questions, call me." Irene left a ten-dollar bill on the table.

Val took it and was about to get up when the spandex-clad Petra maneuvered between the bistro tables toward her. The café's male customers tracked Petra's progress with hungry stares.

Gunnar's ex sat in the chair Irene had just vacated. "I'll make this brief. I've just spoken to the club manager and taken responsibility for the complaints about the food, the water on the floor, and the bug on the salad. I apologize."

Val felt as if she was listening to Petra audition for a part that demanded insincerity. "Is that all you did?"

"My sister was the one who did everything."

Her sister with spiky hair and bulging biceps had certainly planted the worm, but surely Petra had put her up to it, and played some of the other tricks herself. "What about the fish in my car?"

Petra stared at the wall above Val's head. "I guess my sister did that too."

Val didn't believe it. "Why would she do all those things?"

"She thought that by hurting you, she would help me. You'd leave town to avoid the harassment, or you'd lose your job and have to move. Gunnar wouldn't stay in this Nowhere Ville if you weren't here. He'd go back to Washington."

Val caught sight of Gunnar near the café entrance. He watched them with his arms crossed. "How come you're apologizing for your sister?"

"She doesn't do apologies. Or *please* or *thank you*."

"She also didn't cheat on the tennis court."

"I took my name off the tennis ladder." Petra stood up, turned to go, and nearly ran into Gunnar.

He blocked her. "Did you apologize, Petra?"

Her parting words didn't belong in a PG-13 movie.

Val kept a cork on the happiness bubbling inside her, afraid to let it out after the ups and downs of the last few days. "How did you get involved in this?"

"When I stopped by here yesterday afternoon and you weren't here, Bethany told me about the bug in the salad and the water on the floor. I brought in two motion-sensitive cameras. She and I set them up." He tilted his head toward the counter. "Come on, I'll show you them and tell Bethany the upshot of our spying operation."

He pointed out the two cameras. One looked like a CD player on the food prep counter, the other a tiny eye affixed to the TV on the wall. Val hadn't even noticed them, though she might have if she'd spent more than a minute near the counter.

This morning, one camera had caught muscle-woman slipping the nutmeg shaker into her pocket, leaving the café, and returning later to put the shaker back. When Gunnar looked at the video, he recognized Petra's troublemaking sister. With previous arrests for drug possession and theft, she couldn't afford another run-in with the police. Gunnar coerced Petra into confessing to the club manager and apologizing to Val by threatening to show the police evidence of her sister's vandalism.

"Petra isn't all bad," he said. "I admire her loyalty to her sister. Too bad I had to exploit that loyalty. I'm sorry you had to go through this, Val."

"I still think you should check that shaker for poison." Bethany waved a pair of tongs. "I used these to pick it up, in case there were fingerprints. They would sew up the case."

"Thank you both for your help. The case has gone as far as we need to take it." Making a case against a murderer still loomed for Val, and with more suspects than for the nutmeg caper.

"In other good news," Gunnar said, "Mrs. Z is going

to rent me her house for six months. I signed up for an improvisation workshop in Philadelphia this weekend. I'm going to drive up there this afternoon. And I got a part in the Treadwell Players' October production."

"Congratulations!" Val threw her arms around him. He hugged her, lifting her off her feet.

Granddad cleared his throat. "Where's my smoothie and when are we leaving for the Village?"

Val perched on the love seat in Lillian's tiny apartment, barely denting its firm cushion. Granddad sat in one of the swivel barrel chairs at right angles to the love seat; Lillian was in a matching chair across the coffee table from him. She'd given them tall tumblers of ice water.

Val put hers on the glass coffee table and plunged into the questions she wanted to ask Lillian. "What led you to become a geriatric care manager?"

Lillian's hand clutching a glass of ice water froze on its way to her lips. "Nursing. I became interested in eldercare when I worked as a private-duty nurse. How did you discover I'm a care manager?"

"Granddad and I visited the Spring Lake Retirement Community. We're wondering why you didn't tell us you were the care manager for Omar's father-in-law."

The ice cubes in Lillian's drink rattled. "I couldn't tell you without violating a client's privacy rights."

"You also didn't tell us about Scott's connection to a man who'd committed suicide." Val glanced at her grandfather, giving him a chance to say something, but he didn't. She shifted on the hard cushion, angling herself toward Lillian. "How did you end up here, in the same village where Thomasina lives and where Scott was giving investment seminars?"

"Coincidence." Lillian crossed one leg over the other and jiggled her sandaled foot.

Val remembered from her last visit here that Lillian's twitching leg betrayed when she was lying. "You didn't know Scott before you moved here?"

"I knew *of* him. Omar told me the name of the man who bilked his father-in-law. When I moved here, I read that same name on notices for an investment seminar."

Probably true statements, but also evasive. "I'm surprised you didn't report Scott to the staff here," Val said.

"I couldn't prove he was dishonest. And any specifics I gave would intrude on Omar's family's privacy." Lillian swiveled her chair toward Granddad. "When you told me that Scott impressed you with his financial expertise, Don, I warned you against giving him any money."

Granddad put his glass on the coffee table. "How did we go from a warning to an action? I just wanted to throw a dinner party for friends. It was your idea to invite Scott and pressure him into returning Ned's money."

Val had detected Lillian's manipulating hand in the chowder dinner from the start. Granddad must have noticed too, though without admitting it to himself . . . until now.

Lillian thrust out her chin. "You agreed to it, Don. You even invited a reporter who could investigate his scams and put more pressure on him."

No surprise that Lillian had gone on the offensive. Val hoped her grandfather wouldn't cave.

He crossed his arms. "I get to invite people to my own house. You don't get to sneak them in, like you did Omar, for secret purposes. If you hadn't used my dinner as a way to get back at Scott, two people would be alive, and I wouldn't be accused of murder."

Bravo, Granddad.

Lillian leaned forward in her chair. "I'm not responsible for those deaths, and I'm sorry you're in that position."

Not the same as saying sorry for putting him in that position. Val reached for her water glass. The tumblers of ice water, sweating and making puddles on the glass coffee table, reminded her of the water glasses Lillian had put out Saturday night. She'd also filled those glasses. Could she have added an arsenic solution to Scott's tumbler without Granddad seeing her? Would Scott have noticed a slight metallic taste in his water?

Lillian stood up. "I've thought a lot about the dinner since Junie May died. I kept asking myself how anyone could have poisoned Scott's chowder in front of so many people. This afternoon I realized how."

She paced the small living room like a caged animal. When she told small lies, her leg twitched. Did her full-body movement signal a big lie?

Val hoped her voice wouldn't betray her skepticism. "Tell us your theory, Lillian."

"As I said Saturday night, I couldn't recall who wanted what type of chowder. But I know I carried the creamy chowder in my right hand and set both chowders on the end of the table nearest the kitchen.

Thomasina was on the right side of the table. She got the creamy chowder before Scott did."

That tallied with what Val had heard from Irene. "Yes, but then Thomasina changed her mind and asked for light chowder."

Lillian stopped pacing. "So I heard. I brought her a bowl of light chowder and saw her sprinkle salt substitute on it from a small packet." Her tone suggested a dramatic announcement.

Granddad shrugged. "A lot of people use salt substitute."

Lillian looked like a teacher exasperated that her students didn't know an answer. "She might have done the same thing to the creamy chowder, but with a salt substitute packet containing arsenic. It would look similar."

One form of arsenic looked like white powder or crystals, as Val knew from her research. Granddad's girlfriend had apparently done similar research, but that didn't make her theory valid. No one else had mentioned seeing Thomasina sprinkle anything on either chowder.

Granddad frowned. "A mother killing her child is unnatural. Why would Thomasina do such a terrible thing?"

Lillian paced again. "Maybe she depended on him for financial support. He could have forced her to move from one retirement place to another to give him access to investors. He'd gain their trust more quickly with his mother living in the community. As soon as any investor got wise to him, though, she'd have to decamp. If she didn't go along with his schemes, he'd stop supporting her."

Val raised her hand like a student with a question. "Why not go to the police instead of killing him?"

"Money. They might freeze his assets, and she'd be out on the street."

"Far as I know," Granddad said, "Thomasina never encouraged anyone to invest with her son, and she said he was a good son."

"She said that after he was dead." Lillian sank into the barrel chair. "He always struck me as more devoted to her than she was to him. She's behaved oddly for the last few days. If one of my children died suddenly, I'd be in shock and unable to function for a long time. Thomasina played in the Brain Game as if nothing unusual had happened this week."

Grandfather took off his bifocals and wiped them on the bottom of his polo shirt. "She might be in shock and on tranquilizers to help her cope."

Val looked at her watch. How long had it taken Lillian to shift the conversation from her own deceptions to Thomasina's possible guilt? About five minutes. In that time, she'd erected a murder scenario based on a shaky foundation: a sprinkle of salt substitute, which no one else had noticed, onto a soup that hadn't poisoned anyone. "Did you tell the police about the salt substitute?"

"I didn't have the chance. I just remembered it."

Granddad stood up. "Call them now. If you didn't tell them about your connection to Scott, you'd better do that too. I don't like being deceived, and neither do they. Let's go, Val."

Val popped up from the love seat and followed him out. She now knew the answers to all the questions unanswered after her last visit here—where

Lillian had come from, if she had children, what type of work she'd done before retirement, and whether she cared a fig for Granddad. *No* on that last one, and Granddad knew it now, his parting words a sign that her spell over him had broken. "Great exit line, Granddad."

"Hmph. Unless we figure out fast who murdered two people, I'll be taking curtain calls from behind bars."

"Let's go home and figure it out. We can bake a cake. That always helps me think."

Chapter 23

Val smiled when her grandfather joined her in the kitchen, wearing his Codger Cook apron. "You're finally willing to get that apron dirty."

"Who says I'm going to get it dirty?" He pointed to the index card on the island counter. "That's the recipe we're using?"

"It's a slimmed-down version of that rum cake you tried to make last month. Five ingredients." And it had fewer calories than the original.

Granddad adjusted his bifocals and peered at the recipe. "Okay, I'll get the stuff from the pantry."

"Don't forget the spray for the baking pan."

"Wait a minute. That's the sixth ingredient. The Codger Cook's recipes have only five."

"The spray isn't an ingredient. It's a necessity for baking, just like the pan." She took the mixer from the lower cabinets. "Mixing the batter takes no time at all. I'll preheat the oven."

He put the cake mix, oil, and rum on the counter. "You'll have to crack the eggs. I don't want any egg on my apron. I shouldn't use that mixer either. You remember what happened the last time I did."

"Batter on the walls and cabinets, your hair and clothes. How could I forget? Empty the cake mix into the bowl and add the other ingredients. I'll run the mixer."

"This recipe is too simple," he said as she finished mixing and poured the batter into the pan. "You didn't have enough time to think about the murder."

"We have time now. While the cake is baking, we'll reconstruct what happened at the chowder dinner. Why don't you set the dining-room table the way it was on Saturday night while I clean up in here?"

Ten minutes later, she went into the dining room. The table was set for seven. Plates for the chowder bowls to go on, wineglasses, utensils, and place cards. "Where did the cards come from?"

"Lillian brought them with her."

She hadn't brought one for Omar, of course, pretending he'd dropped in. "You forgot the water glasses, Granddad." Val took seven glasses from the china closet and added them to the settings.

Granddad pointed to the bowls and cups on a rolling cart. "We'll use the cart as the kitchen. I don't want to keep running back and forth for this exercise. Let's start. When the gang sits down, I'm in the kitchen and Lillian comes in to fetch the first chowder bowls."

"Hang on a minute. We need to distinguish between the creamy and the light chowder." Val took two bowls to the kitchen, splashed milk in one and water in the other, and returned to the dining room with them. "Lillian sets down the light chowder by

Irene and the creamy one by Thomasina." Val put the bowls where they belonged.

"Then Lillian goes back to the kitchen."

"Irene says she'd rather have a cup of each chowder and hands Scott the bowl of light chowder." Val moved the bowl with the water and went around the table to Thomasina's seat. "Thomasina says the creamy chowder looks too rich for her and passes it."

"Stop." Granddad kept her from moving the bowl with the milk in it. "Don't pass that chowder yet. Let's talk about Lillian's idea that Thomasina sprinkled arsenic on the creamy chowder. She could have done it. Who's watching her? Junie May's probably looking across the table as Irene passes Scott the light chowder. Omar is two seats away from Thomasina, with Junie May blocking his view."

"Or he might have been busy with the wine. You're right that Thomasina had the opportunity to poison the chowder. Let's see if anyone else did."

"Okay. Thomasina passes the chowder across the table to Scott."

"Nope. She gives it to Junie May." Val moved the bowl one place over. "Junie May announces she'd like a cup of each chowder and passes the bowl of creamy chowder to Scott." Val carried the bowl with milk to the other side of the table. Staging the tale of the traveling chowder gave her a better sense of time and place than her table diagram did. "For a while, I thought Junie May could have poisoned the chowder. But it wasn't in front of her for long. Scott was sitting right across from her and couldn't have missed seeing her put something in it."

"Holy cow!" Granddad pointed at Junie May's spot with one hand and Thomasina's with the other.

"What if Thomasina wanted to poison Junie May, not Scott?"

Hmm. A more plausible scenario than Lillian's idea that Thomasina killed Scott, but it rested on the same flimsy foundation of a sprinkle of arsenic that no one saw. "If Junie May was the target, why didn't Thomasina stop her son from eating the chowder?"

"Maybe she was frozen with fear. She talked a lot while we ate the appetizers, but she didn't say much at the table." Granddad took off his glasses and wiped them on his still-clean apron. "I'd sure rather think she killed her son by mistake than on purpose. Why would she want to kill Junie May?"

"Let's not tackle motives yet. We need to figure out who else had the chance to poison the chowder." Val carried the bowl with the milk to the other side of the table. "The creamy chowder's in front of Scott."

"Irene takes two cups of light chowder from the kitchen for herself and Junie May. Lillian brings in the bowls for herself and Thomasina. I bring in my cup of chowder. Before we even sit down, Scott says the creamy chowder is delicious."

"He started eating before everyone else." And finished sooner, slumping over a nearly empty bowl while the others were still eating. "When you sat down, the dog barked."

He grinned. "Yeah, the remote was in my back pocket. I sat on the button that turned Fido on. How'd you know about the barking?"

"Junie May mentioned it. She figured the distraction gave Lillian a chance to reach across Scott's bowl for bread or salt and drop arsenic into his chowder."

Granddad walked around to Lillian's chair. "Nah.

Where's the arsenic? Clutched in the hand she's going to eat with?" Granddad turned one hand upward and made a fist. "When did she put it there? No one knew the dog would bark. It took me about ten seconds to slip my hand in my pocket and turn it off."

"By that same token, Irene couldn't have poisoned Scott's chowder at the table. What's more, she's sitting too far from Scott to drop anything in his bowl." Val sat at Irene's place and demonstrated that she could barely reach Scott's bowl without getting out of the seat. "We can also rule out her putting arsenic in the chowder pot when she was alone in the kitchen before dinner. Only a mass murderer would do that."

"Same is true for me. I had no chance to poison Scott's bowl at the table and no reason to kill my guests. I shouldn't have bothered calling that lawyer. We'll just reconstruct the crime like this for the police." He gestured with open arms toward the table. "Then they'll know I'm innocent."

"Don't fire the lawyer yet." Val's latest scenario— arsenic in the water, not in the chowder—gave both Granddad and Lillian a chance to poison Scott.

"Once we're all at the table, there's only one person who moves around and goes near Scott's chowder." Granddad held up a wineglass. "Omar, when he pours the wine."

"I'd like to see how he could have done that. I'll get a bottle of wine."

Val went to the kitchen and peered at the cake in the oven. Only half baked, as Holtzman would say of her murder theories. She had plenty of them and absolutely no proof to back them up. The doorbell rang as she filled an empty wine bottle with water. She took the bottle and a saltshaker to the dining-room table.

Granddad led Roy Chesterfeld from the hall into the sitting room. "A deputy's here. To see *you*, Val." His tone implied *better you than me.*

Val extended her hand to the deputy with the blond tousled hair. "Nice to see you again."

Roy shook her hand and held it longer than politeness demanded. "I was going to phone you, but I was in the neighborhood anyway. I'm glad I caught you at home."

An excuse to visit the scene of the crime? "Have a seat." She gestured toward the sofa as Granddad left the room, heading for the hall bathroom. She perched on the arm of his recliner.

Roy fingered the deputy hat in his lap. "You were probably right that the murderer took Junie May's notes and computer, but we found her thumb drive. She backed up her documents on it."

"You know what story she was researching?"

"It concerned all kinds of fraud against the elderly. She had notes and sources on telemarketing cons, repair rip-offs, caretakers siphoning money, and investment scams."

"That makes sense." The police must not think that Junie May's research had any bearing on the murder investigation or the deputy wouldn't have told her about it. Or maybe Roy was breaking the rules to find out what Val knew. "A report about the fleecing of seniors isn't huge unless it exposes a case of major fraud. Junie May told me that Scott was one of her sources, but she didn't suspect him of fraud."

"Her notes say otherwise. She tracked down some

evidence against him, and she was looking for more."
Roy scrutinized Val's face. "You look surprised."

"I am. When she told me Scott was legit, I didn't
necessarily believe it, but I thought *she* believed it.
Instead, she was putting me off the scent." And she
was stringing Scott along for her own purposes.

"She kept her research secret from her boss.
She'd have no reason to tell you either."

"She'd have even less reason to tell someone
who'd want to suppress that research. Maybe she
didn't cover her tracks well, and someone found out
what she was researching. Did her notes on investment fraud include Arthur Tunbridge's name?" A
head shake from Roy. So Junie May hadn't dug up
the story of the suicide, or at least hadn't put it in
her notes.

Roy tilted his head sideways toward the dining
room. "Looks like you're expecting company for
dinner. Sorry to interrupt."

Granddad returned to the room. "We're not expecting anyone."

Enlisting Roy's help with the crime reconstruction might give Val a nonchalant way to ask him
about Omar's alibi. "My grandfather and I were
going through what happened at Saturday night's
dinner to see who could have poisoned Scott's chowder at the table. We need someone to assume the
role of Scott. Are you game?"

Roy stood up. "Sure, but I won't eat or drink *anything.*"

"I don't blame you," Granddad said.

Val showed the deputy to Scott's place at the
table. "Here's where Scott sat. My grandfather can
play Omar. He'll pour your wine and try to poison

your chowder to see if Omar could have done it. Here's the wine, Granddad. Where do you want the arsenic?" She handed him the bottle and picked up the saltshaker.

"I can't fit anything but the bottle in my right hand. I guess it's in my other hand."

"Hold out your left hand." Val sprinkled a half teaspoon of salt in his cupped hand. An equivalent amount of arsenic would have killed Scott twice over. "I'll sit where Lillian was."

She took the chair at the end of the table next to Roy. Her grandfather stood on the deputy's other side and leaned over the table with the wine bottle.

As the bottle hovered over the wineglass, Granddad pointed at Val. "There's a spider crawling down your shirt!"

Roy whipped his head toward her. Val pulled her T-shirt away to look down it.

Granddad grinned. "Ha! I just opened my hand and dropped that arsenic in the bowl. And you two didn't notice. All Omar had to do was create a diversion like a magician, point at Lillian, and say something to make Scott look at her. *Presto change-o*— the arsenic's in the soup." Granddad showed them his empty palm.

Roy rolled his eyes. "I can't believe I fell for that."

"I fell for it too, and I'm familiar with my grandfather's wily ways. He proved that Omar could have poisoned the chowder. Junie May didn't say she saw him do it, but she suspected him." Val caught the deputy's eye. "Does Omar have an alibi for Junie May's murder?"

Instead of answering, Roy pointed to his digital watch. "I gotta get back to work."

Val knew it was hopeless to press him about alibis, but maybe he'd tell her a bit more about Junie May's death. She walked him to the front porch. "I've been wondering if Junie May could have been murdered by a woman nearly twice her age."

"Like some of your grandfather's dinner guests? Don't rule them out." Thunder rumbled. Roy looked at the sky.

"If a senior citizen held me at gunpoint, I wouldn't sit there and let her shoot me. Junie May's killer needed to take her by surprise and keep her still for the few seconds it took to simulate a suicide." Val's neighbor in New York had shown her a device that could incapacitate someone, similar to what the police used, but not as powerful. "I knew a woman in the city who had a stun gun that looked like a lipstick. That would keep someone from fighting back."

"You can also buy a stun gun that looks like a cell phone." Roy smiled.

Neither confirmation nor denial from the deputy. Maybe Val had guessed right about Junie May's murderer stunning her before shooting her. "Thanks for playing the role of the victim at the table. My grandfather really enjoyed it."

"Don't tell him, but I noticed when he dropped the salt in the bowl. I didn't want to spoil his fun."

Val wasn't sure whether to believe the deputy, but it didn't matter. "You knew what he was going to do. Scott wouldn't have known to watch his bowl. You're trained to be on the alert and react quickly. He wasn't."

"That's why I didn't bother to stop your grandfather. He made his point. Omar could have slipped something into Scott's chowder, though it would have been risky. Good-bye, Val. I enjoyed my visit."

She shook his outstretched hand. "Did you get what you came for?"

"Sure did. I got to see you."

Flirt. Val went back to the dining room.

Granddad sat in his usual chair at the far end of the table. "We've gone through everyone here and ruled out Irene, Lillian, and me."

Val had ruled out Lillian poisoning Scott at dinner, but that wasn't Granddad's girlfriend's only opportunity. "Were you in the dining room when Lillian filled the water glasses?"

"I was setting up the bar in the sitting room."

Val took the chair the deputy had vacated and fingered the place card with Scott's name on it. "Who put out the place cards?"

"Lillian did. She was following some social formula. Female guest of honor to the right of the host. Male guest of honor to the hostess's right. And so on."

"Did you notice if Scott drank his water?"

"Why would I? He was at the other end of the table, and I was busy eating and talking." Granddad frowned. "You're going somewhere with this."

"Uh-huh. Lillian could have brought a small vial of arsenic solution with her and added it to his water. He might not have noticed its slight metallic taste. You said he was staring across the table during dinner, distracted."

"How could she know he'd drink it?"

"She couldn't know, but it wasn't her only chance to slip something in his drink. Serving him coffee or tea with dessert would have given her another shot at poisoning him if the first one failed." And she'd asked Granddad to wait until after dinner before confronting Scott. Val picked up the bowl from Scott's place setting. "Lillian also got rid of all the leftover chowder, in Scott's bowl and in the pot."

Val watched her grandfather closely. A few days ago, he'd taken the blame for throwing out the chowder, trying to protect Lillian. Would he do it again?

His face screwed up. "So? How does throwing out the chowder have anything to do with poisoning Scott's water?"

No rush to shield Lillian this time. Val exhaled. "Lillian might have thrown out the chowder, not because she thought it contained poison, but because she knew it didn't and wanted everyone to think it did. The chowder could have been a smoke screen to obscure how she really killed him."

Granddad's jaw dropped. "What twisted minds women have."

Val always bristled at his generalizations about women. "Do you mean me or Lillian?"

"Both of you." Granddad stood, walked to the windows, and looked up at the sky. "Storm coming."

But no storm of protest from him over the idea of Lillian as a murderer. Before today, he'd have rejected it without a second thought, but now he seemed to give it serious consideration. He'd lost some of his illusions about his girlfriend.

Granddad turned away from the thunderclouds. "We need some light in here." He clicked on the chandelier, returned to the table, and sat in the chair occupied by his girlfriend on Saturday night. "I can see Omar taking revenge for his father-in-law's

suicide. I can't see Lillian murdering Scott because
she lost a client, no matter how bad she felt about it.
And she had no reason to murder Junie May. At
dinner, Junie May might have seen someone poison
Scott, but she wasn't here when you say Lillian could
have poisoned Scott's water."

Good point. "Junie May told me the night before
she was murdered that she would research Omar and
Lillian. Maybe she unearthed something about—No,
wait." Val flashed back to theories she'd heard but
discarded. "I should have paid more attention to
what Thomasina said. There's another scenario we
shouldn't overlook."

"That someone who didn't come to the dinner is
the murderer? I'd really like to hear that."

"Unfortunately, I'm going the other way—that
two murderers came to dinner."

Granddad groaned.

Chapter 24

Granddad rapped his knuckle on the mahogany dining room. "Two murderers sat at your grandmother's table? They conspired to kill two other people who sat here?"

"I'm thinking about two people who didn't collude. On Wednesday, before the details about Junie May's death came out, Thomasina claimed that Junie May murdered Scott and then committed suicide."

"We know Junie May didn't commit suicide."

"But if Thomasina convinced herself that Junie May did it, she had a motive to murder her in retaliation. I never believed Junie May committed suicide. Neither did you. Thomasina said it, possibly because she'd staged the murder as a suicide and expected the police to fall for the ruse." Val shifted the wineglass and the tumbler into their original spots in the place setting. "What do you think of Thomasina as Junie May's murderer?"

"It makes more sense than Thomasina killing her own son or trying to kill Junie May and doing nothing to stop her son from dying."

The kitchen timer went off. Val sniffed and jumped up from the table. "I've been too engrossed to notice that the cake smells done."

She rushed to the kitchen, opened the oven, and took out the cake. Enveloped in sweet warmth, Val looked around the kitchen she loved. Whenever she baked here, the enticing aromas from the oven conjured up memories of her grandmother. She would never lose her connection to Grandma, who'd taught her to cook, but she never felt that connection as strongly in other kitchens. She would have missed that feeling if Lillian had moved in.

Granddad brought the wine bottle and the salt-shaker to the counter. "When you went out to the porch with that deputy, did you tell him your idea about Lillian poisoning the water?" When she shook her head, he said, "Why not?"

"First, because I have no proof. And second, because I'm afraid Lillian will say *you* filled the water glasses. Your word against hers." And he was the one who'd had arsenic in the house. "That's why you should hang on to your lawyer." A clap of thunder emphasized her point.

"Lillian would only say that if she murdered Scott." Granddad sat at the breakfast table. "We both agreed she didn't have a strong motive."

Bit by bit, his rock-solid trust in Lillian had eroded. Now Val would take a mallet to it.

She sat across from him. "Remember what Gunnar said about con artists having accomplices? Geriatric care managers have access to older people and know their financial condition. Even more important, those older people trust them."

Granddad flexed his fingers. With rain coming, his arthritis might bother him more than usual. "If Lillian helped Scott swindle people—and that's a big *if*—why would she kill him? She wouldn't do it out of greed."

"I agree. As Scott's accomplice, she might have blamed herself in part for Mr. Tunbridge's suicide. She knew the law couldn't touch Scott and wanted to make sure he didn't drive anyone else to suicide." Val waited for a protest from Granddad. None came.

He opened and closed his hands as if clutching at something that wasn't there. She reached across the table and squeezed his arm lightly. The idea that Lillian might have murdered Scott saddened him, but at least he would not protect her at his own expense.

He'd lost his illusions about her, but in making the case for Lillian's guilt, Val had lost something too—her own objectivity. To regain it, she'd have to review with an open mind what she'd seen and heard for the last five days, starting with what she'd observed the night of the chowder dinner.

"What's the bottom line, Val, after our crime reconstruction?"

"We have five possibilities. Three involve a single murderer—Omar, Thomasina, or Lillian killing Scott and Junie May. Two scenarios involve two murderers. Omar killed Scott, and Thomasina killed Junie May. Or Lillian killed Scott, and Thomasina killed Junie May. Bottom line, we have theories, but no evidence."

"We have to find the evidence." Granddad stroked his chin. "Where are you going to look for it?"

"My next stop is the vintage jewelry shop in town.

Scott and Junie May went there Saturday evening. I'll ask if anyone there remembers them or overheard their conversation." Val would need photos of them. Online newspaper articles would probably have photos she could print. She stood up.

"Aren't you going to eat some cake before you go?"

"I don't have time. I want to get to town before the jewelry shop closes. Then I'll stop at the supermarket. We're low on groceries."

"Okay. I'll go to the Village and take Ned some cake."

Val closed her umbrella and shook it at the entrance to the vintage jewelry store on Main Street. The shop's interior reminded her of a restored Colonial mansion. Wainscoted walls, mirrors in gilded frames, Persian carpets on polished wood floors. Salesclerks and buyers spoke in hushed tones.

Val caught the eye of the youngest salesclerk, a twentyish woman who wasn't busy with customers. "I'd like to see any cameos you have. My friend bought a really nice one here."

"I'll show you the case where we keep them." The clerk led the way to the cameo collection.

For five minutes, Val peered at cameos and discussed them with the salesclerk. "I don't see exactly what I want. By the way, were you working here last Saturday at about this time?"

The clerk nodded. "I'm here every Saturday. I work a three-day weekend and spend Monday through Thursday at Dewey Beach."

"That sounds like fun. I don't get to the beach as much as I'd like."

"I'm in a group house," the clerk said, her voice barely above a whisper. "I sublet my room weekends. If you're interested, I can give you a good deal."

"Thanks. I may take you up on that." The clerk now had something to gain by making Val happy. Time to bring out the photos. "Here's a picture of my friend and the man she was seeing. Did you happen to notice them here Saturday, around this time?" Would the clerk recognize the photos as customers or murder victims . . . or both?

"I definitely noticed them. She was looking at necklaces. He called her over to the case where we keep the most expensive rings and told her to pick out her favorite. The one she picked fit her finger perfectly. He said he'd buy it for her as an engagement ring."

"I didn't know they were engaged."

"They weren't. She said he'd have to convince her first that he wasn't a mama's boy. Well, she didn't use those words, but that was the gist of it." The clerk giggled and covered her mouth. "He was kind of old for a mama's boy, but I guess some guys don't grow out of it."

"I'd like to see the ring my friend liked." And its price tag. "She has really good taste in jewelry. Maybe I can talk the guy I'm going to marry into buying it for me."

"It's gone now. Those two left the shop together. He came back without her, just as we were ready to close, and bought the ring. I told him he could return it within a month if it didn't work out, and it's not back yet. They might be engaged by now."

Val hated to spoil the happy ending, but the helpful clerk deserved the truth. "He got sick that night and died the next day."

The clerk's eyes popped out. "Oh no. That's terrible."

Val showed her Junie May's photo again. "You didn't recognize her when she came into the shop last week?"

"Should I have?"

"She was a TV news reporter in Salisbury."

The clerk clapped her hand over her mouth. "The one who was murdered. My mom told me about that. I don't watch the news myself. But the two of them, dying like that, it's like Romeo and Juliet. So sad."

Romeo and Juliet minus suicides and feuding families, but plus a murderer.

An hour after leaving the vintage jewelry shop, Val carried her groceries to the car. Carloads of teenagers and families headed from the parking lot toward Giovanni's restaurant, two doors down from the supermarket. Giovanni made the closest thing to New York pizza that Val had found near Bayport. She would have stopped for a slice, but didn't want to keep Granddad waiting. He was probably back from the Village by now and impatient for her to make dinner for him.

The rain had let up, a lull between storms from the looks of the sky. She stowed the cold items in the cooler she kept in the car during the warmer months.

Her phone chimed as she nosed out from her parking space. She reversed back into the space and clicked the phone on.

"Val, it's Ned. Where are you?"

"At the Midway Shopping Plaza."

"Good, you're closer than me. I'm in Treadwell. Drive straight to the Village. You have to get your grandfather out of Thomasina's cottage." Ned sounded frantic, as if he expected a bomb to blow up the cottage.

His fear infected her over the phone. She pressed the speaker button and pulled out of the parking space. "Okay, I'm on my way."

"Move fast or Thomasina will beat you there."

Granddad was in the cottage and Thomasina wasn't? "You mean she doesn't know he's there? Where is she?"

"She went to the trivia night at a bar in Treadwell. I was supposed to let him know when she left for home. But I arrived late, and by then, the trivia game had been called off and she'd already gone."

"How did he get into her cottage?"

"Um, well, before I bought the hardware store, I was a locksmith. He talked me into letting him in when he found out Thomasina was gone for the evening."

Val felt dizzy. "Why did he want to get inside?"

"To search her place for evidence. Didn't you tell him he needed evidence to prove his innocence?"

"I didn't mean for him to get the evidence himself by breaking and entering." If Thomasina caught Granddad, she'd hand him over to the police. "Did you try his cell phone?"

"He's not answering. That's why I called you. I'm

racing back to the Village, hoping to catch up with her. If I do, I'll stall her."

But Thomasina might have already discovered Granddad in her cottage. "Don't race, Ned. The roads are slick. I'll be there in a few minutes. Thanks." Val tucked the phone in the pocket of her rain jacket and hit the accelerator.

Five minutes later, she pulled into a guest parking spot half a block away from Thomasina's cottage. No sign of Granddad's Buick. Maybe he'd already left. She put up the hood of her jacket, left her handbag in the car, and jogged toward the cottage.

She walked around the garage attached to the house, hoping for a window that would let her see if a car was parked inside. Nothing but solid walls. She mounted the steps to the front porch and peered into the double window. The drapes in Thomasina's living room blocked her view. She was about to ring the bell when she noticed the door wasn't shut tight.

She pushed against it with her shoulder. "Yoo-hoo!"

Val's heart hammered so loud she could hear it. Suppose Granddad's heart had raced after he broke in? Maybe he hadn't answered his cell phone because he'd had a heart attack. She had to make sure he was all right. A quick check to make sure he wasn't there, and then a quick exit.

She crept into the hall, switched on her keychain flashlight, and swept it around the adjacent room. No one there. She crossed to the hall and passed by the bathroom she'd used when she and Granddad had visited Thomasina. The door to the next room was ajar. Her flashlight lit up a large bedroom. To her relief, Granddad wasn't lying on the floor between the bed and the closet. She tiptoed toward the far side of the bed.

A stealthy sound came from behind her. A rustle from inside the closet. She resisted the urge to run. Had to be him in there. Thomasina wouldn't hide in her own closet.

"Granddad?" she whispered.

He came out of the closet. "You about scared me to death," he hissed. "I thought you were one of Thomasina's friends."

"You have to leave now." She kept her voice low too. Trespassing made you want to whisper. "She's on her way. Ned called me."

"Doggone it. Did you shut the front door behind you?"

"No, but who cares? We have to leave now, before—" A noise came from the living room. A jingle of keys. Val's throat closed with fear.

"Climb out the window," Granddad whispered. "I'll handle this."

Before she could protest, he left the room.

"Thomasina!" he said with a booming voice. "Glad you're back."

"What are you doing here?" The woman sounded outraged.

"I came by to visit and found the door cracked open. I called your name. When you didn't answer, I went in to make sure you were okay."

Granddad didn't usually talk so loud. He might be trying to cover up any noise the window might make when Val opened it. She tiptoed toward the double-sash window.

"I'm sure I closed that door," Thomasina said.

Even her low voice carried through the cottage's cheap interior walls. Val positioned her hands on the window, ready to raise it when Granddad bellowed again.

"The door lock didn't catch behind me either," he said. "The lock probably needs adjusting."

Val pulled up on the window. It didn't budge.

"They must have a maintenance crew here, Thomasina. If they can't take care of it, call the locksmith in town."

While Granddad belabored the obvious, Val kept tugging at the window . . . in vain.

"The door is locking just fine now," Thomasina said.

Val felt around the frame, looking for a latch or bar that kept the window from opening. Her fingers touched a small piece of metal with a keyhole in it. *Oh no.* The window wouldn't open without a key.

"Well, thank you for checking on things, Don. Everyone here has been so kind to me."

The quick switch from suspicion to sweetness in Thomasina's tone worried Val. She moved away from the window. She wasn't getting out that way. Maybe Thomasina would go to the bathroom, and Val could rush out. A long shot. Better to invent a cover story like Granddad's.

"We try to be helpful in this neck of the woods, not like city folk," her grandfather said. "You a city gal, Thomasina?"

"I don't like all the traffic and the crime."

As long as Val was stuck here, she might as well poke around while Granddad made small talk. He would have looked in the closet and drawers for evidence, but not under the bed. His arthritis made it painful for him to get up and down.

Val crouched, lifted the dust ruffle, and turned on her flashlight. The suitcase under the bed intrigued her more than the slippers. She tugged at it. Not empty. The case had a luggage tag on it. Her flashlight illuminated the name on the tag—Samantha Lowie. Why did Thomasina have a suitcase belonging to someone else? Or was it her own suitcase, packed for a quick getaway, tagged with the alias she would use next? Aliases often have a connection to the original name. The Brontë sisters' pen names used initials that matched their real initials. Some people change only their last names or their first names. But Thomasina used very different names. Val stared at the luggage tag. On second thought, Samantha, Shawna, and Thomasina did have something in common.

Val stood up and moved closer to the wall dividing the bedroom from the living room.

"Can I get you something to drink, Don? Coffee? Beer?"

"I'd love a beer."

Val cringed. *Don't drink it.*

"Let's have a happy hour," Thomasina said. "I'll get some snacks too."

Don't eat anything.

Time to save Granddad. Val stuck her head out the bedroom door and peeked down the hall toward the living room.

Her grandfather stood near the shelves displaying Thomasina's collection of antique bottles. The vintage glassware reminded Val of her visit to the secondhand shops.

Thomasina was out of sight. Val hoped Thomasina couldn't see her either. She crept across the hall to the bathroom, left the door open, and flushed the toilet.

Two astonished faces greeted her when she sauntered out to the living room. Val grabbed the beer stein Thomasina was carrying. Foam sloshed over the top and spilled on the rug. "Thanks, Thomasina. I've been dying for a beer. I hope you don't mind that I used your bathroom."

Granddad's eyebrows lowered like the thunderclouds outside.

"You've been sneaking around my house!" Thomasina bellowed as loud as Granddad had earlier.

Val tried to look indignant. "I wasn't sneaking. Granddad and I came to visit you. When we found the door open and you gone, we thought you might have an intruder. You didn't, but I really had to use the bathroom."

Fury made Thomasina's face turn bright pink. "You're the only intruders here. You broke into my house, both of you."

A loud pound on the door made them all jump. "Police! Open up!" More pounding followed.

Thank goodness. Val held the beer stein steady and rushed to the door. She flung it open.

Oops. Not the police. Ned.

"Everything okay?" he asked.

Val glanced behind her and glimpsed Thomasina going to the kitchen. "Granddad's here. Don't close the door." She motioned to her grandfather to leave.

Ned came into the hall and stopped dead. His widening eyes focused on something over Val's shoulder.

She turned around.

Thomasina clutched a long-bladed knife in her hand. "You're all crazy. You're trying to kill me, but you won't get away with it. I can defend myself." She pointed the knife at Val and Ned near the door and then at Granddad standing near the fireplace. Back and forth, it went.

Ned stepped in front of Val, shielding her with his body. "Calm down, Thomasina. No one's trying to kill you. We're happy to leave." He spoke quietly, his tone soothing.

"Don't move." Thomasina's mouth with its thick red lipstick looked like a bloody slash in her face. "Close the door."

No way. With the door open, Val and Ned had a chance of getting away. Not Granddad, though. Thomasina stood between him and the door. In her peripheral vision, Val saw him backing away. Diverting Thomasina's attention might give him time to rush to the bathroom and lock himself in. Then she and Ned could run out into the pouring rain and call the police. Well, she could run. She wasn't sure about Ned.

"Someone's coming," she said. Wishful thinking. The downpour made it hard to hear even the sound of a car motor.

"You can't fool—" Thomasina broke off, her expression a cross between rage and amazement.

"Police. Drop the knife or I'll shoot." The voice came from the porch outside the door.

Holtzman! Val never thought she'd be happy to hear the deputy's voice. She was even happier to see his gun. She leaned against the wall near the door, woozy with relief.

Thomasina released the knife. It fell on the carpeted floor. "I'm so glad you're here. These people invaded my house. I was terrified of them."

Holtzman's gun didn't waver. "Step back from the knife, ma'am. Farther. Keep going." As she backed up, he moved closer and beckoned to the deputies behind him.

Val stood aside to let Roy Chesterfeld and two other deputies go by. Chief Yardley came in next, with a young officer Val recognized. Officer Wade had taken her statement about the murder in June. What had brought them all here?

Two deputies Val didn't know flanked Thomasina. Roy picked up the knife.

Holtzman put his gun away. He scowled at Val, obviously not as happy to see her as she was to see him. "I might have known." He joined the crowd in the middle of the living room and motioned for her and Ned to follow him. "What's going on here?"

"That man"—Thomasina pointed at Granddad halfway across the room—"and his granddaughter broke into my cottage. I came home and found them here."

Holtzman pointed to Val's jacket. "You're the hooded prowler a neighbor reported."

As a rule, the report of a prowler probably wouldn't merit his attention, but a prowler at the house of a woman whose son was murdered brought out a lot of law enforcement.

Granddad stood ramrod tall. "She's not a prowler. Val and I saw the door was open. She yoo-hooed, and

Thomasina didn't answer. I went in to make sure Thomasina was okay and nobody had broken in."

Misleading about his motives and the time sequence, but nothing Val would call an outright lie, no facts anyone could disprove.

Thomasina's injured look suggested she disagreed. "I always lock the door when I leave. They jimmied it open." She pointed at Ned with a trembling hand. "And that man barged in here, claiming to be a policeman."

Granddad threw up his hands. "She misunderstood. Ned knocked on the door to tell us the police were coming and we should open it. Then she came out of the kitchen with that big knife."

Ned nodded. "She yelled that we were trying to kill her."

"Of course I had a knife. I was cutting things in the kitchen."

"You came home, found people here who broke in, and went into the kitchen to cut something?" Holtzman eyed the ten-inch carving knife. "What exactly were you cutting?"

He stood equidistant from Thomasina and Granddad, the three forming a triangle. The chief and Officer Wade stood closer to Granddad, while everyone else clustered at Thomasina's end of the room.

Thomasina looked nervously toward the kitchen. "I got it out to slice cheese."

Granddad held out his hand palm up toward her. "See how well she treats *intruders*? She poured me a beer and said she'd fix happy-hour food. Val's holding that beer. I hope you analyze it. I'd like to know if she laced it with anything."

Holtzman looked skeptical, but Chief Yardley spoke up. "It's worth looking at that beer."

At a nod from Holtzman, one of the deputies near Thomasina left her side and took the glass from Val.

Thomasina pointed at Val. "She grabbed it away from me. If it's laced with anything, she drugged it. Why aren't you arresting these people?" With her lips quivering, she looked at Holtzman.

Val groaned inwardly. The man had a soft spot for teary women.

He took a step forward. "This looks like a standoff. Three people who don't belong here say one thing. The one person who does belong says another. This is her property. At least two of you trespassed. Just because a door is open, you don't get to walk in and stroll around. That's a lesson you should have learned, Ms. Deniston, the last time we had dealings with each other."

Thomasina broke into a smug smile, which made Val gnash her teeth. The good news, Holtzman had noticed the smugness.

He stared at Thomasina with narrowed eyes. "You had a weapon in your hand when we got here. No one else did. That changes the equation."

"It was three against one. I was defending myself."

Granddad stepped toward Holtzman. "If you hadn't arrived with your posse, she'd have slashed us. Long as you came this far, take a look around. While I was checking for intruders, I ran across the wig and baseball cap she wore to disguise herself after she murdered Junie May."

Thomasina blinked back tears. "I have a wig in my

bedroom and different kinds of hats. That doesn't mean I murdered anyone."

Score one for Thomasina. If she hadn't drugged the beer, she'd probably get off and file a complaint against the intruders.

If the dish doesn't taste right, add another ingredient. Stir the pot.

Val raised her hand. "Let's not forget the white car."

Thomasina appealed to Holtzman. "I don't *have* a white car."

Val shifted position so she could watch Thomasina's reactions. "Easy for you to rent a car. What name did you use? Shawna Maliote? No, I'll bet it was Samantha Lowie."

Thomasina flinched. Holtzman trained his raptor eyes on her.

Val's turn for a smug smile, but she knew enough to hide it. "A good search of this place might turn up IDs for those and other aliases she's used."

"She might keep her fake IDs in a safety-deposit box," Granddad said.

He could probably show the police exactly where Thomasina kept the safety-deposit box key.

"You can't search my house." Thomasina's calm had returned. "You have nothing on me. You need probable cause for a search."

Roy perched his head sideways and studied her. "Sounds like you've spent time in the criminal justice system."

"I watch *Law & Order.*"

Thomasina had an answer for everything.

Val thought of a way to rattle her. "If someone will

give me a pen and paper, I can write down other aliases she might have used. Maybe you'll find one of them in a database that tracks frauds." And have probable cause, not just for a search, but for an arrest. A murder charge could come later.

At a nod from the chief, Officer Wade gave Val a small spiral notebook and pen. "Here."

"Thank you." Val didn't have the skills Thomasina exhibited at the Brain Game. It would take her longer, but she'd do her best. She wrote Samantha Lowie, studied it, and jotted another name. "Amelia Washton." She glanced at Thomasina's bored face and created another name. "Eloisa Thawman."

Thomasina's eyes flickered.

Val put an asterisk next to the name and kept going, announcing each name after she scribbled it. Mahalia Weston. Athenia Maslow. A twitch from Thomasina on that one—an asterisk. Alison Mae Thaw. Ana Lois Mathew. Natalie Mashow. Sheila Manatow. A tremor seized Thomasina. She clutched the back of the divan, where she'd lolled on Val's first visit here. No asterisk necessary. Sheila Manatow must have done something really bad.

The chief held out his hand for the notebook. "Good enough, Val. I'll run those names." He left.

Granddad gave her a thumbs-up. He'd succeeded in his mission, finding evidence that linked Thomasina to Junie May's murder. But that wouldn't get him off the hook for Scott's murder. A purse on a side table in the living room caught Val's eye, leather with a gold chain strap. Thomasina must have left it on the table when she came in this evening and found Granddad here. The same purse had hung from Thomasina's shoulder at the chowder dinner.

"Something on your mind, Ms. Deniston?" Holtzman said.

She would probably arouse his wrath, but it was worth it to see Thomasina's reaction. "Assuming you do get a search warrant, look for arsenic."

Thomasina looked aghast. "Are you suggesting I murdered my own son? You planted the arsenic. To frame *me* for what *he* did." She pointed at Granddad.

"When did I do that?" Val asked.

"Yesterday when you were in my kitchen."

Roy craned his neck toward the kitchen. "I guess we know where to start the search."

"Handle the salt substitute with care," Val said. "If your kitchen search doesn't turn up anything, check that purse on the table. It may have traces of arsenic inside."

Thomasina collapsed onto the couch. "I want a lawyer."

Chapter 25

Deputy Holtzman allowed Val, her grandfather, and Ned to leave Thomasina's cottage after Chief Yardley reported on the results of running the aliases through criminal databases. Val had no idea what he'd found, but it was enough to tip the balance against Thomasina in the *she said, he said* stand-off. Once outside the cottage, Granddad suggested a fast getaway and invited his partners in crime for a pizza.

They'd driven in separate cars to Giovanni's and now sat at a table for three, facing the parking lot at the Midway Shopping Plaza. The red-checked vinyl table covers positioned Giovanni's in a niche between pizza chains with paper place mats and Italian restaurants with cloth-covered tables.

Val didn't realize how famished she was until she breathed in the scent of Giovanni's hand-tossed pizza. She glanced at the brief menu. "What kind of pizza would you like, Ned?"

"I like everything plain. Some tomatoes on top would be okay."

"Good idea." Val gave her Granddad a *don't argue* look. He preferred pizza loaded with meat, but he owed Ned for abetting his crazy scheme of searching Thomasina's house.

Granddad put his menu down. "Anything except the clam pizza is fine with me. I'm off clams."

The waiter came with ice water and took their order for a large Margherita pizza.

Ned unwrapped his straw. "Why didn't you answer your cell phone when you were at Thomasina's, Don? I tried to reach you and tell you to get out."

Granddad pulled his cell phone from his jacket and punched some buttons. "Yup. Your calls went through. I never noticed because I had the phone on vibrate. I'll put it in my shirt pocket next time."

"Next time, Granddad? You're going to break into another house?"

"He'll have to do it without my help," Ned said. "How'd you come across all of Thomasina's aliases, Val?"

"I made them up, using the same letters she used in the three names I knew about. Thomasina Weal, Shawna Maliote, and Samantha Lowie are anagrams."

Ned frowned. "Which is her real name?"

"They're probably all fake. Remember the trivia question about the alias used by Hollywood directors? Only Thomasina knew the answer—Alan Smithee, which is an anagram of *the alias men*. The names she used are all anagrams of *the alias woman*."

Granddad stroked his chin. "It would have been

smarter to use aliases that had nothing in common. And to answer the Alan Smithee question wrong."

"Thomasina get a question wrong on purpose?" Ned shook his head. "She's too competitive to do that. Anyone who needs that many aliases is up to no good."

Val agreed. "I doubt Scott had to coerce her to help him in his scams. In fact, she might have pressured him to swindle people. I'm really sorry you lost your money to him, Ned."

"He never got any of my money. I wanted to invest twenty thousand, but I didn't have the cash. Your grandfather wrote me a check as a loan until my house sells."

Val turned to her grandfather. "*You* lost money then?"

He poked his straw around his water glass. "Ned got cold feet about the investment. Problem was, he didn't tell me right away."

"I wasn't comfortable using your grandfather's money, but I didn't want to give it back right away. I was afraid he'd invest with Scott, and then it would be my fault if he lost money. I told him I signed his check over to Scott."

"After Lillian warned me against investing with Scott, I moved the money out of my account so the check wouldn't clear." Granddad played hopscotch on the checked tablecloth with the pepper shaker. "I forgot to leave enough in there to cover the bills that get paid automatically. After the chowder dinner, Ned told me what he'd done and gave me back the check."

"I wish I'd known that, Granddad. That overdraft notice had me worried."

"I told you I took care of it."

She might have believed it if he'd given her more details, but he'd expected her to trust him. From now on, she'd try. Just because he botched cooking didn't mean he wasn't competent in other matters.

The waiter set down an elevated tray with the pizza. Val liked how the cheese was dappled on top, not lying like a thick winter blanket over the red sauce. A perfect summer pizza, studded with fresh tomatoes and green basil. They dug in and said little until they'd eaten enough to take the edge off their hunger.

Ned went through two pieces of pizza quickly, leaving the crusty edges uneaten. "Tell me how you figured out Thomasina was the murderer."

Granddad put down a half-eaten slice of pizza. "We reconstructed the murder like they do in the movies and saw that Thomasina had the best chance to poison the chowder. The bowl she started with ended up in front of Scott. She said the creamy chowder was too rich for her and passed it to the person she wanted to kill, Junie May."

Ned wiped his hands on his napkin. "Thomasina never had any problem with rich foods at the Village. Doughnuts. Cheese. Ice cream. She ate 'em all."

"And she asked her neighbor to buy her cream and hamburger meat." Val washed down her last bite of pie with iced tea. "I realized the significance of the food while I was checking out at the supermarket tonight. Her food didn't match her words. Her trivia answers didn't either. She missed a question that anyone diagnosed with gallstones would have known."

"You talked about salt substitute in the cottage. I never saw her use that either."

"Lillian saw Thomasina sprinkle it on the second bowl of chowder," Granddad said. "She must have had a packet with arsenic and one without. In case anyone saw her put the salt substitute in the bowl she gave Junie May, Thomasina had to sprinkle what looked like the same thing on the chowder she ate."

"Did she carry the packets in that purse you saw at the cottage, Val?" Ned asked.

"Probably. Women rarely keep their purses at the table except in restaurants. Junie May had to leave the table to fish her cell phone from her purse on the sofa. But Thomasina had her purse on her shoulder when she left the table. It was with her during dinner so she'd have the packets when she needed them."

"Too bad she didn't mix them up," Ned said. "Did she get the arsenic from a chemical supply place?"

Val shrugged. "Maybe, or it might have come from one of those colorful bottles on display in her living room. I found vintage arsenic in a pretty bottle at a secondhand shop."

Granddad grunted. "And I found some in the attic. I don't understand why Thomasina wanted to kill Junie May."

"I have a hunch," Ned said. "She was jealous. When a woman at the Village praised Scott for visiting his mother so often, Thomasina complained that he didn't spend as much time with her as he used to, because he had a girlfriend in the area."

"Hmph. You can swindle all you like, but you better not neglect your mother."

"Not if she's Thomasina." Val leaned toward Ned.

"I haven't thanked you yet for putting yourself between her knife and me."

Ned patted his middle. "I got more flesh on my bones than you, and you've got more years to live."

"Thank you for being a hero, and may you never have to do anything like that again."

"I'll second that." Granddad signaled the waiter for the check.

After closing the café on Saturday afternoon, Val weeded the vegetable garden, a task she usually disliked. Today she welcomed it as another sign that life was returning to normal. At the club this morning, she'd seen other positive signs. A brisk business for breakfast and lunch, with the summer slump winding down. Her tennis teammates back from vacation and planning the week's matches. Bethany wearing clashing colors instead of animal prints, her caveman diet now history.

Val might even find time to work on her cookbook, now that she didn't have a murder to occupy her. The chief had called with an update on the case against Thomasina to ease Granddad's fear of arrest. Using her Samantha Lowie ID, she'd rented a white sedan the day Junie May was murdered. She also had a fraud charge pending under one of the aliases Val had guessed. While giving no details, the chief had hinted at other evidence tying her to the murders.

Val stood up and brushed off her jeans. Futile. After last night's rain, she had more mud than dust on her. A white sedan with a yellow antenna bauble pulled up to the curb. Lillian. Val resisted the urge to waylay her. Granddad could handle a meeting with his girlfriend without his granddaughter's help.

Two minutes passed before curiosity got the better of Val. She went into the house by the back door, washed her hands, and joined her grandfather and Lillian in the sitting room.

Lillian looked small, enveloped by the old tweed sofa. "I'm glad you joined us, Val. I hear Thomasina's in custody. I owe you both an explanation for what I did, and I hope you'll forgive me. I met with Arthur Tunbridge's family several times after his death. When Omar told me why Arthur committed suicide, I hired a private investigator. He trailed Scott from his workplace to the Village here."

"So it wasn't a coincidence you ended up here. Why did you follow him?"

"I hoped to stop him from swindling other people."

Val understood the impulse to fix a problem and prevent an injustice.

"Did you tell the police about the private investigator?" Granddad asked.

Lillian shifted in her seat, looking uncomfortable. "After Scott was poisoned, I didn't want the police to know about the private investigator. They would have assumed I stalked and killed him. I blamed myself partly for his death, Don. I arranged the dinner and talked you and Omar into confronting him. I figured one of you had poisoned him."

Granddad's jaw dropped. "You thought I murdered Scott? And Junie May too?"

Lillian shook her head. "I knew you wouldn't kill her, and neither would Omar. I should have told the police about the private investigator then, but

I didn't have an alibi for Junie May's murder. Even worse, I matched the description of the person driving away from her house in a car like mine. I was afraid they'd arrest me. I'm sorry that put you in a bad position."

The doorbell rang. Val went to answer it with no worries about her grandfather's infatuation with Lillian. He could decide for himself whether to continue their relationship.

She opened the door to find Roy on the porch, trim and handsome in his uniform.

He broke into a boyish smile. "Hi. You have time to talk?"

"Sure. My grandfather has company, or I'd ask you in. Let's sit on the porch." She perched on the glider and frowned at her filthy jeans. "Sorry I'm not dressed for company. I've been gardening."

"You look great to me." He sat in the wicker chair across from her.

"Are you involved in questioning Thomasina?"

"Yup. She has an answer for a lot of things. She bought the gray wig to see how she'd look if she stopped dying her hair. She got the stun gun we found at her place for her protection after someone pushed her down the stairs. The medical examiner might be able to tell if it made the burn found on Junie May's body."

That burn explained why the police gave up on the suicide theory. Val didn't like the sound of *might*. "Please don't tell me she's going to get off for Junie May's murder."

"She won't. Your list of the possible aliases she used is helping us nail her. When the police first talked to her after Scott's murder, she gave her real name and a story about why she didn't use it. She had a clean record under that name, but we found complaints against her for fraud under three of her aliases. With enough time and resources, we'll probably find the evidence that she helped Scott scam people."

"Given her record, she probably ran those scams. He was a pawn. What about the beer she poured for Granddad?"

"No test results yet. She probably wouldn't have used arsenic again. More likely, she'd have tried giving him something that would result in a heart attack. She had some heart medicine in the kitchen. Your salt substitute tip paid off. We found a half-used packet containing powder that looked different from what was in the sealed packets she had. Assuming it's arsenic, we've got her."

If that turned into the key piece of evidence against Thomasina, Val would have Lillian to thank for it. "Thomasina should have disposed of the arsenic instead of saving it for a rainy day. She was arrogant, assuming she wouldn't get caught."

Roy's stomach rumbled. "Sorry, I haven't had a chance to eat much today." He pulled a protein bar from his shirt pocket and offered it to Val.

"No, thanks. I can get you something more substantial to eat." And tastier.

"I'm good with this." He ripped into the bar. "It would help with the interrogation if we knew why Thomasina resorted to murder."

"I can guess. Scott fell in love with Junie May. Thomasina was losing her grip on her son. The chowder dinner gave her a chance to get rid of her rival. She found out a week before the dinner that Junie May would be there." Val rocked in the glider. "I think that's when Thomasina planned the poisoning. She made up a packet of arsenic-laced salt substitute in case she got the chance to get rid of Junie May. Scott gave his mother an extra incentive to kill her rival that night. He bought an engagement ring at the vintage jewelry shop in town, the last thing he did before picking up his mother for the chowder dinner."

Roy nipped a small piece off the protein bar and chewed it. "We found a fancy diamond ring at Thomasina's place. We'll check with the jewelry store to see if that's the one he bought."

"He left the store happy, convinced Junie May would accept him. By the time he arrived at the dinner, his mood had changed. Everyone said he wasn't his usual charming and talkative self. I think he told his mother his marriage plans on the way to the chowder dinner, and she did not react well. She sprinkled arsenic on the chowder she passed to Junie May, who gave it to Scott."

"Thomasina didn't stop him from eating the poisoned chowder."

"She tried. She asked him to drive her home because she felt sick. He refused, choosing the wrong moment to assert his independence. From then on, she had no use for him. She'd probably say it was his own fault he was dead. He should have listened to his mother."

Roy chewed rapidly. "Once he was dead, why did she kill Junie May? Thomasina wasn't getting him back again."

"Junie May might have figured out the poisoned chowder was meant for her. Besides, Thomasina must have wanted to punish the woman who deprived her of her loyal son and accomplice."

"That gives us some buttons to push when we're talking to her. It sounds like we need a psychiatrist to see her." The deputy stood up. "Thanks for your help. Maybe we can get together when—"

He broke off as Granddad and Lillian came out of the house. The phone rang. Granddad went back inside to answer it, and Lillian approached Val.

Roy excused himself and left.

Lillian extended her hand to Val. "I just want to say good-bye. Take care . . . of yourself and your grandfather. You're good for him."

A final farewell if Val had ever heard one. "He's good for me too. So long, Lillian."

Val sat in the glider. She felt sorry for her grandfather, disappointed in the first woman to capture his heart since Grandma had died.

He came outside, joined Val on the glider, and rocked it. "Did Lillian tell you? She's moving back home."

"It's not that far to Annapolis. You can still see her."

"We agreed that wouldn't work."

Val couldn't tell which of them had agreed first. "Are you going to give up the recipe column now? Its only purpose was to attract her."

"I'll keep it up for a while. Any man who can cook is a chick magnet."

Val laughed, delighted that his experience with Lillian wouldn't make him leery of other women. "Was that a *chick* calling you on the phone?"

"Yes, a reporter for the *Treadwell Gazette*. She wants to interview me about my role in catching the murderer. I sure hope she uses the headline I suggested. CODGER COOK CRACKS CASE. It has a nice ring to it."

Val pulled her earlobe. "A false ring. I know you like publicity for the recipe column—"

"This has nothing to do with that." Granddad flicked his wrist, dismissing his recipe column as a trifle. "I need the publicity to launch my next career—private eye to senior citizens."

Recipes from the Codger Cook

WATERMAN'S CLAM CHOWDER

This simple recipe lets the taste of the clams shine through. If you don't like the briny flavor, you can add milk, cream, or tomatoes at the end and turn it into another kind of chowder. Some folks like to steam the clams first because they're easier to shuck that way than when raw. But if you do that, you're more likely to end up with clams that are overcooked and tough.

  50 littleneck clams
    2 medium onions, peeled and chopped fine
    3 medium potatoes, peeled and cut into
      ½-inch cubes
  ¼ pound diced bacon, salt pork, or pancetta
    1 bottle clam juice
  [Salt and pepper to taste]

Wash, shuck, and chop the clams, catching all the liquid. Strain it through cheesecloth.

Fry out the pork. Add the onions and cook them over medium heat until soft, but not brown.

Put the potatoes in a pot with the pork and onions. Add the clam liquor you saved, the bottled clam juice, and enough water to cover the potatoes and give them a space to swim. Bring it all to a boil, reduce the heat, and cook covered until the potatoes are tender, about 20 minutes.

Add the chopped clams and cook for 2-3 minutes. Don't overcook the chowder unless you want to spend a lot of time chewing on tough clams.

Season with salt and pepper to taste, and serve immediately.

Serves 4 as a main dish or 6 as an appetizer.

Adapted from Tangier Island Fifty-Clam Chowder in *Chesapeake Bay Cooking* by John Shields.

ONE UGLY SPREAD

Why would you serve this ugly glop? Because it's easy to make, and it tastes good. Your guests won't care how it looks if you can convince them to try it.

    ½ cup pitted Kalamata olives drained
    ¼ cup chopped walnuts
    ½ cup raisins
    1 tablespoon olive oil
    2 teaspoons balsamic vinegar

Combine all the ingredients in a food processor.
Chop until the mix holds together enough that you
can spread it.

Put it in a pretty bowl and make it more appetizing
by sprinkling chopped parsley on top.

Serves 8 as an appetizer.

CRUNCHY LIME CHICKEN

*Key lime juice tastes best with this chicken dish, but any
lime juice works. Though the chicken doesn't take long to
cook, you need to think ahead. It marinates in the yogurt
mix for two hours before it goes in the oven.*

>   12 chicken tenders or 4 boneless skinless
>   chicken breast halves, cut lengthwise into
>   quarters
>   ½ cup plain low-fat Greek yogurt
>   2 tablespoons Dijon mustard
>   2 tablespoons of Key lime (or other lime)
>   juice, bottled or freshly squeezed
>   1½ cups of packaged herb-seasoned stuffing,
>   crushed

Preheat the oven to 400 degrees (after the chicken
has marinated).

Combine the yogurt, the lime juice, and the mustard. Marinate the chicken in the mix, covered in
the refrigerator, for two hours.

Lift the chicken from the yogurt mix and let any excess marinade drip off. Roll the chicken pieces in the crushed stuffing, pressing in the crumbs to make them stick.

Place the chicken on a baking sheet and bake it for 10 to 12 minutes.

Serves 4-6.

NO-CRUST NO-FUSS SPINACH PIE

Why would you bake a pie without a crust? Because it takes less time, makes less mess, and uses fewer ingredients. You need a tart pan with a removable bottom to make this spinach pie.

  1 pound baby spinach
  1 medium onion chopped
  2 large beaten eggs
  8 ounces ricotta cheese
  8 ounces freshly grated Parmesan (or similar hard) cheese
  [Optional sprinkles of pepper and nutmeg, no more than ¼ teaspoon of each]

Preheat the oven to 350 degrees.

Steam the spinach until it wilts. Drain it, chop it, and press out extra moisture with paper towels.

Mix the onion, eggs, and cheeses. Add pepper or nutmeg to taste. Fold in the spinach.

Grease the tart pan with cooking oil spray and put in the spinach mixture.

Bake for 30 minutes or until barely brown on the edges. Stick a knife in the center of the pie to make sure it's set. If the knife comes out soupy, bake for another five minutes and test it again.

Remove the pan from the oven and wait five minutes before removing the side of the tart pan. Serve the pie warm.

Serves 4.

Adapted from *Irish Country Cooking: More Than 100 Recipes for Today's Table* by the Irish Countrywomen's Association.

DUMMY RUM CAKE

Any dummy can make this cake. You just throw five ingredients into a bowl and mix. You can make it into a fancier, sweeter, and more fattening dessert by frosting it or drizzling a glaze made of rum, butter, and sugar over it. Or you can eat the slimmer version and take a second helping.

   1 yellow cake mix (15 to 16 ounces)
   3 eggs
   ½ cup cold water
   ⅓ cup vegetable oil (not olive oil)
   ½ cup dark rum
   [Optional cup of chopped pecans]

Preheat the oven to 325 degrees.

Cover the inside of a 10- to 12-inch tube or Bundt pan with cooking spray. If you're using the chopped nuts, sprinkle them in the bottom of the pan.

Mix the other ingredients in a big bowl running the mixer for two minutes. Pour the batter into the pan.

Bake 50-55 minutes until the cake is golden brown and a wooden toothpick comes out clean.

Cool the cake for ten minutes and turn it upside down.

CRUMBLY NUT ROUNDS

You roll the dough for these cookies into balls and put them on the cookie sheet. Be careful not to tip the sheet when you pick it up, or the dough balls might roll away. You can make them stay put by flattening them with the bottom of a glass.

   1 stick (half a pound) of unsalted butter, softened
   ¼ cup sugar
   ¾ cup coarsely ground pecans or hazelnuts
   1 cup sifted cake flour (or 1 cup minus 2 tablespoons of sifted all-purpose flour)
   ½ teaspoon vanilla
   [Optional pinch of salt and sifted confectioners' sugar]

Preheat the oven to 350 degrees.

Cream the butter with the sugar. Stir in the nuts.

Add the sifted flour in two batches. Stir in the vanilla and the salt (no more than 1/8 teaspoon).

Chill the dough in the refrigerator for 30 minutes, covered with plastic wrap.

Shape tablespoons of dough into a 1-inch balls and place them on an ungreased cookie sheet, 2 inches apart.

Bake 15-17 minutes, until cookies are set and just beginning to brown lightly.

Cool on the baking sheet for 5 minutes. Transfer the cookies to a rack to cool further. If desired, sift confectioners' sugar over the cookies.

Yields approximately 30 cookies.

Val's Trivia Questions

1. University of Maryland athletic teams share a name with the diamond-backed turtles native in this region. What is the name?

2. Which of these organs are not considered vital to life—the appendix, the liver, the gallbladder, the spleen?

3. What married couple, both Oscar winners, starred in the 1973 TV movie *Divorce His, Divorce Hers* and, a year later, divorced in real life?

4. What is the official fish of the state of Maryland, also known as striped bass?

5. Some patients in emergency rooms have pyrexia. Is that a burn, an eating disorder, a fever, or a skin infection?

6. Cafe Montmartre opened in 1923 as the first nightclub in what U.S. city: New York, Las Vegas, Hollywood, or Baltimore?

7. Name one of the two major league teams that had a home in Griffith Stadium.

8. Two mothers and two daughters go out for coffee and a doughnut. They spend fifteen dollars altogether and each one spent the same amount. Did they each spend four dollars, five dollars, six dollars, or none of those?

9. The sweet taste of this antifreeze component makes it dangerous to animals and children who might drink it accidentally. Is it isopropyl alcohol, ethanol, ethylene glycol, or corn syrup?

10. What name was used by film directors from 1968 to 2000 when they didn't want their own name to appear in the credits? Was it Stacy Smith, Alan Smithee, John Smithson, or Sandy Shore?

ANSWERS

1. Terrapin
2. Appendix, gallbladder, spleen
3. Elizabeth Taylor and Richard Burton
4. Rockfish
5. Fever
6. Hollywood
7. Washington Senators or Washington Redskins
8. Five dollars (spent by three women: a grandmother, mother, and daughter)
9. Ethylene glycol
10. Alan Smithee

Acknowledgments

I'd like to thank those who shared their expertise with me and answered questions that arose as I planned and wrote this book. For information on murder methods, crime scenes, and forensics, I consulted D.P. Lyle, M.D. I also received helpful advice from pharmacist and toxicologist Luci Zahray, known to the mystery community as the Poison Lady. Cathy Ondis Solberg and Don Solberg answered my questions about investments and financial fraud. My gratitude goes to all of them. Any errors in the book on these subjects resulted from my misunderstanding.

From synopsis through each stage of writing this book, I relied heavily on my friend, writing partner, and sister in crime, Carolyn Mulford. Heartfelt thanks, Carolyn. I couldn't have done it without you. I received excellent suggestions on the manuscript from writers E. B. Davis and Helen Schwartz. Friends and family also read the book and helped me improve it: Susan Fay, Elliot Wicks, Toni Corrigan, Rob Corrigan, and Paul Corrigan. Special thanks go to Mike Corrigan for his insights on the book and for his infinite patience while I wrote it.

Thanks also to my agent, John Talbot, and my editor, John Scognamiglio, and the whole team at Kensington Books. I also want to thank the people without whom this and other books wouldn't exist—readers.

GREAT BOOKS,
GREAT SAVINGS!

When You Visit Our Website:
www.kensingtonbooks.com
You Can Save Money Off The Retail Price
Of Any Book You Purchase!

- **All Your Favorite Kensington Authors**
- **New Releases & Timeless Classics**
- **Overnight Shipping Available**
- **eBooks Available For Many Titles**
- **All Major Credit Cards Accepted**

Visit Us Today To Start Saving!
www.kensingtonbooks.com

All Orders Are Subject To Availability.
Shipping and Handling Charges Apply.
Offers and Prices Subject To Change Without Notice.